Copyright

Copyright © 2024 by Sarah Blue

All rights reserved.

No part of this book may be reproduced in any form or by any electronic or mechanical means, including information storage and retrieval systems, without written permission from the author, except for the use of brief quotations in a book review.

The story, all names, characters, and incidents portrayed in this production are fictitious. No identification with actual persons (living or deceased), places, buildings, and products is intended or should be inferred.

Cover Illustration - amarnouille
Cover Design by - Maldo Designs
Editing by - Kmortinedits
Interior Design - @MarieMackayBooks
Chapter Heads - Turningpagesdesigns

Spotify Playlist

Possum Kingdom - Toadies
Hex Girl - Moon Sisters, The Nostalgia Girls
all-American Bitch - Olivia Rodrigo
All I Wanted - Paramore
I Miss You - Blink-182
Pity Party - Melanie Martinez
Best Friend - Saweetie, Doja Cat
Nightmare - Halsey
Howl - Florence + The Machine
Belong Together - Mark Amber
You Get Me So High - The Neighbourhood
Lost in the Fire - Gesaffelstein, The Weeknd
Meddle About - Chase Atlantic
Judas - Lady Gaga
Season Of The Witch - Lana Del Rey
All Around Me - Fly Leaf
Decode - Paramore
Cadigan - Taylor Swift

Foreword

This book handles topics of abandonment and complicated family relationships including growing up in an orphanage.

There is some violence as well as adult content.

For a full list of all the content in this book, please visit my website.

[Content Page](#)

QR code to content page

Is there knotting in this?

Why yes, honey, do you want some?

Chapter 1

Fourteen years ago

The moon shines brightly over the lake as I climb up the old sycamore tree off the side of the property.

It seems silly to still be hanging out in a tree house when I'm turning sixteen in nearly ten minutes. But, it's become a force of habit, it's a place of comfort in a place rife with discomfort.

This is the one place I don't feel like I'm under a watchful eye from Mr. Mander or the staff he keeps housed on the five-hundred-acre estate.

Don't get me wrong, Mander's Academy for the Highly Gifted and Unhoused—*pretentious fucking name*—isn't the worst place to call home. I know it could be far worse. At least, I can gather it would be worse from the books I've read and the television shows we're allowed to watch. Harrowing tales of children being taken by a nefarious villain, or being discarded completely by the people who are supposed to love them. I guess that second one still rings kind of true in the grand scheme of my life.

At least at Mander's I have three square meals a day and I don't live in fear of not being accepted. Since a young age I've been told

2

I'm different, all that wind up at Mander's are distinct. The outside world is a hard, unforgiving place, one in which none of us will ever be accepted.

It's easy to believe as things can get a little strange around here. Though, most of the oddities are ignored.

When someone does something beyond what is considered normal, everyone just turns the other way. At least I don't have to pretend to be anyone other than myself when I'm here. Not that I know who I am, or *what*. Lately it's felt like there's something more to this school, more to my identity and the other students I'm surrounded by.

I turn the lamp on and open my biology textbook as I wait for Silas to arrive. We're currently covering genetics, which makes me roll my eyes. None of the students here know anything about their genetics. The students of the obscure academy are quite the mystery.

There are those of us who have irregular things happening to us, like myself. Or those who are physically way larger than an average teenager.

Speaking of averagely large teenagers, Silas startles me while hefting his large frame into the entrance and shoving his body into the treehouse. The moon shines behind him, and I have to hide a smile behind my textbook.

My best friend is handsome, especially with the silvery light glowing against his masculine features.

"We need a new meeting spot," he complains as his messy brown hair reaches the ceiling of the treehouse.

"You're the one who needed a tutor," I reply.

We both know he doesn't need a tutor, but neither of us says anything. Silas is the brightest spot for me here, and I love spending time with him. Okay, I more than enjoy spending time with him. I have a ridiculous crush on him, but I don't know if he feels the same. Plus, the last thing I want to do is ruin our friendship. It's not like we go to one of those schools on TV with tons of kids, there are only about twenty of us at Mander's.

He's my friend, my best friend, and I don't want to make things weird.

"We don't need to study tonight," he says softly, shaking back his hair, his brown eyes meeting mine. He's already over six feet tall and is sporting light facial hair that he hasn't quite learned to shave properly. He looks well beyond his sixteen years, and I wonder how much bigger he will get.

I tap my pen against my chin. "I thought you needed to study for the quiz tomorrow?"

A light blush creeps around his neck as he shakes his head and takes his backpack off and pulls out a small plastic container and removes the lid.

He looks shy, which is cute with how much room he takes up in the treehouse. It's part of why I like Silas so much. While he may be large and intimidating, deep down, he's the biggest sweetheart I've ever met.

"I know it's not much, but I made them myself. Jonas helped me," he says.

I look down into the container, seeing bright pink frosting, and smile.

"You made me cupcakes?"

"Almost forgot," he replies, grabbing a candle out of his bag and placing it in the sweet frosting before lighting it on fire. "You have to make a wish," he says.

"It's not my birthday, yet," I reply, looking down at my ancient watch, noting I have two more minutes. "And I don't know what to wish for."

I mean it honestly, I've given up on the dream of finding my family. Most of the 'graduates' wind up just staying here and working for Mr. Mander, anyway. Silas and I have plans to bust the hell out of here when we're eighteen, even if the thought is terrifying. But staying sequestered on this campus doesn't seem like a life worth living.

"What about a pact?" he suggests.

"What do you mean?"

His cheeks are nearly pink and it almost makes me want to tease him more, but I hold back. He's being sweet, and I'm starting to realize that Silas is, in fact, more than my best friend. Perhaps this isn't as unrequited as I thought.

"Like that we'll always stay close and be friends no matter what," he suggests.

"What about when you get a girlfriend?" I ask him and he rolls his eyes, making me bite my bottom lip to refrain from grinning. Is it possible that Silas actually wants me to be his girlfriend? Is that why he's kept up this tutoring farce for so long?

"The candle is dripping all over the frosting," he complains, and I shake my head.

"We need a better pact, Silas. That one is a given."

He huffs out a breath and smiles. My heart skips a beat as he holds his hand under mine, so that we're both holding the cupcake together.

"How about we make a pact that if we're both thirty and single, we'll get married," he says.

This time, I roll my eyes. "There's no way you'll be thirty and single."

"Violet, have you seen yourself? I'm going to have to scare every man away from you if we ever leave this hellhole."

I shake my head at him, and he holds the cupcake toward my

face.

"Make the wish," he grumbles, his voice getting deeper.

"Do you even think you'd be a good husband?" I joke, not caring about the wax dripping all over the frosting.

I like teasing him. I also need him to say that he likes me, likes me, and this goes beyond us being best friends.

"I'd be the best husband, and you know it. We'd be one of those couples who wants to spend all of our time together. You wouldn't be able to resist me. Honestly, the more I think about it, the sillier this pact is, because I think I'm going to convince you to marry me well before then anyway, Violet."

"So confident," I reply sassily, even though my heart is racing a million beats per minute.

It looks like Silas is going to lean in and blow out the candle, but stops a breath's width from my lips and I lean forward as Silas takes my first kiss.

It's short and sweet and when I pull away, his brown eyes are bright with happiness. My heart stills, and there's a slight tingle against my lips that I can't shake. I don't think it's normal, but I have nothing to compare it to. It must just be my nerves or what all first kisses feel like.

"Make your wish," he breathes out.

I close my eyes and blow out the candle. Something deep in my belly warms as I make the wish. Every word of our pact ripples through my mind, almost like a chant. My nerves feel like they're on fire, actually my whole body feels like it's in flames. I've felt a tingling of this sensation before, like something is trying to escape me, but never anything this intense. Fear is licking up my spine and pain rips through me as my vision goes black.

"Silas," I rasp out his name, the cupcake tumbling to the floor as I pass out.

There's a soothing touch against my face. It feels wholly familiar while also being completely foreign.

"I wish to take her home now," the voice says. It's not high pitched, but the authority and primness in her tone is clear.

"The school is a great—" Mr. Mander says, and the woman cuts him off.

"*Please.* Don't pretend you are nothing but a collector of the unfamiliar, Mr. Mander. It's unbecoming. Violet belongs with her people, where she can actually learn who she is, not slumming around with the likes of the other beings you house in this so-called *school*," she says.

I blink my eyes open and glance over at the woman. The moment I see her, I immediately know we're related.

She has stark white hair, which matches the color framing my face. The only difference is the rest of my hair is black, while hers is light over her entire head. I always wondered why it grew like that and no matter what I tried, there was no changing the nearly white shade. But it's unique enough that I know without a doubt she must be related to me.

Her clear blue eyes are exactly like mine, and she's extremely put together, with her hair in a chignon and her simple black dress and cardigan completely in place.

She strokes my hair again and her lips part as she looks down at me.

"You look just like Lavender," she says in a sad voice. Her emotion disappears as she looks over at Mr. Mander. "I'd like to take my granddaughter home now. Please collect her things," she orders.

Mr. Mander looks down at me like he's losing something precious.

THE MARRIAGE HEX

"But—"

"Now, Mr. Mander," the woman scolds.

He sighs, looking frustrated and loathsome of this woman, but tilts his head and leaves the room all the same. Meanwhile, I'm trying to wrap my mind around her words.

Unfamiliar.

Her people.

Beings.

I turn my legs to sit on the bed and blink up at the other woman. "Granddaughter?" I question.

"Yes, well. There will be plenty of time to discuss everything as soon as we leave this charnel house."

"It's a school," I reply in a haze.

"No, it's where *others* go to die."

I blink at the woman who hasn't given me her name and everything she says feels like it means something else entirely. I'm about ninety percent sure she's speaking English, but like she's speaking in a code, I don't understand. "I need to say goodbye to my friends," I say and she shakes her head, her lips in a tight pout.

"I'm afraid that isn't possible. You don't belong here and you surely can no longer be associated with any of these *children*." She shakes her head and crinkles her nose. "I can smell the dog on you."

I shake my head. Am I dreaming? Half of the words she's saying don't make any sense. My fingertips rub against my temples as I try to remember what happened last night. Silas and I were making the wish, and then nothing.

"How did you find me?"

She goes to open her mouth as Mr. Mander hands her a suitcase with my belongings. He gives me one last longing look before leaving the room.

SARAH BLUE

"Whatever spell my daughter cast on you to keep you hidden was lifted on your sixteenth birthday. You'll finally be back where you belong," she says softly. "I'm Aster Delvaux, but you can call me Grand-mére. It's time to go."

"But I need to say goodbye to Silas," I tell her.

He's the only thing I'll truly miss about this place. I still can't wrap my mind around anything this woman is saying. A spell? A dog? Did I hit my head?

All I know is I need to tell Silas that I'm alright, that I'll write to him, or maybe we can communicate some other way.

"I have to say goodbye to him," I repeat. I can't imagine how hurt he would feel if I left without a word.

"I'm sorry, but that just isn't going to happen."

My grand-mére wraps her perfectly manicured nails around my wrist and I'm suddenly ripped away from what was somewhat considered my home. Leaving the school, my best friend, and everything I've ever known behind me.

Chapter 2

VIOLET

Present Day

My heels click along the cobblestone streets as me and my two best friends make our way to one of our favorite local bars. As I hit one of the ancient stones, my heel cracks and I curse.

Looking around, seeing no humans nearby, I pull out my wand and use a repairing incantation to fix my shoe.

Being a witch definitely has its perks. Scratch that, being a witch is fucking everything and I wouldn't trade it for the world.

"Alright, tuck that thing away," Ember says, pushing at my wand as I shove it into my purse.

I can do magic without it, but having a conduit makes things a hell of a lot easier. We're right outside the bar as Iris grins and hands us each a purple vial.

"What is it?" I ask, while Ember takes the cap off and chugs it back without a care in the world. Her reddish blonde hair falls back and her freckled nose crinkles from the taste.

That's always been our dynamic, I suppose. Ember is always willing to take risks, Iris is the calculative one, and I'm the more cautious one.

Since the moment my grand-mére brought me into the coven, Iris, Ember, and I have been inseparable. I never had girlfriends before, and even though they were two years younger than me, we instantly connected. My grand-mére told me female relationships are the basis of a strong coven, and as usual, she was right.

We're forever bonded by magic and kinship, and I can't imagine life any other way. I don't know who I would be without magic or without my coven; they mean everything to me. But especially Ember and Iris. I don't think there's a way to describe how much I love them. It's beyond friendship or blood relation, it's an intrinsic bond that's hard to explain.

"It's a hangover potion I brewed this morning," Iris says, and I swallow the purple potion down with a wince. "Yeah, I'm working on the flavors."

"Fuck, it's crowded," Ember says as we walk out to the back patio.

Iris pulls her wand out behind her purse, her lips moving, but I can't hear the spell. I smile as I watch a five-top suddenly decide they need to leave immediately.

Magic never ceases to amaze me.

"Better not let Aster find out you're using magic in front of the humans," Ember says sarcastically.

"What the High Priestess doesn't know won't hurt her," I say as I wave down a bartender who takes our drink order.

"Keeping secrets from the old witch?" Iris says with an arched brow. She looks beautiful tonight, wearing a daisy yellow dress that contrasts her unblemished umber skin. Her long, thin braids hang over her shoulder, and she's wearing winged eyeliner sharp enough to kill over her long, thick eyelashes.

"She doesn't need to know my every movement," I say as my two friends glare at me. "I mean, I did finally move out."

THE MARRIAGE HEX

They both share a look before looking back at me. "How has it been, living there?" Ember asks softly.

By there, they mean the abandoned mansion my mother left me. The mother that I can't talk about to my grand-mére or the coven; everyone acts like she never existed. My grand-mére swears she's still alive, that she would feel it if she passed, which only saddens and confuses me more.

I've spent so long searching for answers and continually come up with dead ends. Why would she abandon me? Not only that, why would she have taken me away from my coven and suppressed my magic for sixteen years? The only answer I've ever gotten from my grand-mére is that my mom wasn't mentally well before she ran away. I can see the pain on my grandmother's face everytime I bring her up, so I've stopped asking. The coven is all I need, they're my family. Yet… there's still a nagging feeling of loss I can't seem to shake.

I had hoped living in my mother's home would give me answers. But all it's given me is a major magical workout to fix the six thousand square foot dump.

"It's okay," I answer, and Iris glares at me. "Okay, so it's a little lonely, but I needed my own space. Aster has been breathing down my neck about being her protégé and the next steps for the coven. At least I can be myself and feel like every spell I cast isn't being over analyzed. Plus, Walter likes killing the bugs."

They both give me sympathetic nods. They know how hovering the High Priestess can be, and they aren't even her heir.

Ember fans herself with a drink menu and glances around the bar. "Well, don't worry about that tonight. We're celebrating your birthday. Maybe we can find you some hot human to take back to your creepy mansion and have your way with them."

"I'm off men for the foreseeable future. Thank you very much."

SARAH BLUE

"I would be too, after Paul," Iris mumbles under her breath. I went on one date with him, and had to compel him to forget me after the date. It seems a relationship, or even a bit of fun, isn't in my future. When you reach a certain age it's embarrassing to bring up the fact I still haven't been physical with anyone.

"What's even the point, anyway? Witches don't marry, we have our coven, that's all we need," I reply. The line has been engraved in me since the day Grand-mére brought me home from Mander's Academy for the Highly Gifted and Unhoused.

"To come, Violet. That's the point," Ember says, glancing around the bar. "Have you ever done it with a vampire?" she asks, and Iris and I both blink at her. "What? The blood thing is kind of hot. And they're always ready to go."

"If Aster found out," Iris says.

"She won't find out. Plus, it's not like I'm going to fall for a vampire. But we can have a little fun. I mean we all exist, those old hags had to have gotten it in at least a few times," Ember says and I laugh.

But she's not wrong.

The coven is for female witches. If a witch wants to have a baby, well, they do what they have to do to conceive. But in all my years with the Celestial Coven, I've never seen a witch marry or get into a serious relationship. It's just not the way things are done.

"Even Aster has to realize we can have a little fun," Iris says.

"I'm not sure dear old Grand-mére knows what fun is," I say, before clamping a hand over my mouth.

"Let's take some shots to that," Ember says, which makes me incredibly thankful for Iris' potion.

I'm waiting in the never ending line for the bathroom with Iris.

Ember has grabbed some unsuspecting mortal man to dance with as I lean against the wall and push a sticky piece of hair off my face.

Even though it's supposed to be autumn, the humid air is thick, like a blanket over the outdoor bar. The cicadas are screaming their heads off, competing with the live band playing in the corner.

"Aw fuck," Iris hisses.

"What?"

"Moon Walker Pack, twelve o'clock," she says, using her head to point in the direction of said shifters.

I take a quick glance and sure enough, Maddox, Kit, and Selma are walking into the outdoor space like they own it.

Tonight can go two ways. One; we don't interact with any of them and we go about our night enjoying the festivities. Two; everything is about to go to shit.

Just my birthday luck, it appears that it's going to be the latter as Kit approaches us. She's tall, about six feet, with dirty blonde hair and an irritated look on her face. She's pretty, but she isn't a witch, she's a shifter. Shifters and Witches don't mix, especially not in this town.

I didn't understand the animosity when I first got here, but boy, do I understand it now. The origins of the feud are conflicting, but the main story I hear is that the witch created the first shifter as a curse, and ever since then there's been nothing but hatred between the Moon Walker Pack and the Celestial Coven.

Above all, both of us have a strong sense of family, and for generations we've hated each other, and I don't see that changing any time soon.

"Enjoy your last night here," she says, leaning against the wall casually.

"Last time I checked, there weren't any divisions on the mortal lands," I say, eyeing her up and down like she's beneath me.

"Haven't you heard?" Kit asks, looking at Iris and I like we're beneath her station. "There's a new Alpha in town."

Iris rolls her eyes. "How many pack leaders have you had now? Ten in the last twenty years?"

"Yet you both still have the same old hag in charge," Kit sneers.

My hand is on my wand before I can even think as I point it at her chest. She has a whole half of a foot in height over me as she glances down at me like I'm gum on the bottom of her shoe.

"You do not talk about the High Priestess," I warn her.

She smiles, as Iris shoves my hand down to put my wand away.

"She's not worth it," Iris whispers, shoving the wolf shifter's arm away. Iris' eyes flash pale white for only a short moment before her breath hitches and she's ushering me away. "We need to find Ember and get the fuck out of here, now."

"Enjoy your time before the witch hunt," Kit says, waving us off with her fingers.

"What the fuck was that?" I complain as Iris drags me along. "Iris, slow down."

She doesn't slow down, her bright pink nails digging into my arm as she finds Ember grinding on some man, before grabbing her by the back of her dress.

"What the hell?" Ember complains as Iris basically drags us both out of the bar.

"What is it?" I ask as Iris puts the back of her hand against her forehead.

"I had a vision," Iris says, she doesn't get them often.

Her grandmother is a prolific seer, probably the most profound the coven has ever had, while Iris' gift lies more with potions. But on rare occasions, it seems she holds the same ability as her grandmother.

We walk away from the bar, the crowd and band noise slowly

THE MARRIAGE HEX

dissipating.

"We had to leave a night of fun because you had a vision?" Ember complains, feeling totally cock blocked. Sometimes I wish I were more like Ember, that I could enjoy life more easily and not live in my head constantly.

"No, we had to leave because this one took out her wand and pointed at that shifter bitch who was trying to start shit," Iris says, pointing at me.

"Like you wouldn't have done the same if she was talking about your grandmother."

Iris waves me off as she fans herself.

"What was the vision?" Ember asks.

"It's not important," Iris replies.

I stop in the middle of the street and grab Iris' wrist. It's not like us to keep secrets. Well, at least not between the three of us.

"What was it?" I ask.

She swallows and shakes her head. "It could mean anything."

"Iris."

She glances at Ember and then back at me.

"You were in a white dress in the jowls of a dark brown wolf."

Ember gasps. "Like being eaten? I heard that's where this feud started, a wolf killed a witch."

"It didn't feel sinister," Iris says and my brows furrow.

"What did it feel like?"

Iris shakes her head.

"It could mean anything, Violet. The wolf symbolizes so many things; spirituality, adaptability. Maybe it has something to do with your birthday being transformative. I don't think we should read into it."

But Iris looks scared, and Iris is never scared.

"The vision hit you when you touched Kit," I remind her. "Do I need to be worried about her?"

Iris swallows. "I think Kit is the least of our problems."

Chapter 3

SILAS

My muscles tense as I enter the ring against Hoyt. He's been running this pack into the fucking ground, but fortunately for them, I finally found where I belong, where I come from.

I've been waiting for this moment for years. The moment I could claim my birthright, and it's finally here.

"He's weak," Jonas says behind me.

He's my oldest friend, the only friend I could ever truly depend on. While others left me in their wake, Jonas was there, having my back, it's why he will be my second the moment I take over this shambled pack.

Both of our wolves ripped out of us when we needed them the most. We stayed at Mander's for a few years, thinking it was safe for us, until we learned the truth.

We left that hellhole and never looked back. Since then, we've been trying to find the right pack. And it just so happens that this one is tethered to me in blood. And I want what I'm owed.

"We should kill him," Thorin whispers in my mind.

My inner wolf is begging to be let out as he whispers threats of violence in my mind.

"I'll let you out shortly and you can have your bloodshed," I tell him.

"*This pack is ours. Our mate is near. I can feel it,*" Thorin rumbles.

As of late, all the Alpha wolf cares about is finding our mate. The drive has not been similar for me as a man. I just want to finally be a part of something real, somewhere I belong. I can appreciate a woman's beauty, but I've never been drawn to enter a relationship or anything adjacent with one. Being the Alpha of a pack, of my destined pack, has been my only motivation.

"This is bullshit. You think you're going to come into my home and try to take my pack away from me? You aren't even a part of the Moon Walker Pack. You have no fuckin' claim here," Hoyt says in a thick southern drawl.

"If you're such a strong Alpha it won't matter," I say, and his eyes flash yellow.

"He's going to shift," Jonas states the obvious behind me.

Hoyt is ill-tempered, unfit to lead, and clearly misjudging my strength. I've never felt an impulse as strong as I have to take this position from him. The rest of the shifter community stands by, none of them defending their current Alpha. They all just look on with intrigue.

"*He's weak. We should rip out his throat,*" Thorin growls, and I swear I can hear him salivating at the idea.

Hoyt is vibrating across from me, his wolf taking over. What a weak, pathetic asshole. It's been nearly a decade since Thorin involuntarily took me over. We're so in sync at this point in our bond, I'd never look so impulsive in front of my pack.

He rips out of his clothes, shredding them into pieces, and I sigh as the gray wolf in front of me bares its teeth in challenge.

I unbutton my shirt, folding it, and handing it to Jonas, before

THE MARRIAGE HEX

undoing my belt and doing the same with my pants. Having no issue with my manhood, I take off my underwear until I'm completely naked and take one last look at the crowd. My skin is balmy with the humidity, and I almost wish my blood rite was further north, but here we are.

This pack is about to be ours.

The shift is lightning fast, and Thorin takes over.

Chapter 4

I'm nearly twice the size of the insignificant wolf in front of me, and he knows it. The crowd gasps with our shift and they look upon my magnificence.

"Chill the ego," Silas, the man, whispers.

I roll my eyes and dig a paw into the dirt. The man thinks he's in charge, but I just let him think that. We both know that I'm the superior being in this partnership.

Everyone in this pack is about to know the same thing.

I'm nothing if not a complete Alpha wolf. There will be no one above me. It's all or nothing with this pack. Especially if I'm going to impress my mate. I can feel that she's close, and she deserves nothing but the best.

I can feel Silas' irritation with me, but I ignore him, as I do when I'm in my true form.

The other wolf attacks. What an idiot.

I dodge him and bite his hind leg, making him yip and tuck his tail between his legs.

What a pussy.

I spin, using my size to my advantage as I sink my teeth into his neck. He whimpers and cries as his blood fills my mouth.

"Keep him alive," Silas says and I sigh.

He always ruins my fun.

I place a paw on the gray wolf's head as he shifts back into a man; I relent. The medics immediately grab him and put pressure on his throat. I howl into the star filled night sky as the pack descends on their knees.

That's right, bow to your new Alpha.

"Christ," Silas complains and I can feel he's about to take over.

I let out one last victory howl before I regretfully shift back into the man.

Chapter 5

This pack is a fucking mess.

I'm scrubbing a hand over my face as I look over their financial statements and a list of all the members of the pack.

"Ten Alphas in two decades," Jonas complains, as he goes through the paperwork with me along with key members of the pack. His dark brows furrow as he rubs his thumbs over his temples, his light brown skin heating with frustration. "What the fuck has been going on here?"

"We're low on the totem pole here," A man with long russet colored hair, and a beard says. "Maddox," he says his name, like he knows I forgot it. "The witches own the town. Not to mention it's fucking riddled with vampires and a few werewolves who like to give us a bad name."

"Witches?" I question.

"The main coven in the area is the Celestial Coven. We've been at odds for centuries. I don't think anyone knows the real lore at this point, but they're a bunch of self-righteous cunts. They own half the businesses in town, and keep encroaching on our territory."

"How?"

Maddox swallows thickly, he's clearly nervous having my complete attention and one word questions.

"Magic brings a lot of fortune, and with that comes the ability to purchase land, homes, and businesses when they go up for sale."

"Has peace been offered?"

"Peace is for the weak," Thorin rumbles, and I tune him out quickly.

"There is no peace when it comes to this coven. Their High Priestess has been in charge for nearly forty years. Their coven is strong, and they want us gone."

"How many witches are in this coven?"

Maddox looks at a few other members, and they shrug their shoulders. I rub the bridge of my nose.

Morons have been running this pack into the ground. Financially incompetent, weak Alphas have been leading this pack into destruction. Luckily for them, I have amassed a great deal of wealth in my efforts to find my pack. And by that I mean, what was previously Mr. Mander's fortune is now mine.

"I want a list of everything for sale in the area, information on both the witch and vampire population, and I want every single member of the pack present tomorrow at ten a.m."

"Yes, Alpha." Maddox bows slightly, getting out of my newly appointed quarters and leaving with the other scared shitless shifters in tow.

"This is a clusterfuck," Jonas says, running a hand through his buzzed black hair, his dark green eyes scanning all the pack's financial documents. "Things seemed to get really bad about thirty years ago. Looks like that's when the long-standing Alpha and his son died."

"Since then?"

"Everything's gone to shit. They haven't been able to keep a steady leader. Matings are down. Mortality rate is up. We're still eighty members strong, but this is going to take a lot."

I rest the back of my head against the leather chair that's just the right size. My blood ties to the pack are through my mother, who never arose as Alpha. From finding her a few weeks ago, it's clear her being a low-tiered wolf is what got her kicked out of the pack and why she decided to give me up.

I didn't feel much when I found her. There was no strong connection or feelings. If anything, she seemed sad and pathetic. But when I'm here, on this land, with this pack? I feel something so intense I'm not sure how to describe it.

This pack might be a disaster. But they're now my disaster.

For the first time in my life, I understand my purpose. I was born to lead this pack out of desperation and into a new era. One where we're not suppressed by other supernaturals.

Ideally I'd like to consider peace as a first option, but if it's not on the table, then other tactics will have to do.

"Violence?" Thorin chimes in and I shake my head.

Jonas grabs us both a beer from the small fridge and hands me one as he sits across from me and we both take a heavy sip.

"Witches," he grumbles and I grunt in agreement. "Shit isn't going to be easy."

"Everyone has a weakness," I tell him, holding my beer up as he does the same.

"To Pack Moon Walker."

"To Pack Moon Walker," I reply with a smile. "We're finally home."

Jonas gives me a rare smile as we gather everything for the

meeting tomorrow.

The chatter is loud as I hold up a hand. "Quiet," I say in a booming voice, silencing everyone in the hall.

All eyes are on me as I stand at the podium and rest my hands on the edge.

"If you weren't at the challenge the other night, I'm sure you heard about it. My name is Silas, and I'm the new Alpha of the Moon Walker Pack. If you have an issue with this, I have no qualms accepting challenges for the position at any given time."

No one speaks, and I nod my head, enjoying the submission.

"Now, I've run through the financials, I've spoken to involved pack members, and I've come to some conclusions. First and foremost, this pack is running dry on funds. I will be using my personal finances to get this pack on track, but that requires hard work and dedication from everyone. If you are a business owner, I would like you to schedule an appointment with me to discuss your current business model.

"Second, I hear we have a problem with the local supernaturals in town…"

That one has the volume rising as pack members lean into one another to whisper and discuss the ongoing problem.

"While I've been advised that peace is not possible, I'd like to see for myself. I'm going to be holding a meeting with the leaders of each clan in the area. Witches, werewolves, and even the vampires."

"There's no point!" someone shouts from the back of the hall and I lean into the podium.

"Know thy enemy and know yourself," I say, quoting general Sun Tzu. "I understand that I haven't grown up here, that you don't know me. But what you will learn to understand is that I'm dedicated to making this pack what it once was. If we can't come to an agreement with these other beings, then I have no issue keeping them our enemies."

There are chants of excitement, and it's clear the hatred runs even deeper than I realized for the other supernaturals.

What the fuck have I just gotten myself into?

Chapter 6

VIOLET

I arrive at my grand-mére's home wearing black boots, a fit and flare black dress, and a cardigan. I'm already about to chuck off with this heat.

Louisiana clearly has not gotten the memo that it's October.

Her porch is laden with pumpkins, skeletons, and fake cobwebs as I enter the front door, my iced coffee nearly spilling as I step inside.

"This is honestly a waste of time, the only reason I'm even entertaining this meeting is to get a good look at this new so-called Alpha," she says, speaking to her sister, Daisy, who has never spoken a single word since I moved here fourteen years ago.

My great aunt gives me a small smile and a wave. I move to stand by the chair she's sitting in at the window. She's older than my grandmother, but you would think she's far older than her actual age. Time has been hard on Daisy, her hair is thin, her face is gaunt, and I wish I knew why she was withering away. Most witches are able to keep their youth for a considerable amount of time. Supernatural beings, especially ones with magical abilities, are able to live longer and healthier lives.

Every diagnostic I take of her says she's healthy, yet she doesn't talk, and she continues to read by her window daily. Though I always enjoyed the books she would give to me to read, it's almost like she intrinsically knew what I needed to study. I kiss the top of her white-blonde head as my grand-mére's heels click against the tile.

"There you are. We must be going," she says. I put the iced coffee straw in my mouth and suck as much of the liquid in as I can before I take her hand and she teleports us to the meeting place.

I adjust my dress and take a deep breath, wishing she didn't want to bring me with her.

My magic is solid. I've chosen the healing path, which my grand-mére was less than enthused about, but it's where my magic guided me. Casting healing charms, doing diagnostic spells, it comes naturally to me, and I love it. It's just not the typical calling of a High Priestess.

Which is completely fine with me, but not to Aster Delvaux. I should be fluent in every type of magic, which I am. I can handle a potion, but not as effortlessly as Iris. My elemental magic is decent, but nowhere near as fantastical as Ember's.

I love healing magic and everything it encompasses. The only thing that semi keeps her off my back is that no one else in my generation has had the calling to medical magic, so I'm necessary—I'm just not extraordinary.

"You will follow my lead. You're here as a sign of strength, that we have a succession in place whilst this folly of a pack changes paws every turn of the moon."

A blacked out sedan pulls up. The back door opening to a man in a luxurious black suit, popping open a black umbrella. His hands are covered in gloves and his eyes are shielded by sunglasses.

"He invited the bloodsuckers," she whispers, grabbing my wrist to tug me inside of the out of the way seafood restaurant.

It's a neutral place, owned by a human who knows about the things that go bump in the night.

There's a massive crawfish statue wearing a bib and holding a fork and knife in each hand. It feels cannibalistic and tacky, but I shrug it off as she leads us into the event space.

Each seat has a place setting based on which group you're from and we take the two Celestial Coven seats.

I glance over at the vampire in the expensive suit and he smiles at me, his white fang nearly sparkling in the tasteless overhead lighting.

"You know, I could use a witch," he says.

My grand-mére taps her golden wand with thorns and roses against the table. "The day one of my coven helps you is the day I'm rotting in my grave, Warin," she says.

The vampire just smiles, not lowering his sunglasses or removing his gloves. The rest of the supernaturals in the community take their spots as the back door audibly creaks open.

Before he can even face me, I recognize him immediately.

Silas.

My long lost best friend. The one I abandoned fourteen years ago and never even bothered to look back at. The moment I lived under Aster Delvaux's roof, I was taught it was coven or nothing. So I shoved Silas into a tiny little box of things I needed to leave in my past.

He's larger and far more imposing than I remember, but he still has the same handsome features he did when he was sixteen, but now he's a man.

Well, I guess he's more than a man. He's the new Alpha of the Moon Walker Pack.

My first friend, my first kiss, the only boy I ever loved, is now my enemy.

He's flipping through papers and standing next to a man I also recognize. His sharp buzzed hair and eerie green eyes are impossible to miss—Jonas.

There's a part of me that's happy that Silas has had Jonas throughout all these years, that he wasn't alone. A part of my heart breaks as I watch Silas' hard features scan the room, not even a hint of a smile on his lips.

When his brown eyes finally land on me, he stares.

It's like there's no one else in the room as we both take each other in. The time apart has been kind on his appearance, but not on his demeanor as he rubs his chest as he looks at me. It's like every emotion crosses his face: anger, frustration, curiosity, resentment, and something else wholly unrecognizable.

I wonder what he sees in mine. Probably guilt. I've locked Silas away for a long time, not allowing myself to even go there. How could I? Grand-mére explained to me that different un-human beings existed and that when she came to collect me, she could smell that I'd been around a shifter or a werewolf.

So I kept Silas hidden away in my past. Sometimes, when I was feeling lonely or sad, I'd let myself daydream about what we could have been, who we would have been in a different lifetime.

But this isn't that lifetime, him sitting before me as the Alpha of a wolf shifter pack just solidifies that. There is no universe where we're together, or friends again, and it feels like the air is being sucked out of my lungs.

"Are you quite done gawking at my progeny?" she interrupts the moment and Silas' gaze shifts to her.

"My apologies, let us begin," he says, taking a seat and dismissing our perplexing reunion.

He's white knuckling the countertop, and I can't keep my eyes

THE MARRIAGE HEX

off him. If he senses me staring, he doesn't give in, looking anywhere but my direction.

"I want to thank you for agreeing to meet with me. I'm Alpha pack leader, Silas, and I'm hoping that we can leave this meeting with a better understanding of one another and a solution to move forward."

My grand-mére scoffs at even the slightest mention of peace.

"If it's peace that you want, why was this meeting not held at night?" the vampire from earlier asks.

"I apologize for the shortsightedness."

"Hmm. You've apologized twice now during this meeting. Are you also here to apologize for the lives of the witches that ended between the sharp teeth of your pack? Or how about the centuries of crimes against our coven," she says in her rich, southern twang.

Sometimes I wish I spoke like her, or the rest of the coven. Maybe I've picked up some linguistic choices, but I'd never be able to curse in southern sophistication the same way Aster is capable of.

"Please, tell me about these crimes. Ones that are relevant to those living today," Silas challenges her, still not looking in my direction.

What am I going to say to him if I have a chance? What do I even say? I'm sorry I abandoned you. It wasn't my choice, but wanting nothing to do with you now is?

Just the idea of it has bile creeping up my throat.

Her lips purse, like she wants to say something, but by bringing it up it would be showing her cards. Instead, she goes with the low hanging fruit. "We could start with the full moon and how nearly every quarter one of your dogs interrupt our rituals."

"Wolves," Silas corrects her. "Are there treaty lines of where everyone can and can not be on the full moon?"

"Where we roam on the full moon is out of our control," the

werewolf ambassador says. His name is Elias, and he's honestly not a bad guy. Before he was bitten he coached the high school football team, but his life is tied to the moon now.

I suppose it controls all of our lives, in some way.

The vampires thrive under the cover of the night and love the luminescence that a full moon brings.

The werewolves' life is centered on a moon, only shifting once a month, but completely out of control when they do.

The witches use the moon as a source of power, gratitude, and a way of centering our coven.

The shifters tie to the moon is a mystery to me, but they seem to hold something dear to it, with how many times we've had to listen to a cacophony of howls while we set out jars of water to be blessed by the night sky.

"You don't chain yourself up?" my grandmother asks in distaste. I want to sink into the floor.

"Denying the beast only proves to make things worse. When I let him roam, he gets out his energy. I haven't and will never mark someone to have the same fate as my own."

My grand-mére taps her nails against the table, causing Silas to glance at her.

"We can create boundary lines so that my pack and your coven have specific, private areas to convene our monthly rituals."

Her back straightens next to me. She likes what he's offering, but she hates him so much, I don't think she'll accept.

"Why?" she asks him and I sit on my hands, the feeling making my fingers numb. Maybe if I focus on that I'll forget everything that's about to happen.

"Why what?" Silas asks, clearly agitated.

"Why would you come here and embarrass you and your pack with a peace treaty, knowing it's impossible? You have to have something worth trading for peace," she says, standing up and resting her palms on the table and looking around the room. "None of you have anything I want, you're insignificant to me. If I wanted to, I could kill you all with a simple flick of my wrist. Do you know why your pack is still alive, Silas?"

He stares at her, not responding, and she gives him a wicked smile that would normally scare the strongest of men.

"You're alive because I let you live. Because your pack is so unimportant that I barely ever think about you. The history books may be confused about what started this feud, but I don't forget all the things I witnessed at the helm of Alpha Collins," she says.

With that name, Silas tilts his head. That name is new to him.

"I hated that motherfucker, but that man was an Alpha. He brought your sad little pack into the modern age with violence and technology. He killed a member of my coven, not with his teeth like a real wolf, but with something far worse," she says, tapping her nail against the table. "You can forget this silly notion of a peace treaty and prepare for me to take you down even ten times harder."

"It's unfortunate to hear you think that way," Silas says, and my grand-mére already has her wand back out.

It's a stark reality watching how they're both handling this situation, but I shove my conflicted thoughts deep deep down. My loyalty is with my grand-mère, with my coven. Just because I knew him a lifetime ago doesn't change anything, it can't.

"It would be far more unfortunate for your pack to be down yet another Alpha, wouldn't it. Violet, get up, we're leaving," she says.

It feels wrong to leave without having actually spoken to him, but what else am I supposed to do?

"Yes, Violet, run off with your grand-mére. It's where you belong," Silas says and the words hit me square in the chest.

I don't falter, though; I keep my chin high, my eyes clear of any tears as I turn and face him.

"You're right, it is where I belong."

Chapter 7

SILAS

I'm trying to focus and speak to the remaining supernaturals who have stayed for the meeting, but Thorin won't stop fucking berating me in my mind.

"Our mate. Our fucking mate was right there, and you let her walk away. You were mean to our mate. We need to chase after her and show her why we are deserving of her. We could kill her grandmother and put her in charge of the coven."

I try to shake him, but he keeps bitching about it.

"She's so beautiful. It's the girl from your memories. We could have had her as our mate all this time if she wouldn't have left," Thorin says. An immense feeling of sadness fills me as I try to get my shit together.

I can't think about Violet right now.

She's only gotten more beautiful over the years. I can't attest to her temperament, seeing as her grandmother stole the show. But it's clear her loyalty to her coven is the same as my loyalties to my pack. Neither of us are going to be easily swayed on who we support.

The irony of it all is laughable. The girl I pined over for years who ran away without ever looking back is my mate. She's not even a fucking wolf. A witch is my goddamn mate and I want nothing to do with her.

"Speak for yourself."

"Fuck off, Thorin."

My wolf mocks me in my head as I try to listen to everyone else in the room. The werewolves and packs are willing to work together. The vampires are indifferent as long as they can drink their fill of unsuspecting travelers.

"Then we agree to stay out of each other's affairs and hold a united front with the witches?" I ask and get agreements around the table.

The vampire, Warin, stands up. "Next time, pick a family friendly establishment," he says as he passes the crawfish statue, popping a rich black umbrella open indoors before leaving the restaurant.

The rest of the pack leaders and werewolves leave while Jonas and I stay behind to absorb everything that just happened.

"Well, that was interesting."

"Which part?" I ask, rubbing my temples.

"Probably the part about finally finding Violet, only to find out she's now your enemy."

I rest my elbows on the table and place my palms on my forehead.

"She's my mate."

"Thorin confirmed it?"

I nod and groan as my friend smacks my back.

"Well, that's some shitty fucking luck, but hey at least she's still hot."

I pull my hands off my face and point at him. "You will not talk about her like that."

Jonas just smiles. "Yup, definitely your mate. Looks like you have another thing to add on to your very long to-do list."

"Don't fucking remind me."

"But that's in fact my job as the Beta to remind you of your duties."

I sigh and wave him off, remembering her voice. It's still sweet and soft, like I remember, but now there's a slight edge to it. '*You're right, it is where I belong,*' plays over and over in my head.

What if, after everything I've been through, everything I've done, I don't get my mate?

Thorin whines at the possibility, and I push him further back into the recesses of my mind. He can sulk and whine while not forcing me to have to hear it, too.

Instead, I go back to my small cabin that needs to be renovated and think about the things I can do to make sure this pack doesn't fail. To make sure I'm nothing like the grandfather who abandoned his daughter, leading me to be an orphan.

He might be the reason I'm here with this pack, the reason I was meant to be an Alpha, but he wasn't a good man or wolf.

The moment I destroyed Mander and his school, I made myself a promise that I wasn't going to waste this gift. I was a wolf for a reason, and it had to be for good, especially after everything I'd given up.

I pour myself a brandy and sit in the worn out leather chair and think about Violet.

She didn't smile the entire meeting and I try to search my memories and remember what it looked like when she smiled. I can't picture it and it sends a deep feeling of sadness through me.

I never forgot about her, but it wasn't without trying.

Mr. Mander told us her family was found, and she was taken in the middle of the night back to her home. At first I was happy for her, that she knew where she belonged, but that happiness quickly shifted to hurt when I never received a letter or any kind of messages from her.

Despite every file I read at that fucked-up academy, there was never a record of where Violet went. It was almost like she vanished.

Fourteen years later, I find her, and she's the progeny of the witch who wants to destroy my pack.

Mate or not, the pack comes first. The Moon Walker Pack needs true leadership and, if that means sacrificing Violet, then that's what I'll have to do.

Chapter 8

THORIN

Dumb human man. He thinks we can just forget about our mate? Then he's fucking deluded.

My urge to protect and lead the pack is just as strong as Silas'. But the hunt for my mate has been a long and tireless one. Had I known it was the girl from his memories, I would have hunted her sooner.

I had been suppressed for so long inside of Silas, not able to show my true form. That sick man kept us from our true potential.

So, I tore his throat out.

Silas took his money, freed the other beings that were kept prisoner and tested on, and we started our search for a pack.

Nothing besides being an Alpha would do. I could never bow to another wolf. I'd rather be a nomad than dig my paws into the ground and bow to some other motherfucker.

Moon Walker Pack is our pack.

But Violet is our mate.

I'm not as dumb as the man thinking we can't have both. He's not as wise as he thinks he is, anyway, considering I've been shifting into my form at night and doing as I please. It's so much quieter and fun when the man is asleep.

He'll complain when he wakes up, wondering why he's so tired while I rest in the recess of his mind. We might share a form, share our thoughts, but I am the superior being.

The back of the bakery is locked, but I grab the hinge between my teeth and tug before pulling the door open and stroll down the aisle, my nails clicking against the floor.

I may eat my fair share of pralines before grabbing the best looking cupcake that's stored in a plastic container.

My teeth dig into the plastic, despite my efforts to be gentle, but it will have to do.

I have a mate to court, and if the man isn't going to do it, then I need to take charge.

Silas can't recall his memories as I can. As soon as I shifted and was released I spent weeks searching through his most memorable moments. Violet, Jonas, and his wolf, Hyde, were always at the center of his happiest moments.

I remember the date well. October eleventh. It's our mate's birthday, and she needs to know that we're thinking of her. If Silas was being more cooperative, we could have gotten her something nice, but I feel as though the little witch may enjoy my small offering.

I'm deep in the witches territory, it's almost like their magic permeates the air. My instincts direct me to a cottage covered in Halloween decorations, but I quickly realize her scent isn't as deep here. She frequents this place, but it's not her home.

With my nose in the air, I inhale and head north.

Don't eat the cupcake, I remind myself. I should have eaten the bread pudding while I was at the bakery. Maybe after I drop this off, I can swing back around.

Tiny solar lights. No, there has to be magic at play with the

THE MARRIAGE HEX

way the trees cover the walking path, as a massive purple home sits before me. Vines are wrapped around the massive pillars and pumpkins are assorted on the porch.

This. This is my mate's home.

I walk up the stairs and place the container on the mat, using my paw to adjust the plastic as best as I can.

When she awakes tomorrow for her birthday, she'll know her mate is thinking of her. I'll convince Silas to apologize and we'll get our mate back.

It will be simple.

Chapter 9

SILAS

I awake with a pain in my stomach, and blink at the ceiling. I need a bigger bed and need to stop eating so late. My hand rubs down my chest as I sigh heavily.

There's a sensation that licks down my spine as I stand up and dress. My feet move on their own accord, taking me to my motorcycle as I drive through downtown that's decorated with cornstalks, pumpkins, and witch propaganda.

My brows furrow as I park in front of the courthouse, wondering why the fuck I'm here. But my body doesn't even let me take a moment. It's almost like a string is wrapped around my neck and dragging me through the entrance toward the Circuit Courts Office.

As soon as I open the door, I find Violet with her head in her hands. Is she wearing a nightgown?

Her head lifts and her bright blue eyes meet mine.

"There you are," she says in an irritated voice. "We're so fucked."

Chapter 10

VIOLET

I wake with a gasp, clutching my chest as Walter startles next to me.

"Happy Birthday, I guess," he says through our connection, licking his gray paw and curling back up to sleep.

My familiar is ornery on the best day, but he has been crucial to me since finding out I was a witch. He just showed up on my grand-mére's doorstep, told me he was my familiar, his name was Walter, and he doesn't eat cat food.

"Something's wrong, Walter," I tell him, my body moving on its own accord as I slip on my boots.

I try to fight it and go into my closet and change, but I guess whatever is happening is going to happen in this silk, white nightgown.

Walter's ears fly back as he stands on the bed and assesses me.

"What is it?"

"I...I don't know. It's like I need to go somewhere."

"Don't fight it," Walter suggests.

I nod at the wise cat and grab my purse, tossing my wand inside. When I open the front door and look down, there's a smushed cupcake. I inspect the container and it looks like there are teeth marks in the plastic.

What the hell?

I put it back down, not knowing where it came from as my feet take me to their destination. I wrap my arms around myself. The night air is cold. Even when I try to turn around and go back into my house to grab a sweater, my body won't let me. Instead, I take out my wand and cast a warming spell, which works. But when I attempt to cast anything that will stop my momentum or take me back home, the wand seems to be useless.

Could the girls be pulling a birthday prank on me or something?

That's my best guess as I walk down the path of my property a whole half mile until I reach the main street. At least I'm not as cold anymore as the sun rises, and I let whatever magic is affecting me lead the rest of the way.

My feet ache, and all I want to do is go back to bed, but it seems whatever is possessing me has other plans.

Nothing is open yet, as I finally reach downtown and my legs take me to the courthouse.

I glance around as the early birds trickle into the nearby businesses. I sit on the bench outside and shake my foot with anxiety. Deep down, I'm willing myself to get up and go back home, but my feet won't move.

This is not how I saw my thirtieth birthday going. I was supposed to get breakfast with my grand-mére and just relax the rest of the day. It wasn't going to be anything special, but it's what I wanted.

With shaking hands, I pull my phone out of my purse and call my grand-mére. She refuses to reply to texts.

She doesn't answer, and I sigh in relief as I leave her a voicemail.

THE MARRIAGE HEX

"Hey, grand-mére. I woke up not feeling so great. Can we reschedule breakfast? I'll talk to you later. I'm going to try and get some more sleep."

I hang up the phone and just wait. My body is begging to be let into this building, and I have no clue why.

The first government employee comes to the door and glances at me. I must look ridiculous in this nightgown and boots. I didn't even brush my hair.

As soon as the door is open, I'm pushing my way through. I go through security, but they all give me odd looks, like I'm on their watchlist. I probably should be, because whatever is happening to me feels certifiable.

The moment I open the door to the marriage license office, something in me calms down. I still can't leave, and so instead I sit down on the bench and think.

"Interesting wedding dress choice. Will the groom be here soon?" the plain-looking woman behind the desk asks.

"What?" I reply.

"Bless your heart, you're here to get married, right?" she says and I blink at her and look around in the stale government office that hasn't been updated since 1975.

Me? Getting married? What in the seven depths of hell is going on? I try to back away and my body won't let me. It's evident a strong magical force is holding me here specifically.

What could possibly be holding me here, wanting me to get married? This woman probably thinks I'm deranged, wearing a nightgown, boots, and my hair probably looks a mess. I blink a few times and think about the last few days, has anything been different?

My mouth drops. No… no fucking way.

Silas.

SARAH BLUE

"Miss?" she asks, interrupting me putting all the dots together.

"Yes, he'll be here soon," I whisper, looking down at my hands. Not knowing if he will actually be compelled here. Is sitting in the office for marriage licenses for the rest of my life my new form of purgatory?

There's no way. I didn't even know I was a witch when I made that pact with Silas. I didn't have a wand, and I was sixteen, for fuck's sake, I don't even remember what was said. I didn't mean the pact literally.

Well, I guess I did when I said it. But right now, I absolutely need to figure out a way to prevent this from happening.

Luckily, my body does let me walk into the ladies' restroom. I lock myself in a stall and take out my wand. I try every nullification spell I can think of, but the issue is I'm not even sure how I cast the first spell.

That is, if it was a spell. What if I cursed us, or placed a hex on us instead? I'm wracking my brain trying to remember what was said that night, what could possibly undo this very wrong situation I'm in.

It was so long ago, and so much happened that night. I can just remember the basics. We promised each other that if we were single at thirty, then we would marry each other.

Well, I guess that answers my question on if Silas had found anyone in these years apart. We're both single and thirty and whatever my magic did that night has come back to haunt us.

The air in my lungs feels like it's leaking out, and I realize that my body is tired of hiding out in this bathroom. I cast a quick spell to smooth down my hair and reduce the dark circles under my eyes before my feet drag me out of the bathroom with a force so strong I'm not sure how I'll find a way out of this.

I go back to my bench and sit there with my head in my hands.

THE MARRIAGE HEX

Maybe Silas won't have this pull? Maybe I just need to outlast the day and we'll be free and clear.

It seems I'm not that lucky as a messy haired Silas opens the door to the clerk's office and glares down at me. Relief fills me, like I'm no longer in pain now that he's near.

"There you are," I say in frustrated relief. "We're so fucked."

Silas looks around at the humans who are staring at us, wondering what the hell is going on. Then he looks down at my very scandalous nightgown before clearing his throat.

"What the fuck is going on?"

I look around and scoot over on the bench; he takes up most of the space and it's weird having him this close again. His body is basically radiating heat as he crosses his arms, which are very large, not that I really noticed, and glares down at me.

"What did you do? It's like I was in a trance on my way here," he whispers.

"It was the same for me."

His brows furrow, and he rubs his beard. It makes this scratchy sound that I pretend to hate.

"What do you mean? You clearly cast some petty spell to get back at me for yesterday's meeting."

I shake my head and swallow. "No, I cast this spell fourteen years ago, without even knowing it," I say, picking at my black nail polish.

He sits back on the bench, my words clearly not clicking right away.

"The night I left," I say, trying to refresh his memory.

He laughs. He fucking laughs, a deep rumbling sound, but then when he looks at my face, it comes to a halt, all joking slipping from his features as he stares at me.

"You can't be serious?"

SARAH BLUE

"Do you think I'd want to marry you right now?" I complain and I swear something flashes behind his eyes, his dark brown nearly turning gold for a moment. I shift my weight on this hard bench that's making my ass hurt, wishing I was still in bed and this pissed expression wasn't plastered on his face.

"No, just like I don't want to marry you."

"I fear we don't have a choice in the matter," I tell him. Everything in me is tugging me to go to that counter and make this marriage legitimate, even if rationally I want to get as far away from here as possible.

"Well, do something about it. Pull your little wand out and make this go away," he says. It hurts my feelings, even if I do feel the same way.

"I've been here for hours. I don't know what spell I cast, or if it even was a spell fourteen years ago. I didn't even know what I was then, Silas. Everything I know about reversal I've tried. Undoing something like this is going to take time and research."

"Are you really suggesting we get married right now and figure it out later?"

"Do you have any other ideas? You feel the same pull as me, don't you? Like leaving here would be painful?"

He looks around, but nods in defeat. I'm glad I'm at least not alone in this feeling.

"No one can know about this," he says, glancing over at the employee, who is clearly trying to eavesdrop on our conversation.

"We're in agreement about that. We'll just give the hex what it wants and then I'll work on how to counteract it. No one has to know, and we don't even have to see each other while I figure it out."

Silas rubs his chest again, almost like he's in pain, just like he did at the meeting.

THE MARRIAGE HEX

"Are you alright?"

"Let's just get this over with," he grumbles as we both stand and walk up to the woman who's been glaring at me for a few hours.

"You made it. I was wondering if you were getting a case of cold feet. Can I see your IDs and I need you to fill this out. We need twenty-four hours to process your license request and then you can hold a private ceremony and have the officiant sign, or you can book a time at the courthouse," she says.

"No, we need this to be official today," I tell her.

She clicks her tongue, saying in so little words that the government doesn't pay her enough to put up with a weird Bridezilla.

"I'm sorry, unless there are extreme circumstances, we need twenty-four hours."

Oh, fuck it. This is a time where being a witch comes in handy.

"Cheryl, you're going to sign off on this certificate and you're going to get us on the schedule to get married. Today."

Her brows furrow as the grip on my wand tightens as I hold her under my influence. It's not a magic I use very often, but it's one my grand-mére excels at. If she didn't give me private lessons on mental manipulation, there's no way I could do this right now.

Cheryl blinks out her confusion.

"Right. The clerk will take you back shortly. Give this to her to sign," she says, clear confusion written all over her face.

"What about confidentiality?" Silas asks, looking down at me.

I knew when I saw him at the meeting he was far larger than I remember, but standing next to him now feels near comical. An Alpha pack leader indeed.

"We need the record of our marriage sealed."

"Oh, we don't seal marriage licenses," Cheryl replies.

I take a deep breath and focus, my wand being the conduit for this type of power, otherwise I'd probably pass out.

SARAH BLUE

"You will seal this one. It's a matter of safety."

Cheryl blinks at me and scrunches her nose. "Right, I can do that for you. Take a seat, the clerk will be with you shortly."

Some of the earlier tension and unease leaves me as we sit back on the hard wooden bench. I rest my head back in my hands as Silas and I just sit there in silence. If he noticed I had the woman under a spell, he doesn't say anything, and I'm grateful.

There's so much I want to say, so much I want to ask, but what's the point? Maybe we can simply get the marriage annulled, or I'll be able to work backwards in the magic. Either way, we aren't staying married, and we certainly aren't friends.

It doesn't matter what he's been up to for the last fourteen years; it doesn't matter what kind of man he's become, because we're nothing. Well, we may be husband and wife shortly, but not for long.

Chapter 11

SILAS

"Silas Walker and Violet Delvaux," the clerk says as she opens the door and we stand.

"Walker?" Violet says with a scrunch of her nose.

"I was never given a last name, so I took the pack last name," I tell her and she looks down at the floor as we enter the room.

There are no guests, no witnesses, and the clerk calls someone from the office to watch the ceremony.

Violet wraps her arms around her middle, which is terrible, because it presses her silky white nightgown against her breasts.

The naughty little witch has pierced nipples, and I have no clue what to do with this information.

"I know what we should do with that information," Thorin growls in the back of my mind, and I push him out of my head.

The last thing I need right now is my wolf mooning over Violet. She means nothing to me. She was once a friend, once the girl I loved, but now she is nothing.

"She is our mate and our bride, you fucking fool," Thorin says and I push him even further away. He's pissed, but I shake him out of my head as I stare down at Violet.

"Okay, we have our witness. We will keep this short and simple," the clerk says. "Do you have any rings?"

"No," Violet says for the both of us and the clerk looks uncomfortable but agrees, anyway.

She does her spiel and gets to the I dos of the ceremony. I want to bite my tongue. I want to swallow the words back up, but no matter how hard I resist, the traitorous words spill out of me.

"I do," I say against my will.

"I do," Violet says with a little less resistance, and I wonder if it's because she's coming up with a plan on how to get us out of this mess.

"By the power vested in me, I now pronounce you husband and wife. You may kiss the bride."

I shake my head, and Violet does the same, even though our feet move on their own accord, putting us toe to toe.

"This means nothing," Violet whispers.

"Less than nothing," I reply as I bend down and kiss her on the lips.

It's quick, hardly even a friendly peck, but despite this, the same sensation that trickled through me fourteen years ago flashes through me again. I restrain myself, not chasing after that feeling.

Violet Delvaux is my enemy. Her grandmother wants to destroy my pack, my birthright, the people I vowed to take after.

It doesn't matter if she's my mate or my wife. She means nothing to me.

Violet holds our marriage license as we walk outside. A few men gawk at her in the small little white dress and I have to hold myself back from ripping out their eyes.

It's not like I care, it's just a matter of respect.

THE MARRIAGE HEX

"Could you give me a ride home?" she asks, looking around as I reach my motorcycle.

"You didn't fly your broom here?" I ask and she grimaces at me.

"That's not a real thing. And I walked all the way here," she says.

"Well, looks like you'll have an even longer walk back. It's not a good idea to be seen with each other."

She sighs, but nods in agreement.

"I'll let you know when I have information, we can see if the magic will let us annul this tomorrow."

She looks down at our marriage license and then back at me.

"I never meant for this to happen."

"Me either," I reply, feeling like an asshole as I hop on my bike and speed away.

Thorin complains the whole ride home about how I disrespected his mate and how I need to go and apologize right now, but I ignore him.

I have a pack to run, and my morning has already been completely uprooted. It's best we leave Violet to her own devices and act like none of this ever happened.

Pain laces through my entire body as I attempt to lie down in my bed. It's a longing ache throughout every nerve ending that I don't belong in this home. It's wrong, so fucking wrong.

I scrub a hand down my face and turn on my side, every movement hurting. I've fought in this form and my wolf form and never felt this deep of an ache.

Not being able to tolerate it anymore, I stand and pass the small room. It feels a lot like it did this morning, like I need to go somewhere. I just don't know where.

"Our wife's house, you fucking idiot," Thorin says.

SARAH BLUE

I pace more; the tug gets tighter and tighter. It's not like I know where she lives or if she wants me there. Hell, I don't want to be there.

"I know where she lives."

"Yeah, and how the fuck do you know where she lives?"

"She's my mate. It's my job to know everything about her," Thorin says proudly.

"You're fucking pathetic."

"And you're an annoying, stubborn asshole. I bet you'd feel so much better if you just went over there. I'll lead the way," Thorin nearly purrs the notion into my head.

"I hate you," I complain.

"Then you hate yourself, stupid. Pack a bag. We're going home," Thorin says, and I swear I can picture the wolf grinning in the back of my mind.

I park my motorcycle in the gravel driveway next to an older, black Jetta. I'm not sure what I expected Violet's home to look like, but the semi-disheveled mansion in front of me wasn't it.

Parts of it look like it's been repaired, while the rest of it needs serious work.

Is everything in this town falling to pieces?

Part of me wants to get back on my bike and get as far away from this home as I can. Yet, I won't, because being here soothes me already. Some of the uncomfortable achy feeling is still there, but the pain is gone.

With my backpack tight against my shoulders, I sigh and walk up the pumpkin covered steps. There's an uneaten cupcake on the porch, with teeth marks in the plastic. I groan and wipe a hand over my face.

"Did you fucking do that?" I check in with Thorin.

"I don't know what you're talking about," he replies, seemingly going to sleep.

I've never been so out of sync with my wolf, not since the first time I shifted. Thorin is going to need to learn some boundaries or else I may have to take matters into my own hands.

"I'd like to see you try."

I exhale dramatically, tired of my wolf and this ridiculous situation. There are a few real cobwebs in the corners as I sigh and raise my hand to knock on the door, but before I get a chance, Violet is flinging the door open.

Relief flushes over her features. "Hi," she whispers.

"I tried to stay at my place," I say, feeling uncomfortable and vulnerable.

"But it hurt," she says, and I nod in agreement. "Come in," she says, holding open the door.

Unlike the exterior, the interior, or at least this section, is cozy and comfortable. She has candles burning throughout the space, and it smells like violets and jasmine… and muffins? Her decor is every indication that a witch lives here, with crystals, ritual tools, books, and other decor laden all over the place.

I feel at ease in her home, though I shouldn't. She holds out an arm and I sit on her velvet, emerald green sectional. The walls are covered in occult art, and the antique coffee table is covered with open tomes that look ancient.

She flicks her wrist, a few out of place items moving quickly back into place before she comes and sits on the couch, her legs tucked under her. She's wearing a fucking nightgown, again. At least this one is black.

Neither of us knows how to break the silence or talk about what's happening. Whatever spell or hex she cast on us is strong, it goes beyond just the promise of being married.

Violet licks her lips and summons a journal and a pen with a flick of her wrist.

"Do you remember what exactly we said that night?"

"It was so long ago," I tell her and she nods in agreement.

"I'm just trying to figure out what exactly we said to make this spell so strong with such specific requirements. I've, um…never cast anything like this before."

I glance over at her as she taps the pen against her bottom lip in contemplation.

"What do you mean, don't you cast spells all the time, ruining lives all around you?"

She sits up straighter, her dark brows furrowing as indignation takes over her features.

"I don't know. Do you go running around ripping everyone's throat out who dares to challenge you?" she asks.

"Only sometimes," I reply, holding her gaze.

She shakes her head and starts writing in her journal. "I'm the coven's healer," she says softly and I have to stop my lip from twitching.

Violet was always so interested in science class and figuring out where we all came from. It makes sense that would be where her abilities fall.

"We need to remember what was said that night," she says.

"I thought we were going to annul the marriage tomorrow?"

She rolls her eyes at me like I'm stupid and sighs. "The magic forced you to come over to my house with a bag packed. Do you really think it's going to simply let us annul this marriage?"

"I suppose not."

"The less we fight the magic, the better off we'll be. We figure out what curse or whatever was cast that night and we work back-

THE MARRIAGE HEX

wards from there. We keep it a secret until we find a way out of this."

"Agreed," I say, resting my head on the back of the couch.

Exhaustion is heavy in every fiber of my being. But I glance over in high alert as a gray, long-haired cat who looks like it's seen better days jumps into Violet's lap and glares at me. I didn't think cats could glare, but it's like his hatred is palpable in his yellow-stare.

I arch an eyebrow at the small beast, and he hisses at me, showing his small fangs.

"Walter," she says, chastising him, petting down his fur. "That's not very nice."

"You named your cat Walter?" I ask, glaring down at the moody little thing.

"No, he told me his name when he found me. Walter is my familiar."

Thank fuck Thorin is ignoring me right now, because I think he would have some choice words about the creature.

"He looks like he's on his last life," I say and Violet's mouth drops.

She scoops up the cat and glares at me. With her standing, she looks like the powerful witch her grandmother wants her to be as her wand comes zipping through the room.

"You can be mad at me all you want, but you will not disrespect Walter in his own home. There are sheets in the hall closet, unless you'd like to sleep outside like the dog you are," she says, pointing her wand at me.

I hold my hands up in mock surrender. "I meant no offense, Walter," I say, a lie.

The cat bares his fangs to me again as Violet clutches him close.

"I know you don't want to be here. I don't want you here either, but it's clear being near each other is what the magic demands.

This is my house, and Walter is permanent. You're temporary," she says.

Temporary.

"I know, I always was," I tell her and her face falls ever so slightly.

She doesn't respond, just flicks her wand, blowing out all the candles at once, shrouding us in darkness.

"Tomorrow, we'll work on solving the hex," she says as she walks up the stairs with her cat, each step creaking while she goes, her nightdress shifting and showing more of her thigh with each step.

"You're so fucked," Thorin says, and I ignore him as I walk to the hall and grab some sheets.

I get curious as I explore the rest of the bottom level. The place is huge, and as I suspected some of the rooms need some vast remodeling. The kitchen, main living room, and foyer seem to be the only rooms completely finished, while everything else seems to be stuck in the past.

The kitchen in particular looks a mess, like she was baking, and I wonder if she was crawling the walls just as bad as I was.

"Doubtful," Thorin says and I roll my eyes and keep exploring.

One door won't open, despite using all my strength, and I just leave it, taking my place on the couch.

Can a man be in the doghouse when he didn't even want to get married in the first place?

Chapter 12

VIOLET

"He smells. We should kill him," Walter seethes as he sits on my bed retracting and exposing his claws repeatedly, like he could take out the massive wolf shifter downstairs. *"You shouldn't let him stay here. It's going to stink for weeks."*

I pull back the covers and climb into my overly large bed. I had to cast quite a few enchantments to make a mattress fit, but the frame was already here. Why my mother had such a large bed? I have no clue, but I can't deny I love it.

"It's just temporary. Plus, you saw how close I was to showing up at the pack compound to make this feeling go away."

"Killing him would solve all our problems. High Priestess would be most pleased," he says, kneading biscuits into his pillow before lying down to rest.

Thankfully, our communication is when we decide to speak, so he can't hear my thoughts. I might not like the Moon Walker Pack, but I wouldn't wish Silas dead.

"I need to break this hex before grand-mére finds out."

"We're back to my murder plot," Walter says with a yawn. *"You've ruined my rest for two nights now. Go to sleep."*

Walter falls asleep quickly, his eyes doing the weird thing where I can't tell if he's truly asleep because his eyes are partially open.

I hold my covers close to my chest and stare up at the intricate ceiling. Part of me wants to go downstairs and tell Silas everything, that I didn't mean to leave him forever, that I didn't have a choice. I still don't have a choice.

Bringing up the past doesn't matter, only in the context of how we're going to get this resolved. I need to keep this secret from my grand-mère and protect Silas in the process. I might not like him, but I used to know him, he used to be my best friend.

Even if he hates me and the circumstances are less than unfortunate, I don't want him facing my grandmother's wrath because of a stupid spell I accidentally cast.

The ceiling fan above me twirls, and I wonder if I should take a potion to help me sleep. When suddenly, my bedroom door flings wide open, the knob slamming against the drywall, leaving a dent.

A feminine yelp escapes me as Walter jumps into the air next to me, screeching. I hold the blanket close to my chest as the world's biggest wolf stands in my doorway.

I've seen the shifters afar on rare occasions, thinking they were the size of normal wolves, or perhaps Silas' wolf is just abnormally huge. The brown wolf before me stands at what I imagine would be my height.

He isn't snarling or looking threatening as his paws propel him to the bed.

"Stun him, do something, stupid girl," Walter says, but I just lie there frozen as the wolf approaches me.

Deep down, something tells me he means me no harm. Is Silas seeing all this? Or is he completely absent when his wolf takes over? The shifters, like witches, clutch our secrets close, neither group knowing much about the other.

THE MARRIAGE HEX

I grip the bedding like a lifeline as the wolf places his muzzle on the bed, a needy whine ripping through his throat. I swallow thickly as I look into his golden brown eyes. Perhaps the wolf is kinder than the man?

I hold out my hand, going to pet the top of his head as Walter hisses next to me. The wolf glares at my familiar with disinterest as I place my hand on his downy fur, stroking the top of his head and petting back his ears.

The wolf presses further into my hand, like my touch is something to be cherished.

"I'm sorry that grumpy asshole keeps you bottled up," I tell him.

I swear to Hecate, if a wolf can smile, this one just did. I scratch his head, under his jaw and behind his ears, he seems to love it.

"I need to get some sleep," I tell the wolf and he tilts his head.

The wolf doesn't retreat. Instead, he jumps up on the bed and turns three times before lying on top of the sheets and resting his head on my calves. I blink down at him, too afraid to tell him no.

Walter glares at the beast and hisses.

"Get that mangy mutt out of our bed."

I don't want to piss off the wolf, so instead I pet Walter a few times, and he bites my hand.

"Ouch," I snap at Walter, who grimaces at me.

"Now you're rubbing his scent on me. Just tell me you hate me, Violet," the cat complains, jumping off my bed and leaving the room, likely going to sleep in the other guest room upstairs.

I could have offered it to Silas. It would have been a hell of a lot more comfortable than the couch, but I didn't feel like he deserved it. Not after refusing to give me a ride earlier and his sour mood. I did teleport home once it was safe but he doesn't know that.

"Maybe you should stay in this form all the time," I tell the wolf.

He nuzzles against my legs, his eyes closing and I do the same.

I should be scared and unable to sleep with him here. Yet, I doze off nearly instantly.

I'm not sure why, but I get the best sleep I've had in fourteen years.

When I wake up, there are no animals in my bed and I almost wonder if I dreamt last night up. I mean, there's no way that Silas' wolf took over and snuggled me in the night. There's just no damn way. If anything, his beast would hate me more than the man does?

Instead of pondering it too long, I get ready for my day. We have council this morning and the last thing I need is to show up late and raise any flags that something is wrong. Like the fact I got married to the Alpha pack leader. Who slept on my couch, and quite possibly my bed last night.

I shower quickly and cast a quick spell on my hair and face. Beauty charms are one perk of being a witch. I'm able to get ready in a matter of minutes.

The full moon is in five days and we need to prepare, especially after our less than poor meeting with the other supernaturals.

I wear a purple dress with golden crescent moons before sliding on my boots and carefully walking downstairs. Silas could still be here, hell, there could be a wolf sleeping on my couch.

Instead, when I walk down into the living room, I find a shirtless Silas, an arm slung over his eyes as his chest rises and falls. A black sheet covers the rest of his body and Walter sits on the coffee table, staring at the man, and likely plotting his murder.

Silas is lucky that Walter's magical abilities aren't vast, or he would be shit out of luck.

"Do not kill him while I'm gone," I tell Walter in a soft voice.

"No promises," he replies, retracting his claws in and out of his

paw pad.

I sigh and glance at Silas one more time. He doesn't look as angry when he sleeps, if anything he reminds me of the boy I once loved all those years ago. Soft, kind, and gentle.

I'm not sure what he went through, but it's clear that part of him I once adored is long gone. All that's left is an angry, bitter, control freak.

I might slam the door a little harder than necessary before leaving. Walter will ensure that Silas doesn't do any damage to my home. He'd call upon me right away if he was doing anything suspicious. Not to mention the most important things in my home are warded and the shifter wouldn't be able to find them, anyway.

My teleportation magic isn't as strong as my grand-mère's, but it's passable, especially in locations I've already been. After a quick breath, I call on the familiar location and teleport to my grandmother's greenhouse.

"There you are. I tried calling you and stopping by your house yesterday. I know you wanted a low-key thirtieth, but what the fuck, Violet?" Iris says as I happen to pop into existence right next to her.

I dust my dress off and look down at her hands. "Is one of those for me?" I ask with a smile and she rolls her eyes and hands me the iced pumpkin spiced latte. I hum with the first sip. "Thank you, I needed this."

"You're welcome. But you're also not off the hook. You couldn't text back?"

Clearly, I should have thought of my alibi before now. I've been so consumed with needing to figure out this counter curse, hex, spell, whatever the fuck it is, that I haven't thought about how I'm going to keep the coven off my back while I resolve it.

"I was trying to astral project," I lie to her, and she pulls me closer to her body.

"Why, it's been a good hundred years since anyone in the coven has been able to do that?"

"I was hoping to find my mother that way," I say. It's a truth mixed with a lie, so hopefully she buys it.

She furrows her brow and nods. The topic of my mother has always been an interesting one with the coven. Of course, anyone my age or younger knows nothing. But the older witches all have the same story. She was troubled, and she left with me in her belly. No one heard from her again, and my grandmother found me at sixteen. No one's story ever falters.

I've only seen three photographs of her, all in my grand-mère's home. One when she was a young child, another at fifteen, and another at eighteen, when she disappeared.

My grand-mère has tried multiple location spells with a few of my mother's items, and none of them have worked. It's been long speculated that she doesn't want to be found, and I still can't wrap my mind around why.

Why would she abandon me and leave me far from my coven? Why would she never come back around?

Yet, I never act on my curiosity. This coven is everything to me. My loyalty stays with my family at all times. The coven is my family, not the woman who left me alone and helpless.

"We should keep that between us, then," Iris says with a nod.

I want to tell my best friend what's happened, and get her help, but I just can't. As much as I trust Iris, I feel as though only I can fix my gigantic man issue that's currently haunting my home.

"Gather around," my grand-mère says as everyone takes a seat.

The coven is about forty strong, but we network with other covens when necessary. Our family comes first, but we will outreach a hand to another coven. After all, we've all been blessed with the same gift from Hecate.

"Now, as many of you know, the Moon Walker Pack has taken on a new Alpha." Most of the witches seem disinterested, and my grandmother taps her wand against the podium. "Typically, I wouldn't be concerned either. That pack hasn't had solid leadership in decades. But this one is different. I need everyone on high alert. Especially the coming full moon."

She doesn't mention how he wanted peace, and neither do I.

"I fear under this new leadership they will do what they have always done. Taking things that do not belong to them. We must stay vigilant and not engage unless you find it is completely necessary. In the meantime, I'll be looking deeper into their new pack leader, Silas. I believe striking this down by the head will be our best option."

I swallow thickly, knowing she's right, but hating the way it makes me feel.

"Now, let us discuss this full moon's rituals and potions needed," she says, changing pace.

Iris stands up. "I have a few potions brewing that need to sit out in the full moon. I can barely keep the seduction potions on the shelf," Iris says and my grandmother gives her a wide smile.

Iris is not only extraordinarily talented with potions, creams, soaps, what have you, but she also makes a ridiculous amount of money for the coven.

"I'd like to ensure we have a few gallons of water sitting out for the gardens," Ember says from the corner where she sits with her mother.

I lean forward and wave, which she returns with a quick smile.

"Wonderful. We will also use the moon to unify our coven's strength. It's paramount that every witch, regardless of age, is present," my grand-mère says, with no window for discussion.

SARAH BLUE

Let's just hope I'm happily divorced by the full moon…

Chapter 13

SILAS

A door slamming jolts me awake, and I sit up straight on the too small couch. I rub a hand down my chest and frown.

When I pull back the sheet, I realize I'm completely naked. Definitely not the way I slept. Though, it's my preference. I know for a fact I did not go to sleep nude, not here.

"What did you do?" I question Thorin.

He doesn't answer, his voice in my mind completely silent. This fucking wolf is going to ruin my life.

I groan, my body aching from whatever Thorin did, or how I slept on this couch. When I blink away the grogginess, I'm greeted by Violet's pissy cat.

"Did your mistress leave?" I ask him, and he blinks his yellow eyes at me. I already know she's not here. If the slammed door didn't give it away, this aching feeling in my chest would.

I go to grab my phone off the table, but the cat is faster, batting it with his paw, making it clink to the wooden floor.

"Of course, her familiar would be a crotchety asshole of a cat," I mumble, picking up my phone.

I need to be on the compound in thirty minutes. Quickly, I grab the bag I brought and get dressed.

The cat jumps off the table and goes to sit on the stairs, watching my every move and almost ensuring I don't dare go exploring upstairs.

"Tell your mistress to work faster on getting us out of this mess. Then I'll be out of your matted fur," I tell the cat, and I shake my head.

Great, now I'm talking out loud to a cat. Isn't it bad enough I have a goddamn wolf I share a body with.

I grab my boot and slide my foot in. Groaning as my sock sloshes and pools with fluid.

"What the fuck?" I hiss, pulling out my foot. As soon as I sniff, the scent is undeniable.

Cat piss.

"Seriously?" I say, glancing up the stairs. Where this cat slowly blinks at me like he's done nothing wrong.

I curse as I grab my bag and my boots. I flip them upside down once I'm on the porch, watching the liquid drip out.

Violet better be working hard today to figure out how to get us out of this clusterfuck. My back can't handle that couch again, and I certainly don't want another moment with her sadistic cat.

I grimace as I slide on my piss-filled boots, and throw a leg over my bike. There's a sense of wrongness as I drive away from Violet's home, but I crush it down. I have important pack business to handle today.

Jonas clears his throat next to me as I toss my boots onto the worn porch of the Alpha cabin.

"What the fuck is that smell, and where have you been?"

"Cat piss and it's a long story," I reply, turning the shower on and undressing.

Jonas and I have been friends for a long time, shifting for the first time together, taking Mander's over together, and now running this pack. There's no need for modesty or lies between us. Though, part of me wants to keep some things to myself. Jonas doesn't need to know what a nightmare this all is if we're going to resolve it swiftly.

"Thorin riding your ass about Violet?" he asks.

"Something like that."

"I love that you're so talkative. It's probably your best quality." I give him a shitty look before pulling back the shower curtain and letting the warm water wash away the smell and tension from last night.

"The new lawyer has everything written up. As soon as you sign, we own it. Honestly, can't believe the witches fucked this up so bad. I guess they don't operate all the business there, but still."

I smile to myself as I wash my body.

Something tells me I'm not about to have a warm welcome tonight from my little wife.

I turn the faucet off and grab the towel, running it over my hair and beard before wrapping it around my waist and stepping out.

"Let's go show them who owns this town," I tell Jonas, who gives me a feral grin.

"Buy some new boots while we're out," he says, turning to let me get dressed.

The witches didn't want peace? Well, maybe this will change their minds.

The documents are long signed, no doubt the news spreading through town that it's no longer Wedington Properties who owns the main strip downtown. It's Walker Industries.

There are four witch-owned businesses on the small strip. Goddess Apothecary, Lavender and Lime, Cora's Bakery, and The Cauldron.

Perhaps the witches considered owning the building that houses another dozen businesses as a stupid move, or maybe their hatred runs so deep they only cared about buying out land so the pack couldn't get their piece.

For whatever reason, their ignorance is my gain. They're now my tenants and it seems like the price of rent just went up.

I'm trying to stay in my cabin. Desperately trying not to go to Violet's home, but despite all my efforts, I wind up packing a bag and hopping on the back of my bike in the dead of night.

The night air has a crispness that the daytime doesn't offer. I almost feel like I'm shifted and running freely. I sigh as excitement over the upcoming full moon fills me. So many years I've dreamed about what it would be like to run in a full pack. I've had Jonas all these years, and I'm grateful for him, but it isn't the same.

I've finally found my family and I'm not going to let anything destroy it. Especially not a band of self-righteous witches who think magic makes them superior beings.

I'm barely off my bike when the large front door of Violet's home swings open and she comes storming down the porch. Her wand is clutched in her hand, but she doesn't raise it.

"You bought downtown?" she says, raising her voice.

"Seems your High Priestess might not have as much foresight as she thought."

"Where did the money come from?" Violet questions, and I shrug. "You can't kick them out, they've all worked hard to own and run those stores," Violet says.

I take a few steps toward her, towering over her. She seems

THE MARRIAGE HEX

pissed, but tilts her chin so she can glare at me.

"It sounds oddly familiar. Do you know how many businesses your grandmother has torn out of the hands of shifters? Tell me Violet, are you happy to be a bystander to your grandmother's hatred, or are you just as evil?"

"You don't understand, you just got here. This is the way things have always been."

"Been, how? Witches on top and every other supernatural on the bottom next to humans?"

"No," she replies quickly and shakes her head.

"No? Then tell me why Moon Walker Pack has lost nearly one-hundred acres of pack land in the last thirty years. Tell me why our numbers are down, why every member fears your grandmother?"

She doesn't back down, and I'll give her credit for that.

"You heard her at that meeting. Moon Walker Pack killed coven members."

"You're so sure of that?"

She steels her spine and nods at me. "Grand-mère may be a lot of things, but she isn't a liar."

I sigh and bend down so we're at eye level. "I guess some things don't change."

"What is that supposed to mean?"

"That you're still that desperate little girl who would do anything for a family," I say, regretting the words as soon as they slip out.

She holds her wand to my throat, the cold metal pressing against my skin.

"What does that make you, Silas? Don't come here degrading me for my loyalties. Not when you're using this pack as some type of farce as a family. You've been looking for somewhere to belong just as bad as me."

She doesn't move her wand and in that moment, I see her grandmother's teachings, not the sweet girl I met in treehouses who never had a mean word to say about anyone.

"I suppose we both got what we wanted, then."

"You can't kick them out of their businesses," she repeats, threatening me with her magic, which I shouldn't like.

It's the first time Thorin wakes all day, his deep voice rumbling through my mind. *"She's so pretty when she's mad."*

I shake him off and grab Violet's wrist. "I'm not going to kick them out."

"You're not?" she asks, the pressure of her wand slipping.

"Your grandmother said I had no leverage for peace, but now I do."

"That's truly what you want? Peace?"

She lowers her wand to her side as I stare down at her, already mad that I told her I wouldn't kick the witches out of their businesses. She shouldn't be privy to that information or any of my plans.

"I wouldn't have had that meeting otherwise," I say simply.

She crosses her arms over her chest. Tonight she's wearing a pink nightgown. Did they have a sale on these things and she just bought one in every fucking color? Who still wears a goddamn nightgown, anyway?

The bugs are loud and the moon is waxing gibbous, a promise of what's coming in a few days.

"It will never happen," she says, shaking her head and walking back to the porch. She flicks her wand, instantaneously lighting all the carved pumpkins onto her porch.

I have to hold back my surprise at how effortless that was for her.

"Let me ask you this, has anyone from the Moon Walker Pack ever done anything to you personally?" I ask her and she pauses, leaning against the pillar of her home. I crowd her space, my hand well above the top of her head. "Well?"

"Besides unkind words spoken, no," she whispers and crosses her arms. "It doesn't matter, though."

"Why?"

"I know you want that pack to be your family so bad, Silas. But being in a coven? Those women? They mean everything to me and I'd rather die than betray them in any way. Just having you here is a betrayal, sharing coven secrets, talking about my grand-mère? It's been generations of hatred between the Celestial Coven and the Moon Walker Pack."

"Isn't it odd that no one knows the origin?" I ask, tilting my head at her.

"History gets lost, especially when we're all hiding what we are from the real world."

"Or could it be something else? Magical manipulation?"

Her grip on her wand tightens as she glares up at me. "What are you insinuating?"

"Could be nothing. Could be everything," I say, not wanting to show all my cards.

I'm not sure why I want Violet to see reason. It's clear her grandmother has indoctrinated her to some extent. But what if she could see reason? What if everything was different? I groan at myself, knowing it's a stupid idea, it will never happen.

"You ride into town, claim that pack, and you know everything, don't you? Well, you don't know shit about my family or me. It's been a long fourteen years, Silas."

"Very long. It doesn't look like the years were hard on you," I say, pointing around at her house.

SARAH BLUE

"You don't know me."

"Clearly not," I agree, which frustrates her more as she turns and walks through her front door.

Even though this is the last place I want to be, something beyond my control has my feet moving behind her. I do my best not to look at her ass swishing in her nightgown.

If you were to ask me if I glanced, I'd tell you that Thorin made me do it.

When I enter the threshold, her cat is sitting on the stairs, glaring at me.

"Your cat pissed in my shoe," I tell her.

She walks up the stairs, scooping the cat up and kisses his old gray head. "Walter has a great judge of character," she says.

"Any progress on the spell?" I shout as she stomps up the stairs.

"Go fuck yourself," she yells as the front door slams shut, and I'm quickly covered in darkness.

I put the sheets on in the dark and wonder if maybe I can get Violet on my side after all. I mean, the marriage needs to be forfeit, along with the complications of this spell. But she is next in line to be High Priestess. Maybe there's hope after all.

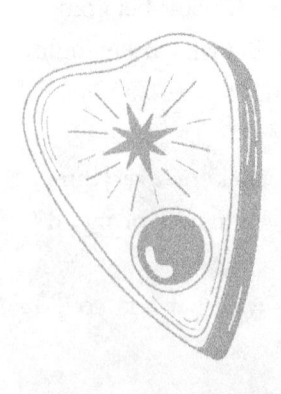

Chapter 14

VIOLET

I haven't spoken to Silas in four days. I just leave my door unlocked, and he comes and sleeps on my couch, giving the hex what it wants as I figure this out.

I'm no closer to anything than I was that day at the courthouse, and I'm not sure what to do next. He can't keep coming over. It's only a matter of time before one of us gets found out, or worse.

There have been no wolf surprises either, just complete indifference between me and my dear husband.

Mason jars are filled with water, Iris' potions are lined up on a table, and there's a clear circle outlined with flickering candles.

My grand-mère approaches me, her hands framing the sides of my face.

"Violet, dear, is something troubling you?"

"No, grand-mère."

"You could tell me anything. You're the most treasured thing in my life. Is this about turning thirty?"

I swallow and nod, worrying that if I say anything, she'll somehow guess what's going wrong in my life. AKA the massive man she hates with a fiery passion being my husband who I left sleeping on my couch again this morning.

"Thirty is young for a witch. Tell me how you feel when you're eighty," she says with a smile. Her fingers stroke my cheekbones lovingly. "I know I've been hard on you lately, but it's because I love you, because you are the successor of this coven. One day I won't be here, but I'll rest in the wind knowing my granddaughter is carrying the legacy of this coven. Just like my mother did before me," she says.

"I won't let you down."

"I know you won't. You're everything I dreamed of." She kisses my head as we enter the circle, every witch of every age holding hands as we begin tonight's rituals.

Iris is on one side of me, her grandmother and mother next to her. My grandmother is on my right, connecting the rest of the coven.

Silas' words ring through my ears, but with the power of all the witches together, they slowly fade away.

This coven is my place, it's my peace. This is my legacy, and I have to uphold everything my grandmother has built. It's my duty.

The magic flowing through me feels cosmic and binding in a way I've never felt before. It's almost like the universe knows I need to be grounded. I need to be centered with my coven. These women are the only family I need, and despite Silas' pleas for us to get along, there's one cold, hard truth.

I'll always choose my coven, and he'll always choose his pack.

Tonight, I'll convince Silas of the one thing I had hoped to avoid. Tonight, we call on the spirits to help us end this farce of a marriage.

There's howling in the distance as we chant, everyone attempting to ignore the noise. It's too loud and frequent to be the werewolves. It has to be Silas' pack.

THE MARRIAGE HEX

Yet, I keep my eyes closed, following the chants and letting the Mother Goddess flow through me. Everything slowly disappears. It's just me and my coven, as it was meant to me.

Feeling rejuvenated after the ritual, I help Ember place lids on the mason jars.

"The Chervil will be ready to harvest soon. So will the Comfrey. I'll bring them over to your place when they're ready."

"Thanks, Ember."

"Things have been slow on your end?" she asks and I nod.

"Nothing major. Sage isn't due for quite a while, so I mostly monitor her. Nothing's required a healer as of late."

"You know, I wouldn't judge you if you wanted to help the mortals too," she whispers, for good reason.

While we might play nice with the humans, sell them goods, and have a friendly outward relationship, our gifts are reserved for coven and coven only.

Helping the mortals in the past has only gotten witches burned at the stake.

"I'll find other ways to help the coven," I say.

Ember shakes her head, her red hair and freckles shining against the candlelight. "I didn't mean it like that. I just worry about you is all. You've been kind of absent since your birthday, I just wanted to make sure everything was alright."

"Yeah, Ember. Everything is going to be fine."

It's late.

Extraordinarily late. But I can think of no better time to connect with the spirits of the afterlife than on a full moon.

I rock back and forth on the white, worn rocker on the back porch, staring at the swampy lake behind me.

Walter slides through his cat door and momentarily gets distracted by a lightning bug before coming to sit on my lap for pets. It seems like he's in a loving mood this late at night.

"*It's so nice not having that stinky man in our home,*" he says, a purr rumbling through his body as I stroke his fur. His body stills the moment we hear a motorcycle in the distance. "*I spoke too soon. Here I thought we were going to have a lovely night together.*"

"Not much longer, Walter."

"*I've only prayed to Hecate every night that he chokes, crashes his motorcycle, or gets shot by a hunter.*"

"That's dark, even for you."

"*A cat can dream.*"

I don't get up to unlock the door, if he's smart enough, he'll come around back. Which he does. His satchel is on his back as he rounds the wrap around porch.

Walter hisses, before jumping off my lap and going back inside.

"You're up late," he says.

"Here," I say, holding out a drink for him.

He eyes me suspiciously, but takes it and sits on the rocking chair next to mine.

"Did you put something in this?"

"No, and trust me, it would make my life a hell of a lot easier if I could just kill you."

He arches an eyebrow, but brings the glass to his lips, taking a heavy sip and sighing.

"What was that?" he says, pointing at the dilapidated structure by the lake.

"A gazebo, I think. Not sure what happened to it."

Four days we haven't spoken and now he's asking me about my backyard.

"I have an idea," I tell him, and he rests his head against the

THE MARRIAGE HEX

chair. He's clearly exhausted after running around with his fellow wolves all night, but I feel it deep inside of me. This needs to happen tonight.

"Can this wait till tomorrow?" he asks, slowly rocking in the chair next to me, his eyes tired, and I wonder when the last time he slept properly was. I may or may not have spelled the couch to be firmer each night.

"It's said during the full moon the veil lifts ever so slightly, letting the spirits engage with their loved ones," I say cryptically, looking at the way the porch lights glow against his sun-kissed skin.

"Okay?" he sighs. I can tell he doesn't want to be here. I don't want him here either.

"I'm thinking the spirits can help figure out our little problem."

"And what fucking spirits are going to help us?" he asks.

"We're not humans. We have generations of witches and shifters in our lineage. Do you truly think we walk this world alone?"

Silas takes a few moments to process my words before sighing and resting his head against the rocking chair, exhaustion clear in the way he slowly shuts his eyes before glaring at me.

"What does communicating with the spiritual realm entail?"

"You're not going to like it," I tell him, standing from my rocking chair and heading to the dining room.

I've already had candles burning on the table and the ouija board set in the center. As soon as Silas walks in, he stops in his tracks.

"Oh, hell no."

"Wait. They have bad press. Humans who don't know what they're doing, inviting the wrong spirits into the world. It isn't like that."

"You can promise me?" he asks and I have to refrain myself

SARAH BLUE

from smirking.

The big bad wolf is scared of my little board.

"I promise. I only need a drop of blood."

He swallows, but holds out his hand. It's large and calloused as I tap his fingertip with my wand, getting a single drop and placing it on the crystal in the center before doing the same to my finger.

"Sit," I tell him, and he actually listens. "We're specifically going to call on our ancestors for help. See if any of them have any guidance on how to break this hex."

I hold out my hand and he glances at it like I have a disease before placing his palm in mine. He squeezes my hand when the flames rise to a higher level around us and I take a deep breath channeling all that was given to me tonight.

I'm not a medium. I don't have the gift of seeing the other side. But I do have magic. I have ancestors on the other side of the veil who are looking after the coven.

I flip the planchette on the side where it says hello, placing it on the middle of the board.

"As friends we gather, hearts are true, familial spirits near, we call to you," I say, and squeeze Silas' hand, arching a brow at him to join me in the chant. He sighs heavily, his gaze searching my home, but reluctantly joins the chant.

We say it six more times before I ask my first question.

"Are there any familial spirits with us?" I ask, moving both of our hands on the planchette as it slides quickly over to the word, yes.

Silas goes to pull away and I hold his hand there.

"Can you help us fix this hex?" I ask.

It quickly slides over to no, and both Silas and I sigh in frustration.

"Can I ask who we're talking to?"

The planchette moves swiftly over the letters. C-O-L-L-I-N-S.

I furrow my brow and glance over at Silas. "Collins?" I ask, and

THE MARRIAGE HEX

Silas frowns before something clicks.

"I didn't think they were in my ancestral line, but my mother was less than helpful when I found her," he says.

"Are you here to help?" I ask.

The planchette zooms over to yes. Silas' concerned brown eyes meet mine. I can tell he's uncomfortable and I'm trying to figure out what to ask.

"What do we need to do?" Silas asks and I roll my eyes.

"You have to ask the spirit simple—"

Before I can finish chastising him, the planchette zooms over the letters again. T-R-U-T-H.

My heart is beating in my chest, and the air around me feels heavy. I was already tired from the long night, but exhaustion is ripping through me like a torrent.

The flames are rising around us, and Silas lets go of the planchette and grabs my wrist.

"That's enough," he says and I shake my head.

I let myself feel the spirit around me. They're sad, lonely in a way. But I just know they're trying to tell me something, something I can't understand.

"Can you show me?" I ask, my hand the only one on the planchette as it shoots over to the word yes.

A quick wind picks up inside of my home and Silas grips the worn wooden table as I hold steady.

"End it, Violet," Silas growls, but I shake my head.

The scent of sulfur is rising in the air as the wind picks up, blowing my hair, and causing an open tarot deck to fly into the breeze. The table begins to shake and a blanket of sadness covers me.

I let go of the planchette and grip the table as the unnatural breeze whips around my kitchen, blowing out all the candles before there is a loud bang and everything immediately stops.

The candles flick back to life and everything stills, like nothing just happened.

SARAH BLUE

With shaky hands, I grab the planchette and flip it over to the goodbye side.

"Goodbye, thank you," I mumble as I look up to a shocked Silas.

"Your nose is bleeding," he tells me, and I bring my wrist up and wipe away the slightest amount of blood. "What was that noise?"

"Let's go check," I say in a whisper.

"Are you good to get up?" he questions and I wave him off as we walk down the hall.

A door is wide open, and I gasp.

"They want us to go into that room?" Silas asks, not understanding my shock.

I glance up at him. "I haven't been able to open that door physically or magically since I moved in."

We both stand at the door frame.

It's a nursery, covered in purple, that looks like it's been preserved in time for the past thirty years.

Chapter 15

SILAS

"Fuck this spooky ass shit. It's too late for this," I say, going to back up and Violet fists my shirt.

"It was your ancestor who brought us here. Stop being a chicken."

"Seriously? You're going to call me a chicken to get what you want?"

"Yes, I undoubtedly am."

"I don't like this," I tell her as I lean my head into the abandoned room.

It was clearly meant for a baby. The white railed crib is full of light purple blankets and different stuffed animals. The mobile above the crib is the lunar cycle of the moon. There's a rocking chair that's similar to the ones we were just sitting on the back porch.

The last thing that catches my eye is a white chest, dead center in the middle of the room.

Violet makes the first step in the room, not sharing her thoughts, but I swear her light blue eyes are watery with tears.

She gets down on to her knees and tugs at the chest, to no avail. She pulls her wand out, placing the tip at the lock and saying words under her breath, and the lock goes flying open.

Fuck it. Tonight can't get any weirder, so I come and sit beside her. Her hands shake as she touches the lid to the chest.

"Do you want me to do it?" I ask and she nods as I push the lid back.

I expected it to be full of stuff, but there's only one thing inside, a legal sized manilla envelope.

Violet's hands are trembling as she reaches in, and swirls the thread to open it, delicately emptying its contents onto the floor.

There's a ripped picture, the half she still has is of a pregnant woman, white blonde hair, cradling her stomach. Violet rubs her thumb over the portrait and grabs the next one.

They're all ripped in half, but all of her mother being pregnant with her.

"She looked happy," Violet whispers.

"She does," I agree.

Violet gasps as she sees a postcard with a picture of the French Quarter that says Welcome to New Orleans on the back.

"Holy shit," she whispers, her eyes scanning the letter over and over.

Her tears threaten to drip on to the page and she wipes them away. "Is there a necklace in there?" she asks and I double check the envelope.

"No," I reply with a shake of my head, and Violet looks up to the ceiling before handing me the postcard.

THE MARRIAGE HEX

My Dearest Violet,

I dream of you every night. I knew the moment the healer told me I was pregnant that your name would be Violet. You're our world and as excited as I am to hold you in my arms, I fear I'll never get the chance.

I hope you're reading this letter next to me on the gazebo on the back of the property. But if what I fear has come true, there's a chance I failed you.

Know that I love you.
Know that magic always binds us.
The moon necklace will always protect you.
I love you to the moon and back.
Mom

I furrow my brows, not knowing what to do. There's a deep part of me that wants to console Violet, my mate. There's another part of me that wants to leave this uncomfortable emotional situation.

Violet flattens all the photos next to each other, along with the postcard.

"They were all taken in the French Quarter," she says, pointing to every single photo.

"Listen, Violet. I'm glad you found something out about your mother. But I don't see how this helps with our situation."

She glares at me before looking back down at the photos.

"That door has been locked, unable to be entered by even the High Priestess. A spirit opened the door and led us to this chest. Are you really that much of an idiot to not realize this means something?" she says, her eyes heavy with exhaustion.

"Let's just sleep and think more about this tomorrow."

"I'm driving to New Orleans tomorrow," she says plainly.

SARAH BLUE

"And what? Walk around one of the busiest places in the country with a thirty-year-old photo?"

She stands, grabbing all the pieces of paper and goes to leave the room as the door slams shut, locking us in.

I groan as Violet tries to tug on the handle. When that doesn't work, she takes out her wand, casting a few spells that even involve sparks.

"You've got to be fucking kidding me," I groan.

I spent hours running as a pack, and now this. Can't a man just get a good night's sleep?

"It's probably because your dumb ass angered the spirit," she says, opening the closet and pulling out all the bedding that's there. I expect it to smell like mothballs and dust, but shockingly, it smells like fresh laundry as she lays everything on the floor for herself.

Following her lead, I grab more bedding from the closet. The room isn't overly large and therefore I have to make my makeshift bed right next to her.

"It will let us out eventually, right?" I ask and Violet curses, casting some spells to make her bed more comfortable. I almost swallow my pride to ask her to do the same for me, but I can't make myself do it.

"I don't know, Silas. You just called the spirit a worthless liar. So maybe we'll just die in here," she says in a shitty tone.

I groan and curse as my back retaliates against the stiff floor.

"Oh benevolent spirit, I didn't mean to disrespect you, it's just been a long night. I'll do whatever you say if you just let me sleep on a bed."

Violet snorts next to me, and damn, she looks comfortable on the bed she's transfigured.

The spirit doesn't open the door and I realize we're going to have to sleep in here.

THE MARRIAGE HEX

"Can you make my sheets like yours?" Feeling like an asshole for asking.

"Will you shut up and listen to me if I do?" Violet asks.

"Fine," I agree.

I think I'd do just about anything for a good night's rest. She arches a brow at me, but takes out her wand, extending her bed of blankets and combining them with mine. The instant relief on my back has me moaning as I shift my weight.

"Thank you," I tell her, even if it hurts me to admit it.

We both lie there, so close, yet so far apart. Even if I'm comfortable, sleep is not going to come easy.

"Did you enjoy the full moon?" she asks in a soft voice.

I smile for the first time since I shifted back tonight. "It's the best full moon I've ever had."

"Is your wolf tired?"

"Yes, why?"

"You could shift to him to sleep if that would be easier. If this is too much."

I tilt my head at her and groan. "He showed himself to you?"

She shrugs, her stark white hair framing her face, while the black parts are splayed against the pillow she made.

"When?"

"The first night, I haven't seen him since. He's quite pleasant though."

I groan and check in with Thorin, who is promptly ignoring the fuck out of me.

"He shouldn't have done that."

"He didn't seem to want to hurt me."

"That's not what I was worried about," I admit.

"Right," Violet says quickly, like the idea of me caring about her safety is ridiculous. Which it is.

SARAH BLUE

"Thorin has a way of doing whatever he wants, not giving a shit about consequences."

"Thorin," she whispers his name, which has the over indulgent wolf perking up in my mind instantly.

"Let me take over. She says my name like a caress," Thorin rumbles sleepily.

There's no fucking way I'm admitting the whole truth to Violet. It doesn't matter that she's my mate. I'm not hers, she's not a wolf. It won't hurt her endlessly when this is over, just me and Thorin.

But it's a pain I'm willing to bear. It's not like I haven't been hurting for the last fourteen years.

"Are all wolf shifters that large?"

"No," I respond.

"Do you hear that? She knows I'm the largest, most capable wolf. Let me shift. Let me comfort our mate. She looks so sad."

I take a deep breath, grappling with my hold on this form. Instead, I switch the direction of the conversation.

"Why do you think finding your mother, or what happened to her, will help with our situation?"

She licks her full lips, clutching the blanket near her chin.

"That night… my birthday. My magic came to me, my grand-mére said whatever spell my mother had cast upon me lifted and that's why she could find me. What if that magic is what caused this in the first place. What if it wasn't my spell, but my mother's?"

"It could have been Mander," I say before even thinking.

"What?"

"Mander had us all on suppressants. Jonas and I didn't know we were shifters until we were eighteen. Do you remember all the medication they had us take at night?"

Her brows furrow, and she shakes her head.

"But then why didn't my grand-mére find me before I got to

Mander's?"

"Maybe it was your mother. I'm just speaking from experience."

"Did you leave at eighteen?" she whispers.

It was always our plan. As soon as we were adults, we would get the fuck out of there and start a life somewhere, even if it was hard, even if we didn't truly understand the outside world.

"No."

"When?"

"Jonas and I left when we were twenty. Took everything Mander had. Destroyed the school and never looked back." I don't mention how Thorin ripped his throat out, or all the horrors we found in the basement.

Her brows furrow. "Four years," she whispers.

"Things got worse when you left. I'm not sure why, but Mander lost it. Thorin got us out of that situation. A pack was all we ever wanted and now we have it."

"Liar," Thorin growls.

"I wanted to say goodbye. I wanted to write to you," Violet admits, her eyes heavy with the need to sleep.

The moon is still shining through the window; the glint shimmering off her cheekbones and I can tell she's being honest.

"But your grand-mére forbid it?"

She looks away, her guilt palpable. The High Priestess didn't forbid it. Violet just made her own conclusion that I needed to be in her past.

"It doesn't matter," I say, wanting to sleep and for this endless night to finally be over.

"Silas," she sighs my name and I shake my head.

"We'll listen to your spirit. I'll go with you to New Orleans. I just need to let Jonas know I'll be gone."

"Thank you," she whispers.

SARAH BLUE

A sensation of calmness takes over me as I fall asleep.

My back doesn't ache in the morning, and the door to the room is wide open. The cat is sitting in the room's entrance making direct eye contact with me as he crunches down on a spider.

I guess I'm headed on a small little road trip less I anger the spirits of my ancestors any further.

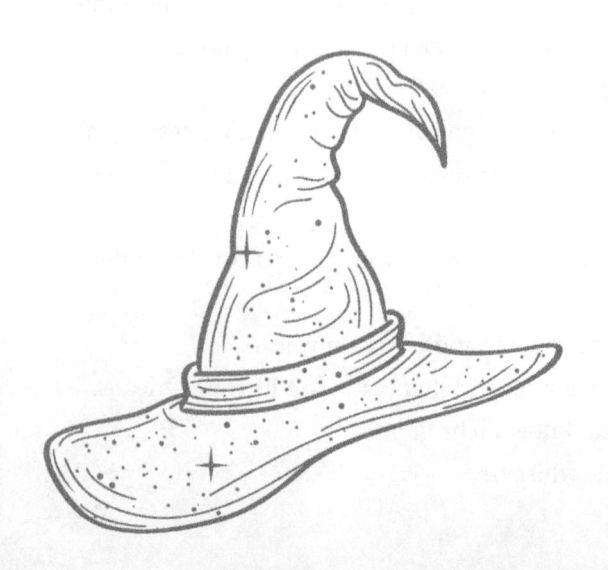

Chapter 16

VIOLET

I stop at Goddess Apothecary before leaving for New Orleans. Someone in the coven needs to know my whereabouts, and there's no one I trust more than Iris.

The bell chimes with my arrival.

"We open in a half hour," she says from the back.

"It's me," I reply, going to the back where she's brewing the potions she had out in the full moon the night before.

"You're up early," she says and I swallow thickly.

"I just wanted to stop by and let you know that I'm going to New Orleans for a few days to help the Salvador Coven."

Her brows pinch and she pauses mid stir of her potion, putting the lid on and wiping her hands on her apron.

"They have two healers," she says and I try to keep my wits about me.

"They've been having issues with vampires and need help on a few cases."

"You're lying," she says, calling me out immediately. "You're not one to keep secrets, Vi."

I look over my shoulder and flick the door shut.

"If I tell you, you need to take a vow of silence," I tell her and her eyes widen.

"Violet, what the fuck is going on? You're scaring me."

"Vow of silence or nothing, Iris."

"Fine," she says, pulling out her wand. Hers is golden, with vines wrapping around, while mine is silver with intricate silver violets and an amethyst at the base.

We hold the tips of our wands together, a golden spark and a purple spark meeting as Iris says the words.

"I vow silence to my fellow coven member and hold her secret with me till death and time separate us," she says and I sigh.

She won't die if she keeps my secret, but the vow will literally demand her silence. My secret is completely safe.

"Now, please tell me what is so important to require a vow of silence. I've never even contemplated that type of magic before."

I take a deep breath and tell her everything. The pact at sixteen, the courthouse, how he's been sleeping at my house, up until last night's encounter. I don't mention his wolf or anything personal, and wonder why I feel like I need to keep that to myself.

She falls back into her chair, her eyes wide as she looks me up and down.

"Holy shit."

"Now you understand the secrecy?"

"You really think your mother is in New Orleans and can help you?" she says, her amber-colored eyes looking at me with pity.

She knows if I don't find her, it will just be another disappointment.

"I have to at least try."

Iris nods, standing up and grabbing my wrists before placing her forehead against mine.

"I give you my protection, and my love. Mother goddess above, keep Violet safe. Protect her against those who wish her harm. Give her guidance and keep her safe," she whispers, and I wrap my arms around her and squeeze her tight.

"I love you, Iris."

"I love you too, Violet. Promise me you'll check in. That you'll be safe and that you'll watch your back," she says and I pull back.

"Your vision," I say with a gasp and Iris' shoulders slump. She looks away and I glare at her. "Iris. Did you see something else?"

"No, I didn't see anything. Just be careful, you promise?"

"I promise."

"Let me send you with a few potions, just in case," she says, handing me all things that could take a man or a wolf out.

I don't tell her that they aren't necessary, but thank her and drive back to my home where Silas waits on the porch.

"I need to hide your bike," I tell him as I get out of the car.

"It won't hurt it, will it?" he asks, and I roll my eyes at him.

"No, a little illusion spell isn't going to hurt your baby," I reply, casting the spell as we watch the motorcycle disappear. "It's still there. It just doesn't look like it is. A little extra incentive to make sure I'm safe, because I'm the only one who can lift the spell," I tell him.

"Give me the keys, I'll drive," he says.

I toss them over to him and grab a few books before taking the passenger side and read while he drives.

It's only a few hours, but each moment in the car feels heavy with words unsaid. We're not talking about the past, and we're apparently not talking about the future either as we finally make it downtown.

Silas parallel parks and for a moment, I'm glad I brought him along. Plus, I'd probably be in physical pain if I left him behind, anyway.

"Any clue where we should start?" Silas asks as we walk down the street. I have her photos in my hand.

"I thought once we were down here I'd have more direction," I tell him.

He doesn't chastise me or tell me I'm stupid, thank Hecate, he just nods his head.

"Should we look for the places in the background?"

So, that's what we do. We spend the day doing an endless amount of walking with nothing to show for it. We've gone through a third of the photos and we're walking down Bourbon Street as the night picks up. It's not carnival season, so it's not as packed, but with Halloween around the corner, it's bumping.

Silas stills a few times while we're walking. Clearly there's a shifter presence here, but none of them approach him. I wonder if they can sense that he's an Alpha, or if they can sense what I am.

"Should we get a drink?" I ask him, pointing over to one of the more empty bars that's trying to entice women to come inside.

"Yeah," he says, everything about him is alert.

It shouldn't be attractive. Because it's not. He's just a big man, I'm only a woman after all, it's not a crime to notice that he's big. Or that his veins are bulging out of his arms, or that he could probably kill someone with his bare hands.

Not hot, just natural. I shake the thought away.

"If you want to go home, you can," I tell him as we each take a stool and Silas holds his hand up to the bartender.

"What do you drink?" he asks.

"Oh, I'll have a hurricane," I say and his lip tilts as he shakes his head.

"I'll have a brandy."

The bartender hands us our drinks as the jazz band plays their music, the bar slowly filling with more people. It's weird, but I find

THE MARRIAGE HEX

myself relaxing more. Maybe it's the alcohol or maybe it's the fact the hex likes the fact that Silas and I are drinking together.

"Two more days. If we don't find anything in two days, we'll leave."

"What did you tell your pack?" I ask, taking a sip of the beverage that's cool against my tongue.

I don't drink often, and I find the cocktail has me feeling loose for the first time in weeks. Shit, I should have gotten a potion from Iris. I'll just make sure to not drink too much.

"Nothing. I'm the Alpha. They don't need to concern themselves with what I'm doing."

I toy with the umbrella in my drink, finding those words attractive. What it must be like to not give a shit what anyone thinks.

"Does Jonas know about us?" I ask.

"Partially," he says, and my brows furrow.

"I'm glad you had him," I say, covering my mouth as soon as I say it.

"Did you just say something nice to me?" he asks with a smirk.

The black shirt he's wearing stretches over his arms so tightly I wonder what size he has to order. Do they have a store for men specifically built like him? Probably not, because I don't think I've really seen anyone else so tall and muscular before.

"Who me? No way," I say with a smile, spinning in my seat. "Can I get another?" I ask, waving down the bartender.

She acknowledges me, and I sit back down on the stool. I feel light for the first time since this ordeal happened, but it's quickly washed away as a hand touches my shoulder.

When I spin around, it's a large man—not as large as Silas. He has short hair, and an irritated scowl on his face. Silas' gaze automatically flings to where the man is touching me.

"I suggest you move your fucking hand," Silas says in a low tim-

SARAH BLUE

bre.

"Why the fuck is an Alpha from another parish here, with a witch? A very pretty witch," he says with a grin.

I shrug and the man only doubles down, gripping me harder. Silas stands, grabbing the man's wrist and squeezing.

"It's New Orleans. I think you're quite used to others passing through," he says, shoving the man's hand off me.

"Not an Alpha and a future High Priestess."

I stand up, feeling incomparably small next to the two men.

"Wait. You know who we are?" I ask. Silas scoots closer to me, his chest nearly pressed against my back.

I hate it. Kinda.

"Word travels fast. Heard about your little meeting all the way here in the big city," the man says with a smile that just looks wolfish.

I pull out one of the photos, even though Silas tries to shove my hand back into my purse.

"Have you seen her?" I ask.

He holds the picture and tilts his head. "She works at the jewelry store on St. Philip street."

"You're sure?" I ask.

"Why are you looking for a human?" he asks, and my heart sinks.

"None of your concern. Once we get what we need, we'll be on the road back to our parish."

"Back to your parish and head your separate ways, I presume?" he asks looking down at me, I'm sure I looked confused. "Bold choice, not marking her with your scent here," he says to Silas who's still behind me.

"We're just passing by. I want nothing to do with your pack," Silas says behind me.

THE MARRIAGE HEX

"No? Not good enough for Pack Corsair? Are we beneath you, Alpha?" he says, and I can tell he's goading Silas, it's the first time I've seen anyone get under his skin in this way, and maybe I'm enjoying it more than I should.

"We'll be going now," Silas says.

"No, wait a minute. The little witch, who smells only of magic, came all this way to the Big Easy. Wouldn't be hospitable of me to let her leave without a reminder of what being around a real Alpha is like. Would the little lady like to dance?" the unfamiliar wolf says.

"No, she would not like to dance. Fuck off," Silas says and I crane my neck to glare at him.

"The little lady can speak for herself. I'd love to," I tell him.

I don't want to dance with him, I just want to piss Silas off as the shifter holds out his hand and I follow him to the dance floor.

My grand-mére would probably go into cardiac arrest if she knew what I was up to right now. Not only am I married to the shifter glaring at me from the bar, but I'm now dancing against some random shifter to piss my said husband off.

"I didn't know witches could be so amenable," the shifter purrs behind me.

I roll my eyes and glance over at Silas whose eyes seem to be almost glowing.

"Seems like your big friend over there is jealous."

"He's not jealous," I assure him. "We hate each other."

"Oh, cher, that doesn't look like hate," he says, his hands sliding down my hips and his warm breath hits the shell of my ear to whisper. "That looks like—"

He doesn't finish his sentence as Silas grabs the man by the throat and pushes him against the wall.

"Oh, my fuck. Stop it, you're going to get in trouble," I plead with Silas, tugging on his shirt.

"Do you want to take this out to the bayou? Should I take over your pack too?" Silas seethes at the man's face and I sigh.

"Just drop it. We got what we wanted," I tell him. Silas doesn't even pay me a single mind as he leans over and whispers something to the other shifter. The man's eyes go wide as he glances at me.

"My mistake. See to it that you're out of town by the end of the week and we won't have any problems," he says.

Silas lets the man go and grabs me by the wrist, tugging me out of the bar.

"Ow. Slow down," I complain, though he doesn't. I nearly have to jog to keep up with him.

As soon as we're out of the bar and making our way down the street, he drops my arm like it disgusts him.

"What is your problem? He gave us our real first lead."

"He was goading me," Silas says, his shoulders tense and he seems even more on edge than earlier. "Fuck," he says in a raised voice.

"What?"

"We need to go somewhere private. Now."

"Why?" I ask, wondering how the normally composed Alpha before me seems to be losing his shit.

"Thorin is demanding to be let loose. I clearly can't do that here."

"Aren't you the one in control?"

"Violet," he says my name in an irritated tone, his eyes glowing again as he looks down at me. "Please, for once, stop questioning me."

I point across the street at the closest hotel. "We can see if they have any vacancy."

THE MARRIAGE HEX

"Quickly," he rumbles.

The inside is nice, though the street noise is insanely loud. A complete juxtaposition from the silence of my home.

Silas is nearly vibrating next to me as I smile at the hostess. She looks at Silas like he might be on something, but she's respectful enough.

"Hello, I was hoping you had two rooms for the night."

"We have one," she says and I groan.

But as I look over at Silas, I know we're running out of time. He pulls out his wallet and slaps his card in my hand.

Well, that's not attractive at all.

"We'll take it," I tell her with a smile as she books us for the night and hands me the keys. I swear Silas looks like he wants to rip her throat out when she goes over the Wi-Fi and breakfast options and busts out a map of New Orleans, giving us that true Louisiana hospitality.

"Have a lovely stay," she says.

I have to jog, yet again, to keep up with Silas. I glide the key over the door handle and it whirls. I step inside, loving the history of the room. They've preserved a lot of the fireplaces and brick walls, the same with the iron banisters out the window.

There's nothing to be done about the noise outside, but it's a place to rest our head for the night.

When I turn around, Silas is tugging at his shirt over his head, basically showing off his big man chest. Right before my eyes, I watch him shift. His clothes rip loudly as his skin ripples into fur, and the large brown wolf I now know as Thorin takes his place.

SARAH BLUE

Chapter 17

THORIN

That motherfucker dared to touch my mate.

In front of me.

I've shoved the man so deep into our consciousness he's nearly scratching my mental walls trying to be present.

I want to leave this hotel, barrel down the streets of New Orleans, and rip his greedy little throat out. Then I want to shift back and force the man to claim our mate so that no one will ever dare to touch what's ours again.

Foolish fucking deluded Silas.

Has he not seen our mate? Of course, she'll attract any hot-blooded male who approaches her. We might be tethered together by her magic, and by the circuit courts. But it's not enough, it will never be enough.

We need our mark on her, our claim on her.

A deep festering part of me considers doing it right now. Sinking my teeth into her delicate throat. But I won't.

A forced claim isn't one worth having, and unfortunately, it can't be me.

It has to be the stupid fucking man who is ruining everything.

Violet holds her arms, palms facing out towards me, like she's trying to calm me.

"Um… hello, Thorin," she says.

My name on her lips is like the sweetest delicacy I've ever had. Better than any sweet praline I've ever tasted.

"Listen. I know that guy made you mad, and maybe I had something to do with that. But I'm really sorry. You don't have to do anything. We can just stay in here and sleep. I do need to get our bags though," she says, trying to pass me to get to the door.

I press my face against her chest, pushing her back, and her body goes rigid, but she obeys.

When I inhale and scent that other Alpha's scent on her, I can't hold back the growl that rips out of me.

I nip at the bottom of her dress and she yelps.

"You don't like the smell?" she asks and I nod my head. "Okay, well, I've got to go get my bag from the car and I can change."

Another growl rumbles out of me. We're parked blocks away and this city bumps with more than just supernaturals at night.

"What would you have me do? I'm certainly not about to hang out with you naked," she says, crossing her arms over her chest.

A shame really.

I think her naked near me would calm me instead of wanting to run into that pack's den and rip out their Alpha's throat.

Instead, I grip the man's shirt in my jowls and nudge it into her chest.

"You've got to be fucking kidding me," she says, grabbing the balled up shirt.

I nudge her toward the bathroom, and she slams the door harder than necessary while I pace outside the door.

She's my mate. Everyone will know this as soon as she and the man see reason. I do not care that she is *different*.

THE MARRIAGE HEX

My mate is perfect as she is. Even if she can never manifest into a wolf and give me what I also need. I shall treasure whatever she gives me.

The idea of never running in the forest with my mate, or sleeping under the stars, is a depressing one. But I'd rather have the company of my mate, her small fingers running through my fur, her scent surrounding me like a caress, than to not have her at all.

The universe has made her ours for a reason. I'll take whatever little she gives me. If my purpose in her life is to just surround her in her sleep so that she's safe, it would be my honor.

She's mine to protect, mine to care for, mine to adore. No matter if she doesn't have a wolf to love me in the same way.

She comes out of the bathroom, her odd dual-colored hair in a bun. The man's shirt nearly looks like a dress on her, but as I inhale, some of the anger and need for violence subsides.

My mate smells like *us*, and it calms me to my core.

I direct her to go to the bed.

"You're bossier than Silas," she says, getting under the covers as I jump on the bed and circle a few times before resting my head on her legs. "I'm sorry about tonight. I won't do it again," she says, running her claw-like nails over my fur.

Yes, even this small affection is worth everything.

SARAH BLUE

Chapter 18

VIOLET

I wake up with a jolt from a horn blasting early in the morning. I blink open my eyes, forgetting where I am for a moment as I glance down and my eyes widen.

At some point in the night, Thorin shifted back to Silas. So now there's a very naked man lying face down with his arms wrapped around my legs. His lips are parted as he sleeps away, but his muscular ass is far too hard not to notice, and I can't help myself when I stare.

Who knew a man could have such a nice butt? One that leads to large legs and a very broad back. Silas doesn't have any tattoos that I can see, only a branding on his left shoulder and a few healed scars. They're all so faintly pink that you can barely see them.

I wonder what healing is like in the shifter world? Is it sped up?

In order to not stare at what seems to be the best looking ass in male creation, I focus in on a scar on his shoulder, dragging my fingertip across his flesh.

He inhales quickly, a surefire sign that he's about to wake up. Instead of making this more awkward than it is, I lie back down, feigning sleep.

I do my best not to tighten my eyes too tightly and give myself away, which is hard, because he's grumbling to himself.

"You stupid fuck. Now I don't have any clothes. What were you even thinking?"

It takes me a moment to realize he's not talking to me. He's talking to Thorin…interesting.

"She's nothing, Thorin, I've had enough," he says, swinging open the bathroom door and turning on the shower.

Well, that was certainly something. I glance at the bathroom door and make a snap decision, grabbing a hotel key, phone, my car keys, and my wand.

I don't give a shit that I'm walking down the street wearing just Silas' shirt. That doesn't even smell that awesome. Maybe earthy, masculine, and rich. But I bet that other Alpha smelled this good, too.

Oh, the lies I delude myself with.

As soon as I get to the car, I grab mine and Silas' bag. Part of me just wants to get dressed and go scope out the jewelry store for myself. But it's clear the city is rife with shifters and after last night, it's evident Thorin and Silas aren't on the same page.

Who would've thought I'd come to like a wolf more than I would a man?

The lock of the hotel room whirls and as soon as I walk in, I'm greeted with a wet-haired Silas, his whole manly chest on display, while his bottom half is wrapped in a towel.

I've seen far too much of this man this morning.

"Where the fuck have you been?" he seethes, pacing, and I can't help but to laugh. "What are you laughing about?"

"You and Thorin pace the same way," I tell him, tossing him his backpack. "Forgive me for thinking you didn't want to walk around naked all day."

THE MARRIAGE HEX

He catches the backpack and looks back at me. "You wore that out?" he says, looking at the way his shirt hits me mid thigh.

"Yes, well, Thorin apparently tore my dress from last night into pieces," I say, pointing over to the corner.

He nods, looking back at my legs again before heading to the bathroom. I take that opportunity to change myself.

I go casual, with high-waisted denims and a black t-shirt with witch's silhouettes on the front that says girls will be girls. I pull out my wand and quickly spell my makeup and hair into place.

When Silas opens the door, he looks me up and down. "Are you just trying to broadcast that you're a witch?" he says, pointing to my shirt.

"Says the wolf shifter wearing plaid. Come on, the jewelry store opens in twenty minutes."

We grab breakfast first, Silas eating an ungodly amount of food while I drink my iced coffee and bite down on a beignet.

"Does shifting make you hungry?" I ask, as we stand across the street from the jewelry store, casing the place.

"I'm always hungry," he says easily, eating his second breakfast burrito.

"You haven't asked me about last night," I question.

I mean, the man was belittling his wolf this morning and reminding him that I'm nobody.

"No need. I know Thorin wouldn't hurt you," he says and my brows furrow.

"How do you—" I stop mid sentence as I watch her walk into the shop. She has a wide smile on her face. She doesn't even look much older than the photos I found in the chest.

She has the familial white blonde hair, my same bright blue

eyes, and the moon shaped beauty mark on the side of her neck.

I toss my breakfast in the trash and barely look both ways before crossing the street and grab the door handle.

A large, familiar scent hits me before his hand wraps around mine.

"We should have a plan," he tells me.

I swallow, watching her through the window as she goes to the backroom, before coming to the front and cleaning some of the glass showcases.

"I imagine she's going to look at me and realize who I am," I tell Silas, who sighs, but doesn't let go of my hand.

"Meeting your family isn't always a happy reunion," he says, and I glance up at him. Now isn't the time or the place to discuss him finding family members.

My mother is right past this door and I'm finally about to meet her. I'm finally about to understand. So, I ignore Silas' caution and swing the door open, a light bell dinging as I walk in.

"Can I help you?" a friendly enough man says, but I shake my head and approach the case near my mother.

She sprays some Windex, wiping any streaks away before glancing up at us with a friendly smile. It's the type of smile you give a stranger you're trying to sell something to, not one of familial recognition.

"Hi there, what can I help you with?" she says in a southern drawl, not so indifferent from my grand-mére's. Her name tag says Laylah, not Lavender.

I'm shocked speechless as I hear my mother's voice for the first time. Her smile falters a little, and she looks above me.

Silas' large hand grips my hip.

"Me and the misses just got hitched, and well, in our haste to the altar, we didn't think about wedding rings."

THE MARRIAGE HEX

I swallow. What? I glance up at Silas and he squeezes my hip again. The touch is for me to play along, to make this encounter last longer so we can get more information.

"Oh, congratulations. You make a beautiful couple. Do you know what you're looking for?"

"I need something simple, durable. And the little lady likes unique, definitely not a diamond," he says.

I can't tell if he's being cheap, or he actually understands my style as she leads us to a case of unique rings before pulling them out.

"Well, we have opal, emerald, and amethyst."

"Amethyst," I whisper out and she smiles, pulling the tray out with amethyst stones.

"Are we thinking big or dainty?" she asks, and I can't help but to just stare into her eyes that are exactly like mine.

"Dainty, she works at a hospital, so something that won't get in the way," Silas says, he's still holding my hip, I nearly forgot.

The ring she pulls out isn't the most expensive. She's not trying to oversell as she holds her hand out. I place mine in hers as she slides the ring on my finger, and I do my best not to cry.

"This one is simple, but timeless," she says as I look down at the rose gold band with an oval amethyst in the middle, flanked by moissanite floral diamonds.

"It's perfect," I whisper, and glance back up at her.

"Wonderful. I love getting it right on the first try." She grabs some rings for Silas and glances at his finger. "Looks like you'll need a larger size, like my husband."

"Your husband?" I question and she nods with a smile but doesn't elaborate.

Silas picks the least expensive ring and slides it on his finger.

"We'll take both of these. How long has this place been here?"

he asks.

He's clearly way better at this whole interrogation thing, but I just can't stop staring at her or making it weird.

"Oh, well, over a hundred years."

"How long have you worked here?" he asks.

Her brows furrow. "Wow, I think I'm coming up on thirty years here soon."

I stiffen and I can't help myself as I grab her wrist. I don't feel her magic, not like I do when I'm around the coven. She feels like any human would.

"I'm sorry, do I know you?" she asks me.

I blink at her, trying to hold it together, but I can't. "No, my mistake."

"Why don't you get some fresh air while I finish everything here?" Silas says, his eyes almost as soft as the boy's I once loved.

I stare at him a moment before I leave. Walking till the Mississippi River stops me. Sitting on a bench created to deter the homeless, I curse as I pull out my wand and melt the iron bars that were splintering the bench into sections.

I sit and stare at the water and for the first time in a long time I cry.

She didn't recognize me. She doesn't seem to have magic. It's not only a dead end to this stupid fucking spell I have with Silas, but a dead end to everything I had hoped she would be.

Is she this way because she left the coven? Witches are not nomadic. Is that the price she had to pay for leaving? Is her husband my father? Or is there so much more going on that I don't understand?

Why did the spirit bring us here? Why now?

I watch as the ferry transfers people across the river and wonder why everything seems to be going to absolute shit right now.

THE MARRIAGE HEX

My life was perfect. All the love, affection, and understanding I needed was based in my coven. Of course, I wanted to know about my mother, but it didn't haunt me like it has as of late. Maybe the moment I moved into her old home was when the need to understand what happened started consuming me.

I look down at my hand, actually loving the ring. My mother picked out this ring, even if she doesn't know I'm her daughter or that my marriage is complete bullshit.

When I go to take the ring off, the magic won't let me and I curse.

"Well, this is just fucking awesome," I murmur to myself.

Silas' large frame plops down next to me and he doesn't say anything right away. It's no surprise he was able to find me, maybe he can scent me, or it's just the power of the magic between us.

"Can't take your ring off, either?" he questions and I nod.

I could bitch about it. Tell him that this is all his fault for coming up with that stupid story. But I freeze. Without him, we wouldn't have gotten what little information we did.

"I was able to gather some more information and something else," Silas says.

I wipe the bottom of my eyes with my thumbs, not wanting him to see me cry as he hands me a necklace wrapped in silk.

"As soon as you left, it was like she remembered something," Silas says. "Her brows furrowed, and she remembered the matching necklace for that ring. It was in the back. It wasn't even for sale."

I look at it. The stone and design is similar to my ring.

"You think it's the necklace from her letter?"

"Could be. I have Jonas doing a background search on her now that I have her name. She said she didn't have any children."

I hold the necklace in my fist. An angry, irrational part of me wants to throw it in the river. But the curious, needing a connection to my mother, part of me shoves it in my pocket.

"Jonas can be trusted?" I ask, glaring at Silas.

"Yes."

I sniffle and rest my head in my hands. "I didn't know what to expect. Is it wrong that I think this would be easier if she was dead?"

"No, because I felt the same."

"You did?"

"Yeah, Vi, I did," he says, splaying his arms out on the park bench as we both watch the ferry.

"What happened?" I ask, wondering if he'll tell me. He surprises me by leaning back and telling me everything.

Chapter 19

SILAS

I'm not sure if it's Violet's half-shed tears, the way this feels like a dead end, or how hard Thorin is riding my ass right now. But I decide Violet should know that she's not alone.

"After Jonas and I took over Mander's, we went on the search for our families. We knew we would have a claim on a pack with ancestral ties. That's usually how things work. But the shifter community as a whole is secretive, most delivering their young at home, lying low, the typical supernatural M.O. So we spent a lot of time traveling around North America. Jonas found his half-brother in Toronto, and we stayed there for a bit, but it didn't work out."

"Why?" she asks, thoroughly engaged in the story.

"His brother was pack Alpha. It took everything in me to hold back Thorin from challenging him. I told Jonas he could stay with his family, but he chose to follow me instead. Eventually we found a lead, and I met my mother."

"What was she like?"

"Terrible," I say with a shake of my head. "She clearly has her addictions. It's why she was kicked out of the Moon Walker Pack and why my grandfather had no direct Alpha heir to pass the claim to, or at least, I thought. It was passed to Collins instead."

"The spirit?" she gasps and I nod.

"I didn't think we were related, but honestly, all the bookkeeping with the pack is absolute shit. He could just as easily be his bastard. Hans, my grandfather, was nearly sixty when my mother was born, and seventy when he passed his claim to Collins. My mother wanted nothing to do with me when I met her, said she didn't know who my father was. I couldn't scent her as a shifter either," I admit.

It's not even something I told Jonas.

Her brows furrow, and she rubs her slender, pale throat. "It can't be this coincidental," she whispers.

"What do you mean?"

"Both of us, ending up at Mander's, both of our mothers no longer a part of their lineage. Something feels off."

I break away from looking at her for a moment, letting the breeze from the river caress my face. She's right, this is all too messed up to not be connected somehow.

"What do we do now?" she asks, looking hopeless and sad.

"Comfort our mate," Thorin whispers, and for the first time since I've reunited with Violet, I agree with Thorin.

"We could go home, try to figure this out, see what Jonas comes up with. Or…"

"Or what?" she asks. The idea of going home doesn't sound great to her either, even though I know my pack needs order right now. But leaving New Orleans with no answers doesn't feel right. Leaving while she looks so sad, doesn't feel right.

"Or we take one day."

"One day?"

"Where you're not a witch from the coven who's trying to ruin my fucking life and I'm not the Alpha of the pack you loathe? Just one day to actually live and then we'll go back to hating each other tomorrow on our drive back home."

She blinks at me, her eyes looking a brighter blue from her tears. She doesn't look at me like she hates me; she looks at me with relief. Like the idea of shedding who she is and what she's going through for just one day will be the thing she needs.

"Okay, let's do that. Oh, let me put an illusion on our rings. Other supernaturals won't be able to see them,," she says, not pulling out her hand, just touching my ring and then her own.

"How do you know it worked?"

"It worked," she says easily.

"So, what would two completely normal people who don't hate each other do for the day in New Orleans?"

A smile takes over her face. Not that I care that I put it there, but it should be noted for the record.

"First and foremost, we're getting on that ferry and getting the best tacos you've ever had," she says, standing and walking, not even caring if I'm following or not.

Just like I found her before, I let the magic between us tighten as I follow my wife to get ferry tickets.

They were indeed the best tacos I've ever had. Who would have thought an old gas station in Algiers, of all places?

I hate to admit that I've eaten eight, compared to Violet's three.

"Shit," she hisses, blotting the side of her mouth. "This might sting," she says, as her wand taps my knee under the table.

It does sting, but only for a moment. When I glance up, I blink a few times as she flips her sunglasses over her eyes.

The woman in front of me looks nothing like Violet. She's a redhead with freckles and an even paler complexion.

"What the fuck?" I say, pulling out my phone and flipping it to look at myself. "Seriously?" I ask, looking at myself.

I look like the security guard at the circuit court.

"It's temporary. I can feel a witch here," she whispers.

"And you think us looking different will matter?" I ask.

"Yeah, I'd say you not looking like a six-foot-seven beast and me not having identifiable hair and features of a High Priestess is a good call."

I don't have anything to say to that, so instead I drink my Coke that came in a glass bottle and consider ordering another taco.

"They'll still be able to sense us," I say and she tilts her glasses down. Her blue eyes are the same.

"Will you eat your taco and stop bitching? Maybe we should go home."

"Miss Delvaux, are you afraid of the coven here?" I ask her, teasing, and she swallows.

"Yes, and if you aren't, you haven't met their High Priestess. If you think my grand-mére is a hard ass, Prudence makes her look like a saint. It's best we go undetected. We definitely won't be caught dead in the Garden District, which is a shame."

"Is that where you'd wanna go?" I ask her and she shrugs.

"Doesn't matter. We could do a swamp tour, a few museums, oh, a ghost tour," she says with a smirk.

"Could you illusion us?" I suggest, and she tilts her head at me.

"Maybe you're not a big dumb Alpha after all," she says. I should be mad, should roll my eyes.

Instead, Thorin is preening in the back of my mind over the fact she said Alpha.

"Let's finish up here, take the ferry back and find somewhere private where I can make us incognito," she says, downing the rest of her drink. "Did you get enough to eat? We can get something

THE MARRIAGE HEX

sweet when we're on the other side of the river."

"Thorin is the one who likes sweets," I tell her, and her brow furrows.

"Did he bring me that cupcake?"

I shrug, wanting to lie, and Thorin pushes at my mind. *"You better tell her I gave her that cupcake."*

"Yes, he did."

"Here, I thought you'd be Dr. Jekyll in this situation. It appears your wolf is."

"You're saying I'm Mr. Hyde?" I say with a smirk, and she looks confused. "Hyde is Jonas' wolf's name," I say, not being able to control my laughter. "I'm going to have to start calling him Jekyll."

That breaks her hard shell as she smiles. "Come on, let's go roam with the ghosts of the Big Easy."

"There can't be that many ghosts," I say, as we walk down the tree-lined streets back to the ferry.

"You were literally locked in a bedroom by a spirit a few nights ago, and you still don't believe in ghosts?"

"What's the difference?" I ask her, not liking that she doesn't look like herself. The red hair doesn't suit her, and I just want her to switch us back.

"Well, all sorts of differences. I'm not a medium, but my great aunt Daisy is, though she doesn't talk. I've always wondered if speaking to the dead was the reason for that. But they all seem to understand her without speaking. She pretty much just reads books all the time though, not sure the last time she communed with a spirit."

She looks both ways, not seeing anyone walking around as she tucks us behind a fence.

"This will tingle, again," she says, her body so close to mine, as her intricate wand is placed between us and she whispers.

SARAH BLUE

The same tingling sensation flows through me, and when I crane my neck to look down at Violet, she's back to herself. Her unique two-toned hair fits her better. It makes her blue eyes pop and frames her symmetrical, heart-shaped face.

She's so close to me right now it's hard to not make a fool of myself. Despite my rational mind, I can't help but crave and enjoy her scent. Against my wishes, she's still my mate and on a biological level, I'm attracted to her scent and looks unlike I'll ever be to anyone else.

"Where do you hide that thing?" I ask as her wand disappears.

"Be nice to me and maybe I'll tell you," she says, grabbing my wrist and dragging me toward the ferry.

Her skin against mine shouldn't feel as addictive as it is. Thorin has shared a bed with her. She's pet his fur. He's made sure to tell me about that multiple times. But her skin against mine feels like an electrical current.

I rip my arm away from her, and she glares as we get on the boat. She automatically picks a seat on the top, her sunglasses on as she looks up to the sky, the breeze blowing her black and white hair.

My wife is beautiful.

It's the worst realization I've ever had.

"Is there something on my face?" she asks, wiping her mouth, and I shake my head.

"No," I reply, and she slides her sunglasses down to look at me.

"Are you going to be weird all day? We're living different lives, remember?"

"Right. We're humans, honeymooners."

She holds her hand out to the sky, the sun dancing against the sparkle of her ring.

"Gotta say, honey. You have taste," she jokes as the old woman behind us coos.

"Oh my, are you on your honeymoon?" the old human woman asks.

"We are. He did a great job, didn't he?" Violet replies.

"How did you two meet?"

"It's a silly story, really. I'm a nurse and Steve here, came in with syphilis. We got him some antibiotics, but I couldn't stop thinking about the slutty man who came in for relief, and, well, the rest is history."

I know my mouth is agape as the old woman's eyes widen and she seems lost for words.

She turns her head, not wanting to ask any more questions about our faux honeymoon.

"I thought we were in a truce," I say, feeling amused, even though I should be more pissed off.

"Do you really think in any reality I wouldn't test your patience?" she says, leaning in. "Mr. Walker, there is no realm where I don't bust your balls." She winks and stands as the ferry parks and we get off to enjoy our day hidden away in the Garden District.

SARAH BLUE

Chapter 20

VIOLET

Knowing that no one can see us makes something shift between Silas and me. It's almost like we truly erased the last fourteen years and are those two stupid kids who would have nightly rendezvous in a tree.

We walk, we talk about nonsensical bullshit. Neither of us tries to talk about this morning, what we're going to do, or what happened in the time that separated us.

We're just a man and a woman leisurely enjoying what this fine city has to offer.

"I think the tour guide could sense we were there, but assumed it was a spirit," I say with a laugh as we leave the cemetery and walk down the stunning streets full of art, architecture, and history.

I only remove the illusion once on our excursion, only so we can eat broiled oysters. The amount Silas eats is honestly astonishing, but as soon as we're done eating, I illusion us again.

The sun is setting as we sit on a fountain lip, listening to the bustle of this part of town quietly and the water trickles behind us. There's too much light pollution here, you can't see the stars like you can back home, but it's still serene in its own way.

When I look over at Silas, it hits me like a ton of bricks.

He's not as bad as I thought he was. He's not so far removed from that sweet boy who would lasso the moon for me. Even if he looks like this big badass Alpha shifter, there's still a softness there.

He didn't need to tell me about his mother, or spend the day with me trying to forget my—our—problems. But he did, with no complaints. Well, no real complaints.

"I never meant to leave you," I tell him, like the honesty is being ripped out of my throat.

"I know," he whispers, resting his elbows on his knees and glancing back at me.

Still the same brown eyes, even prettier now with their golden glow that I now realize is Thorin.

"Do you ever think about what would have happened if my grand-mére didn't find me?" I ask, the vulnerability leaking out of me. Maybe it's because he shared some of himself with me earlier, maybe it's because we're pretending and tomorrow everything will go back to normal. But I find myself wanting to be honest with Silas.

"I thought about it for fourteen years," he says, his gaze not leaving mine.

"What do you think it would have been like?"

His throat bobs. "A lot like today. I think it would feel a lot like today has."

Witches don't cry, I already did enough of that today. His honesty won't make me do it again. But the vulnerability of his answer is hard to swallow.

How can two things be true at once? How can I love my coven so deeply but also crave this alternate reality that Silas is suggesting?

"I think, maybe, we would have been happy."

"I know we would have," Silas says, his eyes boring into mine. I can tell he believes it fully with his heart. "I wouldn't have needed a pack."

THE MARRIAGE HEX

"Witches can't go nomad."

"Says who?" he responds.

My brow furrows and I just let the fountain break the silence for a moment before speaking. "I've never heard of any. You pull your magic through the strength of a coven. I wouldn't be me without my coven."

"Right," he says.

"You really think you could live without ever having a pack? Especially now that you have one?"

He looks down at the cement before glancing back at me. "Now that I have one, no," he says truthfully.

It all comes back to that. He has his pack; I have my coven. They hate each other. There is no brokerage for true peace. Silas might be trying, and maybe he has the upper hand right now with buying most of Main Street. Even if we come to an agreement, there's no world where the Alpha of the Moon Walker Pack and the future High Priestess of the Celestial Coven are anything more than the leaders of their people.

Hell, witches don't even get married. Most of our fathers are unknown to us, or at the very least, unimportant.

"But… if we had run away at eighteen, I wouldn't have needed one. I would have had you," Silas says, and it feels like my heart is shattering into a million pieces of what if's and childhood dreams.

"We're not the same as we were then."

"Maybe. You're still a bit of a know-it-all."

"Am not," I complain too quickly, and he smiles. "Well, you're still enormous and bossy."

He grins at me, and I can't help but smile back. It's like the world around us has paused to let us have just this moment.

Too bad it's ruined by the shifter from last night, with four guys flanking his sides. The Alpha, the man I danced with, has his nose to the air as he inhales.

"He's fucking close," he says and Silas' eyes go wide, the gold shine almost as bright as last night.

I tap my nose, and Silas nods and looks around. He brings a finger to his lips as he stands and dips a foot into the water. I give him wide eyes and he grabs my wrist, ushering me into the water that's too cold even for an autumn night in New Orleans.

He places his massive hand over my mouth as he takes a deep breath and dips us into the water. What feels like an aggressive baptism ends as he slowly brings us back up to the shallow surface.

We both watch as the men's eyebrows furrow as they look around. They know they scented Silas for sure, and suddenly they lost the trail.

"Must be that fucking witch he's with."

My face must read irritation as Silas smiles, even though he looks like a drowned wolf.

"He needs to be taught a lesson," the Alpha from last night growls.

"Felix, it's not worth it. Plus, if he's with a witch, we don't want to piss off Prudence."

"She isn't her coven. She wouldn't care," one of the other pack members says.

Silas' hand is still covering my mouth and the urge to lick his palm is getting almost too much to bear. So I do it.

He doesn't look pissed or move his hand. He just stares at me, and I stare right back as we wait for this pathetic gaggle of shifters to figure out what they're going to do.

They finally give up, jogging in another direction, but Silas doesn't move his hand right away.

Instead, his hand slides from my mouth, over to my cheek, his thumb trailing my cheekbone as he looks at me with awe.

"We would've been something," he says, stroking my skin.

"Yeah, something," I reply, leaning into his touch.

His palm is so cozy and warm compared to the cool water that's currently drenching both of us. The fountain and street lamps glow against his sun-kissed skin and I wonder what it would be like to really kiss him.

Not that peck at the courthouse, the one that was done out of obligation and met with complete disgust.

Silas shakes his head and drops his hand.

"You look like a drowned rat," he says and I gasp.

Cupping my hands with water, I collect as much as I can and splash it in his face. He looks at me with complete disbelief. I go to run away in the fountain and he grips me by my wet t-shirt, tugging me against his chest.

"One little piece of advice, wife?" he says, his warm body heat pressed against me. "Don't run from me."

"Why?" I say breathlessly, my shirt clinging to my front.

He leans in, his nose gliding up the side of my throat.

"Just shut up and listen to me," he says, a common phrase between us that's slowly turning into a term of endearment in my mind.

"I'm not a very good listener," I reply and he squeezes my shirt harder, sending water dripping down my back.

"If you have to do one thing I say, this is it. If you run from me, my instinct will be to chase and claim."

I swallow, looking around at the few passersby who can't see us, but it somehow feels like what we're doing is wrong. I mean, obviously being in a public fountain is wrong, but this doesn't feel as innocent as it started out.

"Chased a lot of damsels over the last decade, Alpha Silas?" I say, knowing I'm pushing his buttons.

I just don't care.

"No, and don't tempt me, witch," he replies, and the way he says witch doesn't have the same bite as I would suspect. It almost comes out as a caress.

His nose touches my neck again and I swear a deep rumble pours out of him, before he suddenly lets go of my shirt, making me off kilter and I go flying forward. I splash against the water and sputter before turning around and gaping at him.

I swear gold flashes before Silas pushes his wolf down.

"Time to go back to reality, Violet," he says.

It's worse than the slap of water I was literally just hit with. Instead, I just nod. Because this was all pretend.

We both have people who need us home. We have a mystery to solve, a hex to unburden us with, and a secret to keep under wraps.

"Today was a mistake," I say and Silas nods in agreement.

"It was. Can you do something about our wet clothes?" he asks.

"I can do something about mine," I reply, climbing out of the fountain and drying myself completely, while Silas stands there dripping wet.

His shirt clings to his skin along with his pants and I smirk. "You look like a drowned wolf," I snap before heading in the direction of my car.

The large man follows me, his shoes squishing with water the whole walk to the car.

He changes on the street as I sit in the passenger's seat, feeling like I lost so much more than I gained from this stupid fucking trip.

I'm no closer to solving our little marriage issue. I have more questions about my lineage than ever. But worst of all, this trip showed me that maybe Silas isn't the sworn enemy I thought he was.

Or maybe the magic between us is confusing me more than I realized.

Chapter 21

SILAS

It physically pains me to hop right onto my motorcycle and drive away as soon as Violet and I get back into town.

But there's no way I can stay here. Not after that trip, not after the day we had together. I need to clear my head and there's so much pack business I need to get caught up on.

This little side quest means nothing. So what we had a good day together, so fucking what Thorin feels more at peace than he's ever felt. It doesn't matter.

Her coven means everything to her and I've pushed myself as pack leader. We both have responsibility and none of those responsibilities are to each other.

"Delusional doesn't look good on you, pack leader," Thorin says, and I shake my head. Shoving him deep, deep down into the recesses of my mind. The last thing I need is his input right now.

As soon as I get back to the Alpha cabin, Jonas is there waiting for me, his laptop open as he glances up at me with a smirk.

"Did you have a good time with your mate?" he asks and I glare over at him as he rolls his eyes. "What am I even saying? Of course, you had a great time. You smell like her, and like some stagnant water, might wanna get that checked out, Alpha."

"Is there a reason you're here at this unholy hour getting on my fucking nerves?"

"Let's see, I remember getting a frantic text asking me to look into a random woman who works at an obscure jewelry store in the French Quarter. Do you want the info, or do you want to chew my head off?"

"Sorry," I grumble, the distance from Violet is riding me.

I can't let it affect my mood. It's the curse making me feel this way, nothing else.

"Laylah Goings, age forty-nine, lives with her husband, Pierre, in a ridiculously expensive home in the Garden District."

"I see," I reply, not wanting to tell Jonas everything Violet is going through.

"Now, the real question is why do you have me looking up someone who is clearly using a fake identity? Her birth certificate is clearly forged. I can't find any schooling information. She seemed to just pop into existence around thirty years ago." I give him a glance and he clicks his tongue. "Figured as much. I've been talking with some elder members of the pack about what happened all those years ago."

"What did they have to say?"

"You already know your mother was exiled before that. Rumor is your father is human," Jonas says gently and I just shrug with indifference.

It truly doesn't matter if I am partially human or not, though I don't believe it. How does a man who is half-human wind up being an Alpha?

Jonas nods, like he knows what I'm thinking. "It's likely rumors. If there's one thing this pack loves, it appears to be gossip."

"What else did you find out?"

THE MARRIAGE HEX

"That's the thing. Everything about the year you and Violet were born is a blur. We know the pack leader and his son left, but no one knows where they went. Everything seems to go to shit from there."

"Violet hasn't been able to get much from her coven, either."

"She's her mother?" Jonas says, and looks at me suspiciously. "I feel like there's something else you're hiding from me, Si. I thought, as your second, we would be well beyond secrets."

He's right, and as the only person I trust in the world, I tell him everything. The court house, the night fourteen years ago, sneaking off to Violet's house every night and a few details of our trip this weekend.

As soon as I'm done, he leans back in his chair and whistles.

"She doesn't know she's your mate, does she?"

"No, it doesn't matter, anyway."

Jonas laughs and shakes his head, standing up and closing his laptop. "You're a great number of things, Silas. But you're not this naïve. Not only is she your mate, she's the girl you've been thinking about your whole adult life. She's the reason you've never had a real relationship. Wolves don't just reject their mates without steep consequences."

"She won't leave her coven."

"Then it sounds like you need to work on brokering peace between us and the witches more than I realized," he says, about to leave the cabin, but stops as he's nearly shutting the door. "I know how much this pack means to you. It's the same for me. We've spent so much time, sacrificed so much to get to this point. But is it even worth it to be miserable in the end?"

He shuts the door and I sit at the kitchen table mulling over his words and actively trying not to drive back to Violet's house.

Could I truly be capable of that kind of change? Could I unite our two species to the point where they would accept me and Violet together? Hell, can I make her like me enough for that? Do I even want to?

I think back to our trip and realize I haven't smiled that much in years. I felt freer than I did during my run with my pack.

This pack deserves a true leader. Which feels like I need to put them above everything in my personal life.

The significance of our lineage and the distance from Violet has me tossing and turning all night. At one point, I even considered shifting to Thorin, so I didn't have to deal with it. Instead, I just got a half-ass night's rest and thought about the consequences and the possibilities.

I came to a few conclusions. One, I'm going to get to the bottom of what happened in this town thirty years ago. Two, Violet and I will work on breaking this curse, and I won't tell her she's my mate. That's my issue, not hers.

Even if I find her beautiful and charming, it will never work, so instead I'll carry this burden for the both of us.

There's a knock on my door far too early in the morning. I curse, putting on a t-shirt and swinging it wide open.

A heavily pregnant wolf shifter I briefly recognize stands at the entryway and I swallow thickly as she rubs her stomach and looks at me with tear-filled eyes.

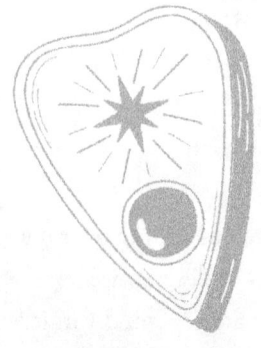

Chapter 22

VIOLET

Sneaking into my grand-mère's house first thing in the morning as the sun rises is probably not my best idea. However, I know her schedule like the back of my hand. It's a Sunday morning, she'll be at Ember's garden praying to Hecate.

I nearly jump out of my skin as the skeleton on her front porch lights up and I give it the finger as I use my key to unlock the front door.

My great aunt Daisy does not share the same spiritual devotion as my grandmother, nor does she like early hours, so I know she's asleep.

I have to be careful. My grandmother is smart and gifted. Anything left out of order will be clearly noticeable.

When her bedroom door opens with an ominous magically induced creak, I glance around, more than familiar with the room. I just have to figure out where she would be hiding something. Where would she have information on my mother?

I feel guilty for assuming she's lying to me about my mom, but something feels off. Even if my mother had lost it, why would no one in the coven go searching for her? She's hiding in plain sight only a few hours away.

I tap my wand on my palm, causing it to glow brightly as I look under her bed and through her closet. I don't find anything and the guilt feels even heavier for doubting her.

My boot hits a floor board that squeaks just as I'm about to leave, so I shift my weight on it, before bending down and using my wand to pull it back.

A large cigar box is in there and I swallow before pulling it out and opening the contents. I pull out multiple pictures of my mother; she looks happy and radiant in all of them, she looks like she fits in with the coven.

There's a rose gold wand that looks similar to my own, which I assume is hers.

"Why?" I ask out loud, staring at the contents of the box as a throat clears behind me.

Fuck.

"Did you find what you were looking for, granddaughter?" she asks and I swallow.

The answer is not really, but I nod my head, anyway.

She sighs and sits on her bed, facing the window and she pats next to her, indicating that I should sit down, so I do, bringing all the photos with me.

Grand-mère smiles sadly over the photos, dragging a finger down my mother's portrait.

"She used to be happy. She loved coven life," she says.

"Grand-mère, what really happened?"

"I've been trying to shield you from the truth," she says.

I take a deep breath, preparing myself for what the harsh reality is, and I couldn't be more shocked by what she tells me.

"Lavender had a wild spirit. She loved to test the limits of things. She wasn't afraid of anything. Not even my disapproval," she says with a laugh, staring down at the photo of her daughter. "She wasn't afraid when she told me she was pregnant, and I wasn't upset. It is unusual for a witch to have a child so young, but growing the coven is always a blessing."

"My father?" I ask, and she shakes her head.

"Some human boy she was smitten with and met at a party. It's our blessing to only bear daughters of magical abilities, but unfortunately we do need human men in that regard," she says with disgust.

"She changed with her pregnancy, her magic depleted, she became sick in the mind and of the body. Our healer monitored her closely, but she was old and not as effortlessly talented as you."

I'm worried she's about to lie to me and tell me that she is indeed dead, but she grabs my hand and squeezes.

"She ran away during her last month of pregnancy, concealed herself with what magic she had left. I'm not sure why. But when I found her months later, she was no longer pregnant, and no longer capable of magic."

I blink at my grandmother. "What?"

"It's very rare, but I fear you ripped your mother's magic from her. When I found her, I asked her where you were and she said you didn't make it and that she just wanted to forget it all. I wanted to bring her back to the coven. She was my daughter. I love her still. Part of being a parent is letting your children make their own choices, so I gave her that wish. I erased everything, and she now lives her life as a human, not knowing our ways or who she once was, or who you are."

"She told you I died?" I ask. Staring down at the photo and trying to make sense of the story.

It doesn't match with that letter I found in the mansion, but what reason does she have to lie to me? A lot of things check out.

Why my mother didn't recognize me, why she has no magic, why she would want to forget me after taking her gift from her?

"I don't know why she told me that. I would have brought you into the coven immediately upon your existence. But I couldn't feel you. Her last act of magic was concealing you from the world, and I still don't know why."

"Have you seen her since then?" I ask.

My grandmother drags a light pink nail across the photo and shakes her head. "It's far too painful. Even seeing you for the first time was painful for me. For all her faults, I love her deeply and she gave me you. I know I'm not overly affectionate, or loving, or even understanding sometimes. Having you in my life has been one of my greatest blessings, if I had to do it all again, I would, only to have you," she says.

Her pale blue eyes fill with emotion. Witches don't cry, especially not Aster Delvaux.

So, I choose to believe her. She's the High Priestess. She's the only family I have. She's the reason I'm in this coven and have found the love and the light that my life is full of. Even with some reluctance, I nod and hug her. She inhales deeply and pulls back.

"This coven needs you, Violet. You're the future. This all had to happen for you to ascend, I'm sure of it. It's time for you to truly prepare yourself to lead this coven when I'm no longer here."

"I think you're going to be around for quite some time."

"Just because I'm alive doesn't mean I should be the one leading. The Celestial Coven has been so powerful because we train our successors properly. We should boost your private lessons with me to two days a week."

"Yes, grand-mère," I say, and she strokes my cheek.

"You're the most important person to me and to the life of our coven. I'm sorry I kept the truth from you. I thought I was protect-

THE MARRIAGE HEX

ing you. You already had such a hard life before we found you. We can't lose you too, not to the past."

I nod, feeling the weight of the coven on my shoulders. Maybe I am cut out to be the High Priestess. Maybe everything she said is true, or mostly true. But she's right about one thing. Dwelling in the past has only made me hurt. It's time to look toward the future. I need to up my studies; I need to get rid of Silas… even though there's a part of me that doesn't want to.

It's the magic, the curse, nothing else.

"I'll make you proud, grand-mère."

"I know you will, it's been foretold," she says and I wonder what Iris' grandmother has seen.

She pats my thigh, placing everything back in its neat little box as I leave the house. I turn back toward the window where my great aunt Daisy is looking at me with an eerie look to her eye.

Instead of reading into it, I continue my walk back to my home, mulling over everything my grandmother said as my phone vibrates in my pocket.

When I pull it out, I roll my eyes. Before Silas left my home, he said he should have his wife's number. I disagreed, but unfortunately it made too much sense.

"What?" I say as I pick up the phone.

"I need you on the pack lands, now," he says, and it sounds like there's a ton of commotion in the background.

"Number fucking one, witches aren't allowed on pack lands, second why the hell would I?"

"You're a healer right, you've made an oath to serve and protect?"

"That's human doctors," I say with a roll of my eyes. "You need to stop watching so much television."

"Violet," he says my name like a plea. "I have a mother and a pup who might die if I don't get some help here soon."

"Don't you have your own medical professionals?" I ask.

"We do, but this is beyond them. Please, Violet."

It's the word please, maybe accompanied by the story that my grandmother just told me that rip at my heart.

"Can you go outside?" I tell him.

"What? Violet, we don't have time for this."

"Just go outside, it's more dangerous if I teleport into a building. But I recognize your signature enough that I can teleport right to you and then that way I don't need to drive into pack territory and get there faster."

"I'll be right back, I'm getting help," Silas says, a door clicks, and he's breathing heavily on the phone. "Okay, I'm outside," he says.

I place the phone back into my pocket and let this pesky magical tether that ties us guide me to where I need to go. With a deep inhale, I pop into existence and right into Silas Walker's arms. I don't dwell on how he effortlessly carries me, or how firm his grip is under my thighs and around my waist.

"Thank fuck," he says, not putting me down and dragging me toward a small wooden cabin.

It's a dark wood, with no Halloween decor whatsoever, which is disheartening. But when he opens the door, there's a woman screaming on his dining room table.

"A witch? No!" the woman shrieks and then cries out in pain.

"She's the only one who can help you right now. Do you want to save your baby?"

"What does it matter?" the woman cries out.

I point to the woman and then arch my brow at Silas.

"It's not mine. It's the previous Alpha's. He skipped town and now it seems the baby shifted in the womb."

My mouth gapes open. "That can happen?"

THE MARRIAGE HEX

"I've only heard rumors, old wives' tales. Most shifters don't shift until they're five, unless their wolf is being suppressed."

"I can't do this," the woman cries.

I pull out my wand and she shifts back. "I'm not going to hurt you. What's your name?"

"Paige," she says softly, sniffling.

"Okay, Paige. I'm going to run a diagnostic on you and the baby. I've delivered five babies so far, well, and one human in the Wal-Mart parking lot."

"Great," she sniffles as the front door opens and I look back, noticing it's Jonas.

We haven't even formally spoken. He was always quiet at Mander's; we weren't close. Especially not the way he was with Silas, maybe I had some resentment when Silas chose to hangout with Jonas instead of me.

He doesn't greet me at all.

Instead, his mouth gapes open as he stares down at the sweaty woman in pain.

"My mate," he whispers, and it's almost instantaneous as some of the fear leaves her and she looks back at Jonas.

"It can't be," she says with a gasp.

Jonas, clearly never having met this woman before, places a cool rag on her forehead and holds her hand, before his eyes turn on me.

"You will fix my mate, now, witch," he says.

"Watch your tone," Silas says, putting a hand on my shoulder. Jonas immediately slightly bows, obeying his Alpha as he goes back to consoling the woman he just met who is apparently his mate, which is important?

There's clearly a lot about the wolves that we don't understand.

"Everyone, just be quiet," I say, holding my wand to her stomach and watching as the bright glow of two diagnostics show before me.

The wolves in the room look on with amazement, not able to read anything. Jonas puts a hand on her stomach and I glance over at them. They literally just met. How can he care for her so instantaneously?

The baby's vitals change at his touch. When Jonas moves his hand, the vitals falter.

"Keep your hand on her stomach. He likes it," I say.

"He?" Paige asks with tears in her eyes.

Jonas tears up as well, even though it's evident this child isn't his. What the fuck is happening?

I try not to focus on everything going on around me and I don't even answer Paige as I glance at the image of the baby in the womb. Sure fucking enough, it's a goddamn wolf pup in her stomach.

"What the fuck?" I whisper to myself, not thinking.

"What's wrong?" Paige asks.

"Sorry, just never seen a wolf in an ultrasound before. He's shifted and I'm worried he might scratch or harm you if we don't get him out soon."

"You need to keep her safe," Jonas says, his eyes glowing with a bit of silver. Ah, that must be his wolf, Hyde.

I direct Silas and Jonas to procure everything I need for a natural birth, or otherwise, as I figure out how I'm going to get this wolf to shift back into a human form. Then it becomes so clear what will work.

Silas is folding a stack of towels and I grab him by the wrist. He looks at me with worried eyes and I fear I may like him more than I can admit. He cares about this woman, maybe because she's pack, or because now we know she's Jonas' mate. Either way, this man cares about their wellbeing so much that he would risk having me, a witch, here to help.

"I need you to command the baby to shift," I tell him and he looks down at where our skin is touching.

I drag him over to Paige and place both of our hands on her stomach. Jonas makes a sound of complaint, but it slowly disappears as I channel Silas through me to the unborn child.

"What do I do?" he whispers.

"You need to command him as his pack Alpha to shift. You just have to think it, not out loud," I say.

Silas takes a deep breath and I channel all his thoughts to the baby. It takes some convincing, the unborn shifter is clearly stubborn as fuck, distressed as hell. I wonder if wolf shifter babies feed energy off their mothers like witches do.

But it eventually pays off, the baby shifting, and Paige screams when it happens. Even though I'm panicked, I do what I've been taught and I bring a crying twelve pound, six-ounce wolf shifter into the world crying in what sounds like a howl.

Chapter 23

SILAS

Violet delivers the boy, washes her hands, and immediately leaves the cabin without a word.

I look over at my closest friend, who just somehow gained a mate and a child in a matter of moments, and he looks happier than I've ever seen him.

"Tell her I said thank you," Jonas says, touching the massive newborn and his new mate.

I nod and go outside, expecting her to be gone, to have popped out of existence, and headed back to her large, lonely home.

Instead, I find her on the edge of the woods, her hands shaking as she holds her head in her hands and sits on the bark of a fallen tree.

I sit next to her, and as soon as I do, the dry, rotted bark breaks and sends us crashing to the ground. I fall on my ass and knock the air out of my lungs, but when I glance over at Violet, she's laughing with tears in her eyes.

"You're so big you broke the tree," she says, wiping the tears away and letting out a breath of air as we stare up at the tree covered sky. A good number of the leaves have fallen, but it's nothing like the crunchy leaves you see up north.

We don't even bother getting up from the forest floor.

"You did good back there. Thank you," I tell her and she looks at me with an expression I wish I could read.

"I've got to say, that is by far the most dramatic, intense birth I've ever seen. Not to mention the first boy, and the first one over nine pounds. That poor woman."

"Witches only have girls?" he asks.

"It's our blessing," she says with a smirk, and I shake my head. "So, are we going to talk about the fact that your best friend found his mate while she was giving birth?"

"What's left to say?"

"His devotion toward her was instant," she says and I nod, trying to fight my own instincts and devotion toward the witch next to me. Her coming here and helping my pack has unfortunately only endeared her to me more.

"That's typically how matings work."

"Do all wolves have a mate?"

"Yes, and no. I suppose we all have a mate. I'd say about a quarter or so find mates. Others have chosen mates."

"So you have a mate?" she asks, and I brush it off.

"It doesn't matter, being the Alpha these people need is more important. What you saw today was a small portion of it. We can go to human doctors for most things, and we heal incredibly fast naturally. But taking Paige to the hospital would have exposed us, which, as you know, can't happen. These people deserve more than just making ends meet. They deserve someone who will stand up for them. If I have to give up my own wants and needs for them, I will. That boy you just brought into this world should grow up knowing how to be a man, not scraping by and figuring it out as he goes."

Violet looks at me like she understands completely and goes back to looking up at the sky.

"You turned out pretty okay, Silas."

"You turned out pretty okay too," I tell her, grabbing her hand against my will and squeezing. She doesn't shrug me off and I realize if this is the only touch I ever get from her, then I'll cherish it for the rest of my life.

Despite having had time with Violet today, my body still demands that I go to her house, so I do as I have the nights before and pack a bag and make the drive to the massive purple home. I park my bike in the same spot, and it immediately disappears before my eyes.

All the pumpkins on her porch are already lit and before I can knock on the door, it's swinging wide open on its own accord. No Violet insight.

Just her demon of a cat, who blinks at me with its yellow eyes.

"Hello, Walter," I tell him and he hisses, before retreating upstairs.

I walk back into the kitchen, the dishes are being washed with no one in sight, just a sponge in midair with a plate, before a rag dries it and it is placed on a drying rack. A timer goes off and I watch in complete fascination as the oven turns itself off and the door pops open, a tray of muffins floating on top of the stove.

I can't deny that the magic is impressive and captivating.

She's not in the living room or dining room.

Instead, I look out the back window and find her barefoot, wrapped in a blanket, sitting on the ruins of what was a gazebo from the photos we found. The moon is in its last quarter, but the glow of solar or magical powered lights leads me down the path.

The frogs are croaking obnoxiously loud near the water, but I can see why sitting out here would be peaceful.

Violet glances up at me, but doesn't speak. She looks pale and worn out and I can't stand it.

"Are you okay?" I ask, not knowing what else to say.

She sighs and puts the necklace that's wrapped in silk on the ground of the wood base, that I'm not one-hundred percent sure can hold my weight. I look down at the familiar necklace and back up to her.

"You haven't put it on yet?" I ask her.

"It's not an amethyst," she says matter-of-factly. "I wondered how it was so bright, and the more I looked at it, the more I realized it's moonstone covered in magic."

I furrow my brows and sit down, the wood complaining as I plop my weight down.

"I mean, I don't think either of us is surprised it has some magical qualities?" I reply.

"No, I just—I feel like when I put this on, everything is going to change."

"I don't know about you, Vi, but I'd say the last couple of weeks have been pretty wildly different from our normal life."

"Part of me thought about tucking it away, forgetting about it."

"You're good at that," I say, feeling like an ass as soon as I do. But Violet doesn't argue, she just nods with a shrug.

"Compartmentalizing helps protect myself. I had to put you in a box, Silas. Or I wouldn't have been able to live. I've kept my mother in a similar box, taking my grand-mére's word, my coven's word. I don't know if it's because I moved into her house, finding her, but both boxes I kept firmly shut have both exploded in my face."

"You think this will explode in your face?"

THE MARRIAGE HEX

"I can feel it. Maybe it's a witch's intuition. But this necklace, it's more than jewelry. It's not protective magic, it's something else," she says, glancing down at the hypnotizing purple and opalescent color of the necklace.

"Should you have a coven member here?" I ask, hating the idea, but if she's that worried about the magic, there's only so much I can do.

"No, I just need you to make me a promise."

"Aren't we in enough trouble for making each other promises?" I ask.

But she doesn't laugh, doesn't smile.

"You'll subdue me if anything goes wrong," she says, handing me three things. "This one is a powder, in case you can't get close to me, it will knock me out. Enough time to take the necklace off and take me to Iris. This one is oral. If I'm with it enough, I can down this and it will do the same. But if things go really bad," she says, pulling out the smallest little dart. "Hit me with this."

"Maybe you shouldn't put the necklace on."

"I'm tired of not knowing the truth," she says.

"And you think a necklace will give you this truth?"

"In her letter, she said *the moon necklace will always protect you*. I've got to hold on to that."

"Is there something you're not telling me?" I ask her, and she doesn't look at me, so I grab her chin. Her soft skin feels like silk against mine. "Violet?"

She looks like she wants to say something, but tightens her lips.

"I just…I just need to know the truth, Silas. Promise me you'll make sure I'm okay. I know we don't always get along, that you're still mad at me and we're trying to figure out how to get ourselves out of this mess, but I know you'd never hurt me. So just promise me, that whatever happens when I put on this necklace, you'll make sure nothing bad happens."

Her mind is made up, I can read it in the seriousness of her face. She's putting this necklace on no matter what I say. I mean, the thing looks harmless. Her mother gave it to her. Not that she knew who she was giving it to, or maybe some small part of her did. There was something intrinsic in the way she knew Violet needed this necklace, and she gave it to me to give to her.

"I'm going to be really pissed if I have to shoot you with this, Violet."

She smiles and takes a deep breath. Her fingers shake as she grabs the chain, unclasping the mechanism before putting it around her neck and clasping it. The blanket falls, showing that she's wearing a purple nightgown.

Fucking nightgowns.

"I like the nightgowns," Thorin says, unhelpfully.

The glowing stone rests right above her breasts, and nothing happens. We both take a sigh in relief, and she picks it up between her two fingers and sighs.

"What did you think was going to happen?"

"I don't know, some major magical power trip that leads to me destroying the world," Violet says, and I can't tell if she's serious or not.

"Let's go inside and talk about what I learned from Jonas."

"Okay," she says and we both stand.

We glance up at the disappearing moon and Violet stills for a moment before she collapses against the cold hard ground. Her nails dig into the dirt as I crouch next to her.

"Violet?" I say her name with panic as her body trembles.

It's like she's being possessed for a moment until a scream so intense rips out of her and her head arches to the night sky.

A scream I remember all too well.

Her bent over body trembles more as I watch the telltale signs of a first shift. Her nightgown rips down the back, exposing her spine that now ripples and repositions to that of a wolf.

What was once her unblemished skin now turns to fur. She cries out in pain again, but before the sound can finish, it's cut off with a howl of frustration.

I blink twice as the small wolf in front of me cowers.

She's smaller than some of the adolescent wolves in the pack, but completely unique in her coloring.

Her face is stark white, glowing bright blue eyes framing her face. The white is spotted with black on her neck, until the rest of her form is completely black, minus her two front paws.

The wolf whines and gets down close to the ground in fear and panic.

"It's okay," I say, going to stroke her head, but she backs away in fear. "Violet, it's okay. It's going to be okay."

The wolf yips and I sigh, knowing what's about to happen.

"Finally," Thorin whispers, and before I can even undress, he's taking over, ripping my favorite pair of jeans in the process so he can meet his wolf mate he didn't know existed.

Things just got fifty times more complicated.

Chapter 24

THORIN

She's as magnificent as she is scared.

I approach her; I know my size is daunting, but surely the small wolf will recognize me as her own quickly.

Her glowing blue eyes blink at me from where she lies on the ground, in a frightened position.

"Do not worry, little mate, I would never hurt you," I tell her. "Is Violet sharing this moment with you?"

"The woman?" she asks. Her voice is sweet in my mind.

"Yes, is it just us?"

"I... I think so. I don't hear her."

"It's scary shifting for the first time. You did wonderful, little wolf."

"Who... who are you?" she asks.

"I am Thorin, your Alpha, and your mate. May I know my mate's name?" I ask her, to know my mate's name would mean everything to me.

I love Violet, I even love the man. But the wolf before me is my everything.

"Azure," she says and I raise my head to the sky, letting the beauty of her name and the sound of her voice wash over me.

I thought I was lucky to have a mate in any form; I didn't believe this was possible. But here she is. Magnificent doesn't even begin to cover how gorgeous her pelt is.

The moon has chosen wisely, but I already knew that.

"I'm scared," Azure says, and I lie down next to her, my paw over hers.

"You do not need to be scared around me or the man, we are devoted to you, though I am the more superior one."

"I can feel her, Violet. She wants to shift back," Azure says.

"You don't have to listen to her. In fact, I think we keep this mate business between you and me," I tell her.

"Why?" she asks with a precious tilt to her head.

"The man and the woman aren't as wise as us. They complicate things, though I believe they will come to terms with reality soon. For now, we can just be mates when we're in this form and leave them out of it."

"What if I'm locked in again?" she says.

I rub the top of my head against her own and she calms. Her fur is soft, and she's perfect.

I'm a lucky wolf.

"I will not let that happen. You'll never be locked away again, my mate."

"You promise?" she asks.

"I promise. Would you like to go for a run?"

"A run?" she says, standing up straight. Her legs are slightly wobbly, like a child shifting for the first time, I find it adorable. "I think I'd like that very much."

I howl at the moon and I run around with my mate all night, living the life I only ever dreamed of.

Chapter 25

SILAS

It takes what feels like forever to wrangle Thorin back. I gave him time and tried to pop in and out of his conscience to see what was going on.

All I see is the repressed wolf finally finding his mate, and I can't take that away from him.

Especially if this is a part of Violet she wants to keep tucked away in another box. I don't know how much time Thorin will have with her, so I wait and wait. When Thorin is wrapped around the wolf, I now know is named Azure, both of them panting heavily from their run, I know I can push the shift.

"Don't take her from me," Thorin asks.

"I need to make sure Violet is alright. You know how hard the first shift is."

"What if she doesn't want to shift back?" I don't have an answer for him and he whines. *"You need to tell Violet what she is to us. You need to stop these lies you tell yourself. They are ours. Be the man you need to be or I will take over for both of us,"* he says sternly.

But after he lashes me with his tongue, he gives up control. My naked body lies next to the small wolf who sleeps, and I groan.

I lie there for a moment, wondering what the fuck just happened. How Violet being able to shift changes everything. She's not just a witch, she's the only hybrid I've ever met and I'm not sure if it's possible.

Can she only shift with the necklace on? Was her wolf suppressed, and the necklace unlocked it?

I look down at her white head and realize her hair was an indicator of who she was this whole time. The white blonde from her witch family and just like Jonas, the black inky portion is from her shifter family.

This whole fucking time she was like me and neither of us knew it. It's why she's my mate, it's undeniable for me at this moment.

I could never pull Thorin away from Azure, not only because he would likely shift and never let me out, and because this has been his dream.

I never let myself actually dream of a mate, but now… now I wonder if it was more than just the hex Violet cast unknowingly on her sixteenth birthday. It all feels like so much more.

Azure is completely out, exhausted from her first run with Thorin. But I keep an eye on the wolf when I run into the dining room and grab a pair of sweatpants and an extra blanket.

I toss the blanket on top of the wolf and stroke her soft fur once before waking her up.

She doesn't look as afraid as when she first shifted, but still leery of me.

"Azure, I need you to shift back to Violet," I tell her.

She plops her head back down on the patio, ignoring me. Great, two disobedient fucking wolves to contend with.

"Azure, I'm your Alpha. You must shift back." She fucking huffs at me, no care in the world, and I sigh. "I promise I'll talk to Violet and make sure she lets you out to see Thorin."

Her eyebrow shifts, her bright blue gaze not knowing if she should trust me or not.

I reach for the necklace, and she nips at me.

"I can see why Thorin is so besotted," I tell her with a smile, stoking her fur. "If you won't shift back, you at least need to come inside."

The she-wolf glances at the house and groans before the shift happens. Violet's hair splaying on the cold hard ground of the porch while the blanket hides her modesty.

I wrap her up in the blanket, not touching her skin as I bring her to her bed. As soon as her head hits the pillow, she wraps a hand around my wrist.

"Stay," she whispers.

So I do. Hoping that maybe she means forever and not just the night.

Chapter 26

VIOLET

"You want me to stay?" Silas repeats and I tuck the quilted blanket around myself.

He's shirtless, which I've seen before, but somehow it never gets old. It's like his body was made out of bronze and carved with the female gaze in mind. His sweatpants are tight around his waist, and I try not to stare at what is definitely an impressive bulge.

I scoot over and he joins me in the bed, both of us feeling stiff and uncomfortable for a moment.

"Am I…"

"Half-wolf shifter, undoubtedly. There's no magic that I have ever heard of like that. I don't know if you can only shift with the necklace, but it clearly unlocked her. Do you hear her in your head?" Silas asks, his amber eyes looking at me with caution.

I breathe in and out and try to get in tune with my inner wolf. It's weird, foreign, and I'm not sure how I feel about it.

"You will not take me from Thorin," a soft voice whispers in my head and my eyes go wide.

"She just told me I won't take her away from Thorin. What does she look like? What's her name?" I ask, wishing I could remember a single moment when I shifted.

All I remember is pain and lethargy.

"The more you shift and become one with your wolf, the more you will be able to be present when you're shifted. However, it's nice to just let them run wild from time to time. She said her name was Azure, and she was beautiful."

"She was?" I ask, grabbing the necklace so hard it feels like my palm may bleed.

"She was. Thorin was very smitten."

I snort. "I bet he was."

With a heavy sigh, I turn on my back and look at the ceiling. "Everything is a lie," I whisper, and I truly cry, letting tears roll off the side of my face.

Deep down, I didn't buy what my grandmother was saying. It felt like a half-truth. I've put so much of my identity into being a witch, into what I can give my coven, my grandmother. Yet, it's all been a fucking lie.

"I don't know who I am," I whisper, nearly forgetting that Silas is next to me.

"Hey," he says in a deep gravelly tone and I turn to face him. His massive hand cups my face and he wipes my tears away. "This changes a lot, but it doesn't change who you are."

"How can it not? I'm a witch, it's who I am, it's what I've held onto for the last decade and a half."

"You're still a witch."

"They...if they find out," I gasp and sink further into the sheets.

Will they cast me out of the coven? Will I end up like my mother—that I'm now certain never wanted to be forgotten and magic-less. A life without Iris and Ember sounds meaningless.

My whole identity is wrapped up in my coven. Who am I if not a fully pure witch?

THE MARRIAGE HEX

All the excitement from the transformation slowly is turning into pure panic and Silas can see it in my eyes as he grips both sides of my face, forcing me to stare into his eyes.

He looks like he wants to say something, but stops himself, licking his full lips. I find myself tracing the motion, fascinated.

"You're still kind, loyal, and brave. You have and will always be that girl who met me in a treehouse to tutor me. Still the girl who I trusted my secrets with, who remembered my birthday, and always gave me her leftovers."

I laugh at the last bit, trying to calm down.

"You really see me that way?"

"Even when I don't want to. You're even more beautiful to me now," he says, his thumb still stroking my cheekbone.

I'm not sure why I do it, maybe because I need to feel something other than this bubbling panic, or because of his pretty words.

I lean in and kiss him.

It's not a peck like in the treehouse or at the courthouse. This is a *real* kiss, and it automatically soothes me. Those same butterflies I felt fourteen years ago—that I've never been close to recreating—are back in full force.

He kisses me back eagerly, hungrily. A near mirror reaction to this cosmic feeling flowing between us.

I've never kissed anyone with a beard before, but I find that I enjoy it. I like the way the soft hairs brush against my face as our lips meet and he holds my face close to his.

A masculine noise seeps between his lips and I don't think I've ever heard a sexier sound in my life as I tangle my fingers in his soft hair and hold the back of his head against mine.

No kiss has ever felt like this.

Nothing has ever felt like this.

The taste and feel of his mouth against mine is addictive, and my heart is thundering in my chest. My breathing hitches as his one hand slides from my face, cradling the side of my neck. He isn't grabbing me or holding my throat, just tenderly caressing the flesh of my collarbone and neck.

As his thumb runs lower on my throat, I realize that I'm completely naked. I should feel scandalized, not only because I've never been naked in a bed with a man before, but I don't, because it's Silas.

His tongue swipes in my mouth and I moan at the sensation, gripping his hair harder. Silas is warm, large, and perfect.

"Violet," he whispers my name like a prayer as he rests his forehead against mine. "I can't."

"What?" I say, pulling back and blinking at him.

The best kiss of my life—even if I don't have many to compare it to—and he's telling me he can't?

"I want to, believe me. I want to rip that blanket off you and do so many things. But I can't do this…not if you're not sure. Not if this is all because of the heightened emotions of what just happened, or because of some fucking spell pushing us together. You can't kiss me and walk away again," he says, and my hand slips out of his hair and I clutch the blanket closer to my chest. "I'm not scolding you. I'm not bringing up the past. I just can't have you giving me any more pieces of you if you're going to take them away again."

It's not a scolding, but it feels like one, and I scoot just a little further away from him.

"You think I kissed you because of the spell?" I ask, immediately feeling defensive. "How do I know you're not here because of the fucking spell, too?"

He takes a deep breath and flips onto his back, so I do the same.

"It's not the spell," he says.

"If it's not the spell for you, then why wouldn't it be the spell for me?"

THE MARRIAGE HEX

"You just learned you're a hybrid, the only one I've ever fucking heard of. Your life just got flipped upside down and I'm the only one here."

"Get out," I say, turning on my side.

I feel like I'm going to cry for the second time tonight and I'm doing my best to shut it down, though I think the catharsis would be good.

"Vi, I didn't mean—"

"Get out, please," I repeat, staring at my nightstand, of the photos of me and my coven.

What the fuck am I doing?

"You can sleep in the guest room down the hall instead of the couch. Just please, get out."

"Violet," he says again, trying to touch my shoulder and I shift away.

He makes a noise of protest, but I eventually feel him shift off the mattress. He doesn't shut the door right away, which is odd, but then eventually I hear the click of the knob.

A soft weight jumps on the bed, and I immediately know it's Walter. He isn't always cuddly, but he immediately walks over my body, his paws feeling like a million pounds each, until he's cuddled against my chest.

"It appears I'll have to get used to the stench of dog," he says, and I let out a small laugh before the tears start falling. *"Oh, this is terrible. Please stop,"* he says, putting a paw on my chin and pushing away.

Now I have two creatures talking directly in my mind. At least Walter can't hear my thoughts. Well, I'm not even sure if Azure can, either.

She stays silent and Walter bats at my necklace.

"I'd remove this, unless you'd like to accidentally go mongrel on us again," he says.

I sigh in agreement and place it in my nightstand drawer.

SARAH BLUE

"Shall I piss in his boot again?" Walter says, rubbing his forehead against me.

"No, that's okay. "

"It's really no hardship. I could also chew on his phone charger, or scratch his satchel to shreds."

"I appreciate it, Walter, but we have bigger issues here."

I scratch his fur, and a low purr takes over his chest as he relaxes against me.

"If it's just the necklace, you can hide it away. We can destroy it and never look back. No one except the stinky man down the hall will ever know. Plus, we could still kill him, toss him in the swamp and let the alligators eat him. Then there will be no witnesses."

"I don't know if that's what I want. I definitely don't want Silas to be alligator food."

The cat sighs, wiggling out of my grip and going to sit on his pillow. Apparently, that's as much affection as I'll be getting tonight.

"You're still a witch, my witch above all else. The universe sent me here as your companion. I'll be by your side no matter what, even if you smell horrible."

"Thanks, Walter. I love you, too."

"Don't get all soft on me now, witch," he says. *"Get some rest."*

I try to sleep, but all that plagues me is nightmares.

Nightmares that feel a hell of a lot like visions. A black and white wolf convulsing alone in a forest.

It feels like an omen, and I'm not sure that necklace was made to protect me, after all.

Digging into the past may just ruin or deny me my future forever.

Chapter 27

SILAS

Sleep evades me. All I can think about is everything that happened last night.

The necklace, Azure, Violet's tears, the kiss.

That fucking kiss.

"You're such a disappointment," Thorin says, and I groan, rubbing my eyes so hard with my palms my vision has dark spots.

I wanted it. Part of me hates that I stopped, even if it was the right decision.

I wanted to kiss her before I found out she was a wolf, as much as I hate to admit it. But now that I know we're true mates, in every sense a shifter can be, everything has changed for me. There are more possibilities now than there weren't before. Now we're physiologically matched, though not completely on the same page.

She's still a witch, that hasn't and will not change. What she decides to do with this new information, this new part of herself, will decide everything.

If she abandons her wolf, then I'm not sure what will happen. There's no way Thorin would stand for it, and I'm not sure how I could move on. I'd live the rest of my life as I already have, celibate and alone.

Violet has some serious choices to make when it comes to her coven and my pack. They are her choices and hers alone.

No matter how fucking badly I want to sit her down and lay out everything for her. That she could be the person, the thing, that brings the shifters and witches to peace. That she has to realize she's been lied to by her grandmother at the very least, some truths have been withheld.

I thought I could fight this tether between us, look past the fact she was my mate because it wouldn't really work. But the universe has a way of making me swallow my own words.

The resentment of the way she left Mander's is slipping away the more I get to know her and learn about her life.

She didn't want to leave me. She hid me away in a mental box, not because she wanted to, but because she felt like she had to. We would have been something. We could still be something.

Even with all these revelations I still realize that I'm the only one winning in this situation. I get everything, keeping my pack, peace with the witches, and my mate.

Violet could possibly lose everything she's known in her adult life. That… that is precisely why I had to stop that kiss, no matter how good it felt. As much as I meant what I said, I can't go through the torment of losing her again. I also can't let her choices be based on me, this hex, or the tug she may possibly feel from this unmet mating bond.

Maybe since she's only half, she doesn't feel it as strongly as a full-blooded shifter would. Her wolf, however, would undoubtedly have been able to feel it.

"She did. She's beautiful, my mate," Thorin says as five loud bangs jolt me out of the bed as I rush down the hall to the top of the stairs.

Violet looks at me, blinking away her sleep, it appears I'm not the only one who didn't get much sleep last night.

"Violet Delvaux, open this fucking door right now before I blow the hinges off," the voice says and Violet rolls her eyes, flicking her wand, which effortlessly smoothes and ties her hair into a bun.

"I'm coming," Violet yells as she descends down the stairs.

When she swings open the door, there are two women on the other side. One I recognize, but haven't actually met. Violet just used her face when she was hiding from the other witches. Her hair is a long blondish-red, and she wears heart-shaped sunglasses and a pink sundress. The other witch is taller than the other two, with long braids that hit her mid back, she's wearing a simple black t-shirt and jeans.

Both of their gazes look up the stairs and they just stare.

"Go put a shirt on," Violet says waving a hand at me.

"Oh my god, did you two sleep together?" the redhead asks.

"No, Ember. Jesus. What's with the wake up call and the inquisition?"

"I don't know, maybe because a few days ago you spilled all your secrets to me, which I physically can not tell Ember, and I haven't heard from you since, which then made me take matters into my own hands. This isn't like you, Vi," her other coven member says.

"I'm sorry for not getting in touch, Iris," Violet says, feeling properly scolded. I grab a shirt, tug it over my head, and go to meet my wife's best friends.

It only takes me a few minutes to join them in the kitchen, all three of the witches turning their gaze on me. The redhead I know now as Ember's mouth is wide open. It seems Violet was able to get the basics of our situation out while I was upstairs.

"You're married. Like, full blown husband and wife?"

"Yes," I reply.

"For now," Violet says.

Iris watches both Violet and me extremely closely, like she's fitting all the puzzle pieces together, though there's no way she can know the complete truth about everything.

"And the hex is forcing you to live together?" Iris asks.

Among many other things.

"Yes, and we're working on breaking it. There's no reason to tell the High Priestess," Violet says, while pretending to be busy in the kitchen.

Iris stands, her fingertips balancing on the table.

"When you're ready to be honest and tell us the truth about everything, let us know. Ember, let's go," she says and Violet's eyes widen.

"Wait," she stops her coven members, and they sit back down on their seats. As she leans against the wooden counters that still look like the original ones built in the home, I perch my own ass against the counter and wonder if she's going to make her decision right now.

"I found my mother," she says instead, clearly not going the route of complete honesty.

"Shit, you did?" Ember asks, her deep green eyes full of pity and sadness for her friend.

"She didn't recognize me. She has no magical signature."

Iris's brows furrow, and she glances down at the table.

"What did Aster say?" Iris asks.

"She said that I took her magic from her when I was born, and she decided to live a human life. That she probably put me up for adoption because she couldn't handle what I did to her."

I glance over at Violet. She hadn't told me this yet. It doesn't match the same mother who set up a nursery, wrote letters, and clearly worked very hard on a necklace to preserve her other half.

THE MARRIAGE HEX

"You don't believe her," Iris says and Violet shakes her head.

"It just doesn't make sense, none of it. Why can no one truly remember my mother?" Violet asks.

The two other witches look contemplative.

"You told him this before us?" Iris asks, and Violet shakes her head.

"No, he didn't know what grand-mére said before now."

Iris looks at me, her eyes going hazy for a moment, and she quickly looks away.

"How can we help?" Ember says in an upbeat voice that makes Violet smile. I eye the witch, wondering why she's so suddenly eager to help Violet and not concerned about going behind her High Priestess' back.

"Grand-mére can't know what we're up to. We can't bring anyone else in from the coven, not yet. I need to work on getting this issue resolved," she says, shoving a thumb in my direction. "I also need to find out what really happened."

"Is it not in the past?" Iris asks.

Violet simply shakes her head no, and Iris sighs.

"Ember can look through the archives. Her grandmother has some of the best kept histories of the coven. I'll help with this situation," Iris says, glancing at the two of us. "What do you have so far?"

Violet blushes, and it's endearing. "Not much."

Iris rubs her temples, clearly frustrated with the lack of initiative on our end.

"I have an idea. I need to talk to the shifter alone," Iris says.

Violet looks panicked, but Ember takes her hand as they go out into the backyard. I watch from the window as Ember uses her gift to regrow and revive some less than fortunate plants in her backyard.

SARAH BLUE

"Are you going to be a hindrance in reversing this spell?" Iris asks.

"Wouldn't dream of it," I reply, and she narrows her eyes at me. I cross my arms over my chest and she mimics the motion, not backing down for a moment.

"We could lock you up and toss you into the basement."

"This house doesn't have a basement, and I'd simply shift and free myself."

"We could confine you to the house."

"You could," I reply, staring down at the formidable witch.

"Violet is a lot softer than she looks, if you think I'm going to let you fall back into her life and tear her apart again, you're dead fucking wrong."

Confusion is riddled on my face as I speak. "She left, not me."

"Please, as if she had a choice. The first months she was here, all she would do is cry over you and endlessly talk about you to the point where I would wish for my hearing to give out. She's my sister and I'll have her back no matter what. That includes ruining you if you hurt her."

"We're working towards dissolving this marriage," I remind Iris, who rolls her eyes.

She pulls out her wand, just toying with it, not threatening me directly.

"Aster is going to ascend Violet within the next decade," she says, and I know the confused look on my face feels permanent. "Violet missed out on a lot of basics being away for so long. No matter how she may think of herself, she is actually extraordinarily gifted as a witch. I don't think anyone else with only fourteen years of training would be where she is now. The High Priestess is hard on her, because she wants her to be the best, to continue the Delvaux dynasty."

"What are you getting at?" I ask.

Her bright amber eyes glance up at me. "If you had to wait a decade for there to be a change in hierarchy within the coven, would you?"

She's being serious, and so my answer is just as real.

"I've waited fourteen. What's another ten?"

She nods, tucking her wand away. "I'll get to work on getting rid of this legal problem of ours. You work on not making a mess of things, and we'll get our house in order," the witch says, and I wonder why she isn't in charge of things.

Iris smirks, as if she knows what I'm thinking.

"Witches who have the gift of foresight can never lead a coven. Understanding the future is both a blessing and a curse," she says with one final glance as she goes to the backyard to speak with her two friends.

I scrub a hand down my face and fill a glass of water for myself and wait for Violet to return.

The cat jumps on the table and sits in front of me, staring at me with his freakishly yellow eyes.

We just sit there in the stalemate, until he sticks his paw into my glass of water and then licks the droplets off his nails.

I realize that I somewhat have her friends on my side, now it's time to tame the small magical beast.

SARAH BLUE

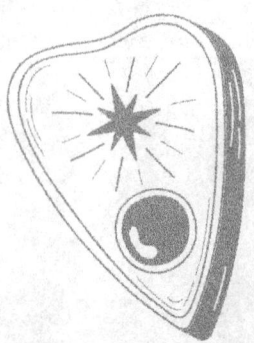

Chapter 28

VIOLET

Ember takes the vow of secrecy, and we all make plans to solve my problems.

Even if Iris looks at me like I'm still keeping secrets.

Which I am, but I just can't bring myself to admit this piece yet. They accept my whoopsie of a marriage, and my wanting to go behind my grandmother's back to find out my history.

But admitting to them that I'm part shifter, or that I have the ability to shift with a necklace, is just too much. There's only so much acceptance I can ask for and I worry this may be too far. Or maybe it's all just because I haven't accepted it yet.

I hug them both as I head back into the house. Silas is sitting in a dining room chair as he and Walter have a staring contest.

He grabs a piece of a muffin that I made last night and puts it down for Walter. My familiar seems confused at first, and eyes Silas suspiciously before bending his head, never taking his eyes off Silas and eating the pastry.

It's the first nail in the *'I'm falling for Silas Walker'* coffin.

That's probably a lie. These pesky feelings have been riding my ass longer than I'd like to admit. But this is all post enlightenment, post me knowing most of the truth.

"What did Iris say?" I ask, and both Silas and Walter glance over at me.

"Typical witch threats," he says, and he gives Walter some more muffin.

He's buttering up the cat and me. I'm fucked.

"You took the necklace off," he says in an even tone.

"Yes, well. I don't know if it's the necklace itself that allows me to… change. Or if the necklace was just a key unlocking a very dormant lock."

He nods and takes a sip of coffee. The coffee I made for myself. Mentally I use a crowbar and unhinge that aforementioned nail in the said *'I'm falling for Silas Walker'* coffin.

"I'll see if Jonas or I can find anything in the pack's archives."

"Isn't he busy with his new mate?" I question.

Something in me feels uneasy about the very little knowledge I have of shifters and mates. I shifted, yet as I stand here in my kitchen, I don't feel any different.

It's not like I'd want Silas to be my mate, anyway.

Oh, the lies I keep telling myself.

"He's busy with Paige, the baby, and other tasks as my second."

"Did they give him a name?" I ask, making myself another cup of coffee. Honestly, it's very mature of me to not complain that he stole mine. Go me.

"Ryden," he says. "Ryden Walker."

I glance back at him with a furrowed brow. "I thought you said Jonas found his family. He didn't take their surname?"

"No," he says simply, and I turn back to the coffeemaker. I'm just as protective of Iris and Ember.

Fuck. He's just struck the second nail.

Unfortunately for me there are a series of events that have me feeling a particular way about my dearest husband. Feelings that I shouldn't be having when I haven't made a decision about my wolf, my coven, or literally anything.

The only clear decision I've made in the recent days is that my husband is fucking hot.

I'm sitting on the porch, it's nearly twilight and the air around me smells like fall as the harsh sun slowly slips away. But it's not the fading sun against the red maple and black willow trees that are catching my attention.

No, not even close.

It's my shirtless husband raising an axe behind his head and easily slicing wood that has my full attention. Sweat beads are trickling down his muscular back and I have the abhorrent thought that I would eagerly lick it if he'd let me.

I've never looked at a man the same I do as Silas, let alone have such illicit thoughts. I'm truly not sure what to do with all of this energy.

When he lifts the axe and cuts through the wood, I realize I have to stop watching him, that I'm actually getting physically worked up. Part of me wonders if this is his own way of letting out frustration over our situation. It feels like the spell is getting stronger, like we aren't giving it what it wants. Which I worry is because our marriage isn't consummated.

His stack of wood is large and I figure if I get some of this tension out, maybe I wouldn't be sitting here basically degrading the man into a sex symbol.

Though, I imagine masturbating to your husband, who's not really your husband, is no better.

Yet, I find myself with a cracked nightstand drawer and a vibrator down my panties. The visuals I come up with are more than enough to have me nearly coming instantly.

Me wrapping my arms around his waist and grazing my fingertips along his rippled abdomen before going further and grabbing what I'm imagining is a very large cock.

In my fantasy, I'm confident as I stroke him outside of his pants. A low moan rips through his throat before he turns around and cups my jaw before leaning down and kissing me. His massive arm wraps around my middle as he hefts me up to deepen the kiss before carrying me to the porch and into the back of the house.

We're ravenous for it, knocking all the candles and trinkets on the dining room table before he's sitting me on the edge and ripping my dress in half. I'm panting in the fantasy and on my bed as I move the vibrator to the right spot.

The noise that falls out of me is obscene, and I come before I can picture him touching me, my back arches off my bed and I squeeze my eyes shut as my release hits me.

It's decent, but it still doesn't feel like enough. I curse, walking to the bathroom and washing the toy before leaving it on the counter to dry.

This is all so fucked up. I shouldn't be incorporating Silas into my masturbation material, let alone getting off on it before he even slides his hand below my collarbone.

When I go back to the kitchen, I use this energy to make some more sweet tea, along with another batch of muffins. But unfortunately, I don't really need to do much when magic handles most of the legwork.

So I just stand by the window, getting my fill of Silas chopping wood, but he's already making his way back into the house. In an effort not to look awkward, I look exceptionally awkward as he comes through the backdoor and his eyes pan directly to me.

A smirk takes over his face and I clear my throat.

"What are you working on out there?" I ask.

"Not as important as what you're working on in here," he says slyly.

No fucking way. Can this shifter scent what I just did? Oh, Hecate, does he know I just masturbated after watching him cut wood?

"What?" I say, busying my hands.

"More muffins. The last batch was delicious. I'm going to go shower," he says, though there's a glint in his eye and a smug smile on his face.

I can't help but find it attractive.

The third nail aggressively bangs itself into place.

It feels like we're getting nowhere. No one can find any information that isn't already speculated from thirty years ago, and Iris doesn't seem to have any idea on how to reverse this spell either.

So, I spend my days pretending that everything is fine, even if the necklace in my drawer haunts me daily. I continue my lessons with my grand-mére, I do my daily duties as the coven's healer. But most notably, every night, the sound of an old Harley down my driveway lights a fire in my chest.

Sometimes we eat together, sometimes we say nothing. But lately it's like a craving is festering away at me.

I need a distraction from my husband.

So, I bought a puzzle. A puzzle is a completely unsexy way to share the same space and not be tempted to touch.

Silas made himself clear. Unless I know what I want. AKA if I'm going to embrace my wolf, or accept him wolf and all, then there's no point to this attraction.

I'm no step closer to a decision. Even if I have been tempted to put the necklace back on. It's evident that the necklace is what ties me to my shifter side, because Azure has been silent. I don't hear Azure the way Silas hears Thorin, and I haven't felt the ache to shift.

I could toss the necklace away, destroy it and my life would go back to normal, just as soon as we get a divorce.

Is that what I want?

The alternative could be losing my coven and not being accepted by the pack. I could have Silas, but I'd lose everything else, and I'm not sure I can make that decision either.

I need this hex removed so I can fucking think clearly.

It's easier to just sort the puzzle pieces by exterior and interior so that's what I'm doing as Silas walks through the door. A gash across his face, trickling blood down his neck and over his lip.

"What the hell happened?" I ask.

He waves me off and sits down on his chair at the dining table. When he claimed a chair, I'm not sure, but that's the one he sits in now.

"It will heal by tomorrow," he says, as I grab a washcloth and cover it in warm water before coming to stand between his legs and press it against his face.

"What happened?" I ask again softly.

"There was a challenge for being Alpha."

"And they did this?" I ask. He doesn't even wince as I clean up the blood, just stares at me while he speaks.

"You should see the other guy. When I fell, I hit my head on a branch. It's just a scratch."

"Why were they challenging you?"

He shrugs and I sigh, grabbing my jar of healing salve before setting it on the table.

"Why?" I ask again.

"Because they don't agree that we should make peace with the other supernaturals. They think we should be pack strong and that's it."

I stick my fingers into the pinkish wax like salve before grabbing his chin and putting it along the gash.

"Can I ask you something?"

"Yes," he replies.

"If I wasn't in the equation, would you still want harmony with the other groups?"

"Yes. Why wouldn't I? Getting along with everyone who will outlive humans, who has to keep the same secret, it's a good decision."

"But most factions don't get along."

"Mostly over historical bullshit no one can remember. If we're united as supernatural beings, it can only benefit all of us."

I concentrate on his wound and process his words. Words I agree with. Words that my grandmother would hate to hear.

"My grand-mére will never see it like that."

SARAH BLUE

"What if she wasn't High Priestess?" he says, his large hand grazing my thigh, which sends a tingle down my spine. "What if someone with a more open mind was leading your coven?"

"I...I'm not ready." I mean it more than I care to admit. The idea of being High Priestess so soon is terrifying, and I don't know if I'm cut out for it.

"I'm not pushing you, but could you imagine a world where you're accepted for who you truly are? Your two friends that were here the other day. I know they wouldn't turn their back on you if they knew you were half shifter."

I go to step away, and Silas grabs the back of my thigh, keeping me in between his legs.

"She's my family," I whisper.

"And shouldn't your family love you regardless?" he asks and damn it, I hate how emotional I've been lately, how confused I feel over everything.

Because I know he's right, that my grandmother's love has conditions. What does it mean that I'm willing to hide who I am to appease her?

I look away from him, and his hand lightly rubs the back of my thigh. Despite the heavy conversation, I lean into his touch.

"My acceptance of you comes with no conditions."

I scoff. "Only because you know I'm part wolf now."

"It doesn't hurt, but let's not deny there was something between us before that, Vi. It might have taken me longer if you never shifted, but you can't deny what's between us doesn't feel cosmic."

"It's the hex," I reply.

"Or is it just fate?" he asks, tapping my thigh, and I move out of the way so he can stand. He towers over me as he looks down at me, cupping the side of my face with his large hand, which is warm and calloused, and unbelievably comforting. "Don't deny yourself of who you are. Haven't you already given enough?"

He walks away, and it's like the coffin seals itself shut.

I want my husband, but I can't have him. Not until I make some very serious decisions.

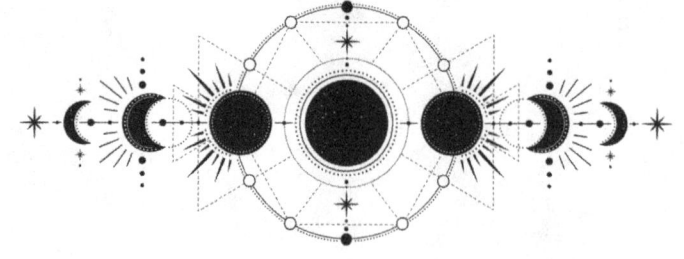

Chapter 29

AZURE

If this bitch doesn't let me out soon, I'm going to have to take matters into my own hands.

Chapter 30

VIOLET

It's Trunk or Treat for the businesses on Main Street. It's not really Trunk or Treat. I guess they don't know how to advertise that it's trick or treating from business to business.

I help Iris every year alongside Ember, who already used paint to make the storefront design. It's a mixture of black cats and orange pumpkins. We even splurged for full size candy bars this year.

The only problem is the property is now owned by Walker Industries, which means Silas is currently across the street at Howl at the Moon, which has always been a dive bar. It's just under a new name and management now. The shifter presence in town has increased exponentially and everyone's noticed.

I curse as my grand-mére approaches us, glaring across the street at the walk-through haunted house the bar has.

"This is just ridiculous," my grand-mère says.

"It hasn't changed business. If anything, I've sold more this month," Iris says, tilting her witch's hat back.

"It's because it's October. Main Street used to be our territory. A wolf wouldn't dare to come here. Now they're everywhere," she complains, crossing her arms.

"They're just people, grand-mère."

"Tell that to your dead coven members," she snaps back.

I'm not sure why I grow a spine at that moment. Maybe it's because I know she's lying, or Silas' words from last night.

"You know, I can't find anything about coven members being attacked in the archives. Nor can I find any reason why we've been feuding with the wolves for so long."

"You know our records are mostly verbally based to protect the sanctity of the coven."

"I also note that every single Celestial Coven owned business on Main Street has done better since Walker Industries took over, and they haven't raised any of their rents."

"Yet, he hasn't raised it yet."

I cross my arms, realizing that my witch outfit is a little too tits out for this argument, but I don't care.

"He offered peace. You didn't take it. Maybe the coven is the problem here."

My grand-mère's clear blue eyes flash and she rests her hand on the table in front of us, pushing aside the Kit-Kats and Sour Patch Kids.

"Do you need a reminder of why and who we are? All the witches who died at the stake so that you could sit out here dressed like a stereotype and live amongst the greedy, stupid humans? Or must you be reminded of your conditions prior to this coven? I am your blood, the reason you get to practice magic and flitter around that decrepitate disaster of a purple monstrosity every day. Perhaps you don't have what it takes to lead the coven one day. Perhaps I made an error in my judgment. Surely Iris is more cunning, Ember more relatable and good with the soil. There's also Hazel and Rosalee. Their devotion to the coven has never come into question. Act like a respectable witch or I shall show you nothing but the harsh real-

THE MARRIAGE HEX

ities of what it is to be on my wrong side."

I swallow, my confidence leaving me immediately.

"Yes, grand-mère, I understand."

She lifts her hands off the table, straightening her dress and looking across the street.

"I'm going to retire for the evening. Do make sure the patrons of Goddess Apothecary know we are the best and only place to get their beauty and health needs," she says, glaring one more time across the street.

Where Silas is staring at us, no doubt listening in. Can wolves hear that far?

My grandmother walks away, and Ember has a hand on my back.

"Are you okay? That was a bit of a reaction," Ember asks.

"Do you think she's onto us?" Iris asks.

"I don't think so. I'm just going to get some fresh air," I say.

"Violet, we're outside," Ember says and I wave her off as I walk a block down and slip through the alleyway.

The cool, rough brick presses against my back as I wrap my arms around myself.

I realize I can't live this way. I can't live a lie.

Not only the lie of who I really am, but I can't blindly follow my grand-mère anymore. The wolves' distrust of witches is just as backward as ours of the wolves. But with Silas at the helm of the pack? With the coven discovering that the modern world is beyond ourselves? Real change feels possible.

Change doesn't happen in a day, far from it.

I need a plan, a real plan on how we can make the coven see the light and how the hell I'm going to come out with my own secret.

Something tells me that my mother is the key to solving all of this, and that's where I'll have to start. Along with dissolving this hex with Silas, even if I've made my choice, I need to know that what's between us is real and not the magic I unknowingly cast as a teenager.

"Are you alright?" his familiar voice says, startling and comforting me at the same time.

"How much of that did you hear?"

"All of it," he says.

"I think you're right," I tell him as he comes next to me, leaning against the brick, his side briefly touching mine.

"I'm right about most things."

"Doesn't mean you need to be an ass about it," I say, bumping his hip.

"That's exactly what it means. But, really, are you okay?"

"I think she's on to me," I sigh and look up at Silas, who is undoubtedly staring down my dress right now. "My face is up here, Alpha," I say.

The sound that ripples through him is purely masculine and borderline animalistic, as he spins, putting a hand above my head and another on my hip as he looks me in the eyes and down at my breasts again.

"Did you wear this so I would stare at you all Halloween, Vi?"

"Is it working?"

"I wanted to smack the teenager dressed as the Joker that was staring down your dress," he says, his fingertip touching my collarbone and ever so slightly trailing my skin to the top of my breast. "I hope you have a decision soon."

"I have a decision," I tell him breathlessly. His hand slides up to delicately rest against my collarbone.

"Is your decision for me to finger fuck you in this alleyway? I can scent your arousal, you know?" I gasp and blink at him while he smiles. "Should I go chop some wood to get you in the mood, wife?"

I wrap my hand around his wrist and lick my lips. I should let him, no, I definitely shouldn't let him. Anyone could see us together and report back to my grand-mère.

"Only if we still feel this way when the hex is lifted," I say, trying to be strong and not admitting to the other parts.

He leans in, his nose trailing my jaw, like he's scenting me.

"I'm patient. Very patient," he says, kissing the side of my throat, before adjusting his very large cock in his jeans, winking at me, and walking away.

I slump against the brick wall and take a few breaths.

He's going to come to my house tonight and I'll only be able to think about his hands on me, how he wants me. This is bad, I need to keep my wits about me.

I pass all the other Halloween tables. Kids are meddling about dressed as their favorite characters and supernatural beings. If only they knew we were right in front of their faces.

As soon as I'm back at Iris' table, she knows something's up.

"Why are you flushed?" she asks.

No point in lying now. "I need something to curb my libido," I say.

Ember looks like I'm delusional, and Iris just laughs.

"Hate to break it to you, but no one comes shopping for a dry snatch. The only thing I have are some oils to help things run smoother."

I plop into my chair and rub my face. "I fear I want to fuck my husband," I say on a sigh.

"Pft. Do it, it's not like you haven't done it before," Ember says and my cheeks heat even redder. "Wait. Violet. No. Seriously?" Ember asks, going through all the emotions. She grabs at my skirt. "Have you checked for cobwebs?"

SARAH BLUE

I smack her hand away. "Stop it. The opportunity never came around and then time just went by and it felt like I didn't need it. This is the first time I've actually wanted to."

"You should check with your great aunt Daisy, I'm sure she can give you a ritual or something so you won't throw yourself at the man," Iris suggests as a group of girls dressed like princesses grab some candy with their sweet rounds of 'trick or treat.'

"Grand-mère is probably out praying to Hecate for my obedience. She probably isn't home. I'll give that a try," I say.

Iris clicks her tongue. "Or, you could give into something you want for the first time in forever."

I give her a small smile. "I can't. Not until I know it isn't the hex."

"If that's what you need," Iris says.

"Do you two have everything handled here?" I ask and they both nod.

"Just to put my two cents in, I think you should ride that ride and then come back and tell me what wolf dick is like," Ember says and I toss a bag of M&M's at her, before I pay my great aunt Daisy a visit.

When I enter the home, she's where she always is, at the window reading a book. I grab one of the red velvet chairs with gold filigree decor and slide it next to her. She pauses on her page, touching my face gently with a smile.

"Hey, Aunt Daisy," I tell her and she smiles.

Her face is wrinkled with time, but her pale blue eyes are always expressive.

"I'm hoping you have a particular spell. One that would… um… make someone…" I didn't think about how exactly I was

THE MARRIAGE HEX

going to ask her for a spell or ritual on how to not be horny before I got here.

She taps my hand twice, and two books come flying at her small oak table at once. They both look ancient as the top one opens, the cover slapping as the pages turn on their own accord.

I read the pages it lands on.

The Ritual of Virtue.

I skim the pages, not really liking the solution, but it's better than nothing.

"How did you know?" I ask her in embarrassment.

She cups my face and for the first time it looks like she wants to talk, but can't. My great aunt sighs, and just taps on the page twice. I collect the book, but she smacks her cane twice against the wooden floor. I glance back at her and she holds the second book.

I don't know why she wants me to have it, but I take it, placing a kiss against her white, thinning hair. She touches my face one more time as I leave the house.

As soon as I'm out of her wards I teleport home, working on everything I need to build a fire. Thankfully, my dear husband chopped me plenty of wood.

Tonight is not going to be fun.

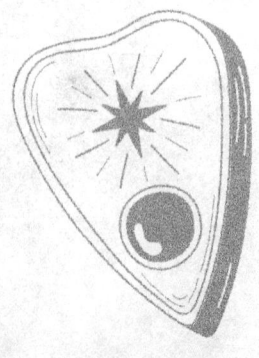

Chapter 31

VIOLET

I didn't expect to spend my night building a fire.

Thank goodness for magic, because without it I probably would have given up after carrying one log. But with feather light spells I'm able to bring everything I want into the woods.

It's still technically my property, but it's deep enough you won't be able to see the fire from my back porch. At least I hope.

It just so happens that I'm in luck with the waning moon. The new moon starts tomorrow, which means this spell has a three-day window, and today happens to be that day.

I scatter the cymbidiums into the growing fire as night takes over. I'll be able to perform the ceremony in about fifteen minutes. Until then, I stare at the flames and consider everything I'm going to have to do.

Going behind my coven's back isn't something I would have considered a month ago. But it has to be done.

The truth needs to come out, no matter what it is.

Part of that is denying myself this one thing I want. I've waited thirty years for this. What's a little bit more time?

I groan, hating that I'm being impatient, hating that I want him so badly.

The idea of desiring a man before felt frivolous and kind of disgusting. Men as a whole are rather irrelevant, but Silas is something else. Now here I am performing a ritual on Halloween night to prevent myself from climbing that giant man and experiencing how good he can make me feel. Just like he rationalized the night we kissed, I need to know this is real.

Just as much as Silas can't let me walk away again, neither can I.

I look up at the stars and the moonless sky and sigh—it's showtime. I take off my nightgown, tossing it to the side before placing the white pedal of a carnation on my tongue as I hold my hands in the sky and begin the ritual.

The flames are hot and have my naked body dripping with sweat as I perform the ceremony.

You're supposed to do the chant one-hundred times, which seems excessive, but I'm going to follow it to a T.

I'm at chant eighty-nine when a stick breaks behind me, breaking my concentration.

My head snaps to the side, some of my hair sticking to my neck as glowing amber eyes stare at me. I swallow thickly, unmoving, as the wolf steps toward me.

This isn't sweet Thorin, who lies on my bed for snuggles or forces me to wear a shirt that smells like him. No, he looks like the true predator he is and it only takes a moment for him to shift back into Silas.

Seeing a naked, slightly sweaty Silas approaching me does not help when I was mid ritual.

His cock is already hard, huge, and different?

I tilt my head to the side, noticing the bulge at the base of his hard shaft. My gaze trickles down to his large muscular thighs and then back to his face. All I see there is hunger.

I don't know why I do it. Maybe it's insanity. Maybe I fucked up the ritual. But I do the stupidest thing possible.

I run.

Fallen leaves and twigs fracture under my feet, and my chest heaves as I take each step, knowing I'm not going to get far.

When I turn my head, my hair sticking to my skin, he's closer than I thought.

Fuck.

My pulse is racing with a mixture of desire, fear, and excitement. He warned me not to run, told me exactly what would happen. I'm either hard-headed or I wanted him to chase.

It's the latter and I'm more than slightly embarrassed to admit it.

I'm getting more turned on as I circle back toward the fire, the large wolf shifter behind me is chasing me and I'm not even sure he's going at full speed.

I glance back at him, and nearly trip. Two large arms wrapping behind me, his hard cock pressed against my back as he lifts me off the ground. One hand is secured around my waist as the other wraps around my jaw.

He doesn't speak right away, no; he licks a line down the side of my neck, up to my ear.

It's hotter than I ever expected it to be. I never thought licking someone could be so erotic, but wasn't I just envisioning myself doing the same thing only a few days ago?

I grip his forearm that's holding me, my nails digging into his skin as he rubs his nose into my hair.

"I can smell how wet you are, little wife. Let me take away the ache."

A big part of me breaks at that moment. He told me not to run, it clearly brings out a dominant possessive side of him. But I know that if I told him no, if I asked him to walk away, he'd let me.

It's why I stay and give him the slightest nod.

The sound that leaves Silas is masculine and deep, making my legs shake as he holds me closer to his body. He's so big and warm, and it's almost like I'm consumed by him. I've never been this turned on, I've never wanted to be with someone so desperately.

A little voice in my head is nagging me about the hex. But fuck it. I've spent my entire life being cautious. This is the one thing I want, and you know what? I'm going to let myself have it.

"I told you not to run from me, little witch," he whispers against my ear as he carries me easily over to the fire. "Did you want to be caught? Is this what you need?" he asks, grabbing my breast with his hand and I moan.

"Yes," I whisper, and he groans.

Silas sets me down on my feet and turns me so I'm facing him. I'm greeted with a direct view of his chest, and he tilts my chin up, forcing me to look into his eyes.

"Tell me you ran because you wanted this too," he says, his thumbs rubbing soothing circles on my cheekbones.

I decide I'm quite tired of him asking me the same question over and over, so instead of a verbal response, I wrap my hand around his cock. Even if I don't feel particularly confident about my skills, the sound of pleasure that spills out of him has my ego inflating immediately.

His hand wraps around mine, tightening my grip, and I swallow. I avoid the base of his cock, and I'm not really sure how to bring up that situation there, so I ignore it for now.

"I want you, Vi," he says and I sigh with relief. It's not another question of consent, which he already fully has.

His hand leaves mine and I swear it shakes as he grabs me by the hip and draws me in for a kiss. I lose all my momentum at that point, and eventually give up. It's like I can't think when he's kissing me.

That same electric energy fills me like it has the other times we've kissed and I know without a doubt there's no turning back. Though, I think deep down, I always knew that.

Silas bends further down, grabbing the back of my thighs to bring me down to the ground. I whisper a quick spell for the grass to be soft and clean as he crawls on top of me, taking in every inch of my body as he does.

"Do you know how beautiful you are?" he says.

"No. Tell me," I whisper, as bats flap wildly in my stomach.

He smiles. His body is on top of mine, and I'm eager for it. I'm not afraid.

"You're the only woman I've ever dreamed about. The only one I ever wanted this with," he says, kissing down my neck as his hand squeezes my breast, his thumb toying with the piercing I got on a whim at twenty.

"I haven't… nevermind," I say, as his brown eyes meet mine, an over confident smile taking over his face.

Smug bastard.

"Neither have I. Was waiting for you, wife," he says.

My heart thunders in my chest. No, surely he doesn't mean what I think he means? My brows furrow and he leans forward, sucking my nipple in between his lips before pulling back.

"Really?" I ask. Maybe it's because I feel insecure about my situation, but he waited? For me?

He just makes a grunt of acknowledgement as he kisses down my stomach, his hands gripping my hips tightly as he shifts down my body. My breathing is labored in a mix of excitement and nerves.

Silas kisses the apex between my thighs, causing my back to

arch. The fire crackles beside us, but all I can hear is my heartbeat. He slides his finger from the top of my pussy, collecting an obscene amount of wetness before sliding two fingers inside of me.

I gasp, and before I have a moment to revel in the sensation, his lips are on me.

Oh, my fucking stars.

Silas goes down on me like I'm the best thing he's ever tasted. He's messy with it, not caring about the sounds or any semblance of politeness. I feel devoured in the best way possible.

I thread my hand in his hair, and he groans against my clit, before redoubling his efforts to make me come. His fingertips are digging into my flesh and I find I like the little bite of pain against the pleasure he's currently bringing me.

He curls his fingers inside of me, sucking down hard on my clit, and I fall apart. Screaming into the night air as he holds my legs, keeping my thighs tightly pressed against his face.

My legs are trembling, my back arched against the ground, as my eyes close in ecstasy.

This is what I've been missing all this time. I mean, I'm no stranger to getting myself off, but this is something wholly different. It's addictive. No, being with Silas is what's addictive. I can almost guarantee it would never have felt as good with someone else.

He kisses his way back up my body, wiping his mouth off with his forearm, before bracketing me with his big body. I spread my legs wide, making room for him as I wrap my hands around the back of his neck and bring him in for a kiss. The salty but clean taste of me is fresh on his tongue, and it only makes me want him more.

I've denied myself happiness for so long; denied myself of having Silas for even longer.

"Please, let me fuck you," Silas says, his body nearly shaking with an energy I can't explain. He presses his forehead against mine.

"I want you," I tell him honestly and hope he understands the double meaning of my words.

He pushes some hair out of my face, cradling the back of my head as he kisses me roughly. His beard is soft against my face, but there's nothing gentle about the kiss. It's hard, needy, borderline feral as he dominates my mouth.

His other hand grabs his cock, gliding the tip against my wet entrance as I wait in anticipation. His fingers grip my hair, like he's searching for some sort of control.

Silas lines his cock with my entrance and slowly pushes in. My head falls back to the sky, but not for long as he tugs my hair, forcing me to look at him. His eyes are glowing brighter than usual as he looks at me.

The noise he makes I can only describe as a masculine whimper as he pushes into me—not all the way.

"Don't worry, baby, I'll work you up to taking my knot. You want it, don't you?" he asks, his fingers laced in my hair and his cock deep inside of me.

I nod, the motion straining my neck and he smiles, before leaning in and kissing me.

"Do you know how fucking long I've thought about what it would feel like being inside of you? Better than I could have imagined," he says.

He hitches my thigh up, the wetness that was coating his fingers is now sticky on my thigh. It allows him to go deeper. He's bigger than any toy I've used on myself and I embrace the stretch.

I dig my nails into his broad, thick shoulders, and can't help but to look down, admiring the way we look together.

His abdominal muscles flex, as the hair that trails down his stomach presses into the softness of my skin with each thrust. The dark patch of hair above his length hits my clit with every flex of his hips, and I'm close.

"Silas," I say his name. I'm not sure if it's in praise or a forewarning, but he clearly likes his name spilling from my tongue while he's deep inside of me.

"Make a mess on your m—husband's cock," he tells me.

He forces my mouth back to his, kissing me hungrily as he pushes in and out of me, his pelvis rubbing in just the right spot.

"You own me, Violet," he says, and it has me falling apart, hitting my second peak of the night.

My walls tighten around Silas' length and he's moaning with me while I let it ricochet through me.

"Come inside me," I grate out.

I swear it wasn't a spell, but it almost feels like it the way he immediately presses harder into me, coming with a curse, and a firm hand tightening in my hair.

He doesn't pull out right away, and all I can think is this was one-hundred percent worth waiting for.

Chapter 32

SILAS

I stroke her soft skin, her bright blue eyes scanning my face, and I wonder exactly how we got here and where my patience went.

My plan was to wait, to make sure she was ready for this—that I was ready for this. But when she ran from me, something snapped. I had to claim my wife, my mate.

My cock is still deep inside of her, and I regretfully have to slide out. I wince at the loss of her wrapped around me, but don't stop staring at her.

She's beautiful. Perfect. Usually, nothing in our lives is ever done the *right* way. But this felt right, the only thing that would have made it more perfect is slipping my knot deep inside of her. But I know, the moment I do that my teeth will be deep inside of her neck marking her as mine.

I push some sweaty hair off her face and press my lips against the warm skin of her cheek, taking in her scent, the soft touch of her fingers on my shoulders, how small she feels beneath me. I don't want to move or face reality.

Can't Violet and I live in this moment forever? Where nothing is weighing over our heads and it's just us? I kiss her one last time before looking into her eyes, needing to know that this moment was just as salient for her as it was for me.

"Okay?" I ask her and she nods.

"Yeah, more than okay," she replies and I stroke her cheekbone with my thumb.

"You're sure?"

"More than sure, Silas. It was amazing," she says, her bright eyes sparkling back at me as I lick my lips and consider where we go from here.

"What were you doing out here naked, anyway?" I ask, glancing over at the fire that's still going on.

She laughs and shakes her head. "It was supposed to be a spell in virtue, in not giving into physical desires."

I laugh and smile at her, which is contagious. "Didn't go so well for you."

She uses her nails to scratch through my beard. "I think it went the way it was supposed to."

"Stay my wife," I blurt out, more as a statement than a question. Maybe I'm feeling vulnerable and needy at this moment, but I need more assurance that she isn't going to up and leave me again. I can't lose her, I can't give her this piece of me and have her walk away again. I need Violet tied to me every fucking way imaginable.

"What?" she says, blinking.

"If you need to break this spell, even if it is a real thing, then so be it. But stay my wife. Stay mine."

She licks her pouty, soft lips and all I want to do is kiss her and fuck her again.

"There's a lot more that needs to be figured out," she says and I sigh, feeling overwhelmed.

"When the dust settles. After your coven is sorted and you decide what you want your role in the pack to be, I still want you as my wife."

"And if I don't want a role in your pack?" she questions.

"I don't really care. If you want to keep your wolf a secret between us forever but work on pack and witch relations, I don't care. I just need you to be mine."

"Are all wolves this possessive?" she asks, resting her wrists behind my neck as her fingers toy with my hair. The sensation is soothing and I realize now how rarely anyone ever touches me, not that I would want them to. I only want Violet to ever touch me again.

"I don't care about anyone else besides us. Me and you, we're going to make peace in this town and you're going to stay my wife, because you know you want to. Nothing has ever felt as good as this, nothing has ever felt more right."

"Okay," she whispers, tugging me closer to her body.

I have to use my elbows to keep some weight off of her. The fire crackles behind us as the frogs in the distance bellow and the lightning bugs around us sparkle.

"It's you and me against the world," I tell her, and she kisses my neck and holds me closer.

"It's you and me, Silas," she says, and for just a moment, I let myself believe her. Right now, everything is perfect, a world where no outside factors are controlling us. "I'm on a potion, by the way," she says, and it takes me a moment to realize she's talking about pregnancy.

"Unfortunate," Thorin purrs, and for once I share the sentiment.

At this moment, I feel a happiness that has always evaded me. An emptiness that has always consumed me seems to be disappearing. The anger I've held on to for years is so far gone, all I can think about is the way she feels in my arms.

"Should we get out of the grass?" I ask her, and she shakes her

SARAH BLUE

head.

"Just a few more minutes," she says, and I fall to my side so we're both staring at each other.

"I'm not going anywhere," she promises.

I can't decide if I'm stupid for believing her or not.

What they don't tell you about finally having sex, it's like lighting a field of tires on fire, the burning sensation of need never stops. Now it's all I can think about and all I want.

Considering I'm in a continuous rotation of meetings with different wolves makes this fact rather annoying.

"Oh, poor Alpha Silas," Thorin whines to me.

I sigh. He's been slightly insufferable, begging me to convince Violet to put the necklace on and let Azure out. As much as I understand his frustration and want, Violet needs to come to terms with her wolf on her own time.

"I'm going to rip out the throat of the person who tied her wolf to that necklace," Thorin says, and I rub the bridge of my nose.

"Silas?" The man in front of me says my name, trying to get my attention.

"Sorry, where were we?" I ask, and he hands me a stack of businesses that need more attention than others.

"We need to decide what should potentially close and if we should reopen something else."

"Close the beauty shop, everyone goes to Goddess Apothecary in town, only the wolves shop there. We should add a laundromat downtown. The tattoo shop needs a rebrand. I went there the other day, and it was disgusting."

"Yes, Alpha," the man I know as Bruce, says.

"Bruce?"

"Yes, sir."

"Do we have a list of all the births in the last three decades?" I ask.

"Of course," he says, standing up and opening what appears to be an ancient filing cabinet and pulling out multiple files. "Here you go."

I specifically pull the year Jonas and I were born, wondering if Violet is also listed, but I'm met with confusion.

"It says no males were born this year," I say, pointing it out, and Bruce puts on his glasses and nods.

"Yes, no males." His brows furrow and he clears his throat. "I believe a few pregnant women left that year. Their children must not have been cataloged."

"What was the climate with the witches back then?"

"Oh, that was a terrible year. Atticus Collins was a great Alpha, his son, Oberyn was set to take over, but he disappeared. That year was when the witches started really eating up downtown and pushing us out. We had shitty leadership after that, no one fit to lead. You can see the way births have gone down since then."

"Do you have Oberyn Collins' family chart?"

The older wolf scrubs his beard and looks around at the massive stacks of files and cabinets.

"I'll have to search around for it. Though I don't think you're in his line."

"Thank you Bruce. If anyone has any issues with my ideas, please feel free to send them my way."

The old man smiles, his eyes crinkling. "You're a lot like your grandfather, but better in the ways he lacked," he says and I tilt my head.

None of the other elders have freely mentioned him, and I didn't want to push it.

SARAH BLUE

"Hans was too hard. Some joked about how he didn't have a heart. He led the wolves into a strong era. We avoided the witches, and I'll give him credit. He handed the torch to Atticus when he was getting too old. But you're not self serving. You're strong, but you still have a heart."

I'm not sure how to take the compliment, and I nod at Bruce instead of saying thank you or letting his words go to my head.

"We are an excellent Alpha," Thorin says, having no issue at all with the compliment.

"Also, I have a few granddaughters your age, all unmated, beautiful. Well, maybe not Seline, but the other three are."

"Thanks for your help, Bruce," I say, ignoring that he just called one of his granddaughters ugly. I scoot my chair back and wonder if Jonas and I were the only males cast out of the pack at birth.

What had everyone so scared thirty years ago?

When I arrive at Violet's home later that evening, she's in the black nightgown, the silk clinging to her body like it loves her, as she eats a bowl of noodles at the table. She has two ancient looking books open in front of her, magic turning the pages while she reads.

"Hi," she says, putting the chopsticks down and standing up.

The dress tightens against her chest and I lose it, grabbing her by the hips and tossing her over my shoulder.

She laughs and wiggles as I slap her ass and carry her into the bedroom. I plop her down on her massive bed, loving the way her hair splays against her soft purple sheets.

"Long day, honey?" she jokes and I nod.

"Been thinking about how I'd come home and fuck my wife," I tell her.

THE MARRIAGE HEX

A coy smile takes over her mouth as her nightstand drawer flings open. Her vibrator floats in the air, until it lands in her hand.

"What if I already took care of that itch?" she asks.

"We both know that you need more than one, little witch."

"Hmm, do I need a man for that?" She spreads her legs, toying with me.

She's wearing no panties and her scent fills me as I look down at her pretty pink cunt.

"I don't know, do you?" I ask, unlatching my belt, and sliding it through the belt loops, dropping it on the floor, before taking off my shirt and pulling out my length and stroking it.

"How does that"—she points to my knot—"work?"

"It swells when I come," I tell her easily.

"Why?" I shrug and she frowns at me. "Has it always been there?"

"No," I reply quickly, climbing onto the bed built for a king. "Now, are you going to fuck yourself and let me watch, or are you going to let me make you feel good?"

She tosses the vibrator on the bed, and I pick it up.

"Something you should know about me, wife? I don't take threats lightly," I tell her before flipping her easily onto her knees and pushing the silk to bunch around her hips.

I fist the material with one hand as I slide the vibrator over her clit with the other. Her shoulders and face are pressed against the mattress while she moans and fists the sheets.

"Hm, how many times can I make you come before you're begging for my cock?" I ask her.

She grumbles something against the sheets, and I smirk, shifting the toy to a higher setting, making her jolt. I rein her back in with my hand on her nightdress.

"Always teasing me with these dresses, and how sweet you smell when you're turned on," I tell her.

Her breath hitches and her thighs shake as her first orgasm hits her. I don't move the toy and she tries to get away from me.

"What have I told you about running? Oh, are you trying to get me to fuck you? But you wanted to tease me with the toy."

"Fuck, please. It's too much," she says and I smile, holding it tighter against her clit. Wetness is sliding over my fingers and I have the urge to take a moment and lick them clean, but resist.

She moans, and attempts to shut her thighs and push away from me, but I hold steady, keeping the toy on her pussy, making her writhe and whine in pleasure. Violet quickly breaks apart again, shaking and arching her back as she comes.

"Has my poor baby had enough?" I ask.

"Please, Alpha, please," she says.

Any resemblance of control I have breaks as I fist my cock and shove it into her roughly. Her perky ass bounces with each thrust as she moans into the bed, taking me so beautifully.

I need her closer. I need the feel of her skin against mine.

My hips snap against her ass one more time before I wrap an arm around her chest and tug her back against my front, kissing the side of her throat.

One day…one fucking day, I'll claim her there.

Her nails dig into my forearm as I slide in and out of her. Violet's head tilts back, resting on my shoulder, and all I think about is how I want all of her, and to give her all of me.

But she's not ready.

She's given me her body, her promises, but she's not ready to embrace everything that comes with her wolf. If this is all I can have right now, I'll take it greedily.

"So good. Fuck, give me one more," I tell her, balancing her with one arm as my hand slides between her legs, feeling where we're connected and the way her pussy coats my cock in her essence.

"I…I…Silas," she whines, as I toy with her pussy while still filling her up.

Her body is so over stimulated she rests most of her weight on me as I fuck her to release.

"Nothing feels better than coming inside of you," I tell her as I come deep inside of her, satisfaction flooding me completely.

We both collapse onto the bed, and her head rests on my shoulder, my arm wrapped around her as she traces a few scars on my stomach.

"Feeling good?" she says, and I grunt, kissing her head. "Good, because I've got to go to New Orleans tomorrow."

"Um, what?" I say, and she kisses me to shut me up before sliding down the bed and licking my cock. That's already getting hard again. "Violet?" I say her name and she shushes me by sliding her lips around me and sucking.

For the first time in my life, I forget everything and let this tiny yet powerful moment silence me.

Chapter 33

VIOLET

"Okay, run me through this again?" Silas asks as Ember pushes her overly packed suitcase into the trunk.

I hold the ancient tome against my chest, before leaning it forward and flipping the pages.

"My great aunt Daisy gave me this book along with the other one when I wanted to do my little ritual," I say, and he smirks, likely thinking back to that night. "I hadn't really thought about why she also gave me this book, but when I flipped through, I found this."

I point my finger over the title of the ritual, and he reads the heading.

A Remembrance Rite.

"It calls for a minimum of two witches, but I figured the three of us would make this easier."

He grabs my elbow, dragging me over toward the porch. "I'm coming too."

"I don't need a shifter bodyguard," I tell him, clutching the book to my chest.

"I know you don't. But I don't feel comfortable with you going there when there's a pack who doesn't like us, among other things."

"What are these other things, Mr. Walker?" I ask him, blinking my eyelashes.

He sighs, scratching his beard, making sure my friends can't hear. "You're my girl, hex or not, right?" he says with a smile. "Then that's reason enough. I'll pack my bag."

My mouth gapes open as he jogs up the steps into the house.

"Good luck fitting his crap in here. Hecate, Ember, we're going for a day. What did you pack?" Iris says, having to use magic to shut the trunk.

"You always have to be prepared on a trip like this," Ember says.

"We'll work on your transfiguration spells when we get back," I reply as my boots rustle against my stone driveway. "Are you two really okay with him coming?"

"Every mission could use a little muscle," Ember says.

"Daisy said nothing else? Just gave you the book and expected you to figure it out?" Iris asks.

I nod with a sigh. "I think she's taken a vow of secrecy. Maybe that's why I've never heard her speak. This was her way of getting around that. I'm not sure how she knows what I've found out, but it's the best we have. If we can reinstate at least my mother's memories, then we can figure out where to go from here."

"Are you sure this is a door you want to open?" Iris asks.

I glance up at the house, where Silas has his satchel thrown over his shoulder. It's more than knowing I want to be with him. I'm falling for him, or maybe I already have. He wants a better world for his pack, and it's what I want too. A peaceful life between the witches and shifters. But more than anything, I need to know the truth.

"I'm sure."

Silas joins us, and I hand him the keys to my car.

"Thanks for letting me join your trip, ladies," Silas says, as I take the passenger seat and Ember and Iris slide into the back.

Ember starts immediately with the questions.

"How old are you when a wolf first shifts?"

"It depends," Silas replies.

"Are you in control when you're in wolf form?"

"No. The wolf part of me is."

Ember leans into the center console with wonder on her face.

"So, you're two different people? Personalities? Is he around when you're in human form?"

"Sometimes."

"Fascinating," Ember whispers in excitement.

"So, what's the plan? Are you going to kidnap her after her shift at the jewelry store?" Silas asks, probably to stop Ember's inquisition.

"No, we're going right to her home," I reply, my leg shaking anxiously in the front seat.

What if we can't restore her memories? What if it's another dead end?

Like he isn't even thinking about it, Silas' hand lands on my thigh, stilling my leg as he squeezes gently.

"Whatever you need, I'm there."

He keeps his face on the road, and I stare at his beautiful profile. Maybe I don't want to break the hex after all, not if every moment with him can feel like this.

It feels off putting being in the Garden District, and I can tell Ember and Iris feel it too. It didn't feel this way when Silas and I were incognito last time. No, this feels like a warning, like the magic of the coven who lives here is telling us to get the fuck out.

"Why in all of New Orleans does she live here?" Iris asks and I shrug, because that's a good question. If she has no memory of who she is, why is she surrounding herself with witches?

"I don't smell any shifters nearby," Silas says and I give him a nod.

We're a block away from her home, before the High Priestess of the Salvador coven and two younger witches materialize in front of us. I feel Silas grab the back of my dress, but he doesn't make another move as the witch looks me up and down.

"Miss Delvaux, I don't believe I've had any communication with the Celestial Coven granting you access to my territory. Not that it stopped you a few weeks ago," Prudence says, a smile wrinkling her eyes.

The High Priestess is stunning, with luminescent dark brown skin and greenish-brown eyes. I couldn't guess her age, not with the spells and potions she uses, but there's no doubt despite her appearance she must be close enough in age to my grand-mére.

"I apologize for not giving notice. We're here to meet a human friend, and then we will be on our way."

Prudence laughs, throwing her head back, before taking a step closer to me. Silas' grip on my dress gets tighter and I really want to smack his hand away, but I don't.

When her face is close enough to mine that I can see the creases around her eyes, I swallow in fear.

"You know, all those years ago, I thought I was doing Aster a favor. Her progeny had lost her magic, had lost herself. She wanted her daughter to live her life as a human, while still being protected. Witch to witch, I took her word for it, and granted her this favor."

Prudence touches the ends of my hair, twisting the white-blonde strands with the black.

"In New Orleans we work alongside the shifters, you know," she says, still holding on to my hair and glancing up at Silas. "It's how it should be. Protecting each other from the humans while knowing we're far better than them. Fighting each other only causes more damage. But I suppose you and your Alpha friend here know that."

"I just need to know the truth," I tell Prudence, and she looks me up and down.

"I will let you pass as long as when you ascend to the High Priestess of your coven, I have your true alliance. Not this farce your grand-mére has conned me into."

I hold out my hand. So does Prudence, as I grab her forearm and she grabs mine, a whirling of magic surrounding us, cementing our agreement.

She sighs after the magic settles and glances at the four of us. "Her and her sleeping wolf live in the house with the pink shutters," she says, and as quickly as she came, she leaves, all three of the witches disappearing in front of us.

"I thought she was supposed to be cutthroat and vicious," Iris says.

"Add it to the things we've been lied to about," Ember replies.

Silas' grip on my dress loosens, but he doesn't let go. I shouldn't like it, but it's the first time I've had someone this physically possessive of me, and I enjoy it.

My heart is racing in my chest when we get to the front door, and I can't bring my fist up to knock. A large arm reaches up as Silas knocks on the door above my head.

It only takes a few moments before my mother is answering the door.

"Sorry," I whisper, before taking out my wand and paralyzing her.

Silas catches her, and we bring her to the center of their living room. I grab a throw pillow and place it under her head as he lays her body on the large Turkish rug.

"I'm not going to hurt you, I promise," I whisper, as a tear trails down her cheek.

Ember's luggage finally comes to use as she unloads the vast amount of candles and lighting them quickly with her magic.

Silas watches from where he's leaned against the wall, not putting in any input, just fascinated with the setup and the effort that goes into preparing the room.

It's nearly nightfall by the time we're done. My poor mother is terrified on the floor as Ember, Iris, and I get on our knees and hold hands as we surround her.

"I promise this will all make sense soon," I say, pushing back her light hair as she looks at me with fear.

"Ready?" Iris asks quietly and I nod my head, squeezing my two best friend's hands.

They know what we're doing is right; they believe in me; they love me. I take a moment to let the reality of all the different types of love that are in this room. I'm not sure if it's because the truth is at the tip of my fingers, or that this moment proves that Iris and Ember would never turn their back on me.

But I make a choice at that moment. Once I know the full truth, I will be giving it to them in return. I can't tuck away Azure forever. She's a part of me.

We begin the chant, a low breeze whips around the room as we close our eyes and anchor ourselves to the spell. I pour everything I have into the spell, needing for it to work.

The wind around us is caressing my face as we say the chant one last time, the last word slipping from my lips like a prayer.

I take a deep breath and open my eyes, dropping my hands out of Ember's and Iris'.

My stomach feels upside down as I look down at my mother,

who stares at me. I release her from her paralysis and she sits up, her light blue eyes blinking at all of us. It's the longest few moments of my life as we wait to see what she says.

Her eyes connect with mine and her brows furrow.

"Are you with the Salvador Coven?" she asks, and I glance over at Iris.

"No. We're with the Celestial Coven," Iris answers for me.

"She sent you to take me away?" My mother asks, dragging a hand down her torso, and she gasps. "My baby. Where's my baby? What have you done with her?" she says scooting away.

I can't move or speak. I'm in shock.

"Fuck. It worked, but it seems like she only remembers up to before your birth," Iris says, and my mother looks at me again. This time, she really looks at me.

"What's your name?" she asks me.

"Violet Delvaux," I say softly and my mother covers her mouth and shakes her head. Her bright blue eyes wide as she stares at me with confusion and frustration.

"This can't be," she gasps. Her hands shake as she covers her face and looks around the room. "How old are you?" she asks, her eyes nearly crystalline as they fill with tears.

"Thirty," I reply, my own tears threatening to fall.

Tears stream out of her face as her hand comes to cup my cheek. "Thirty years? I've lost thirty years with you?" she asks.

My own tears fall at this point and she uses her thumb to brush them away, as a caring mother would.

"What happened?" she asks.

"That's what we're trying to figure out."

Her hands shake as she touches my skin, making sure that I'm real. "You're beautiful," she says, her fingers touching my two-toned hair and her fingers graze over my cheekbones.

I'm not sure what to say, or where we go from here. It's obvious that this is a lot on her, it's a lot for everyone.

We stare at each other for a few long moments before the front door flings open and a shotgun is aimed at us. A man with short black hair and deep brown eyes threatens us.

Silas looks ready to kill him as my mother holds up her two hands.

"Oberyn, no," she says. "They aren't here to hurt us."

The man's brows furrow. "Who the fuck is Oberyn?"

My mother sighs and glances at me. "Stun him, you're going to need to perform the same spell. This is your father, Oberyn Collins."

The man cocks the shotgun, but before he can do anything, Silas is grabbing it and pointing it to the ceiling, while Iris incapacitates the man that's apparently my father.

Chapter 34

SILAS

The tension in the room is thick as we all sit at the large dining table. Violet's father, Oberyn, glances at me now and then and I can feel the edge of him being an Alpha as well.

It's hidden deep within him, but it's there.

Violet's mother keeps touching her, like she isn't sure this is all real. I suppose even being supernatural, this all seems far-fetched.

I've kept quiet, letting Violet take the lead, which is hard. I can tell she doesn't know where to start. Honestly, no one sitting around the table does.

"The necklace. I gave him the necklace," she says, glancing over at me. "Is he truly your husband?" she asks and Violet nods, and eyes her two best friends before swallowing.

She's going to do it. She's going to tell them everything.

"Yes, he's my husband. Yes, I still have the necklace."

"I'm sorry I hid that piece of you. I had too," Lavender says. Her husband places a hand on his wife's neck as he looks at his daughter. The man hasn't said much and I wonder if he's quiet or this is all just too much.

"What necklace?" Iris asks, and Violet licks her lips.

Lavender cups Violet's cheek as tears fall from her eyes. "We never meant to leave you. Everything we did was to protect you, but at what cost?" she asks.

Violet wipes a tear from her eye and tells them everything. How she spent sixteen years in a fucked-up orphanage, how Aster picked her up on her birthday and she had a happy life with the coven, then her hex with me and the spirit that visited us in the mansion.

"I didn't realize at the time that Collins was my ancestor," Violet says looking at her father.

"My father thought you would solve everything. Aster thought differently," Oberyn says, and Violet's brows furrow.

"His spirit led us here. We visited the jewelry shop, and we brought the necklace back home."

"Did it preserve your wolf?" Lavender asks. Both of the other witches' heads quickly turn to Violet, who looks shy and scared.

"It did," she says, glancing over at her friends.

"You're both?" Iris asks, her voice soft. "You can shift?"

"Only with the necklace on," Violet says, searching her friend's reactions. "I didn't know how to tell you."

Iris nods, and Ember smiles. "This changes nothing," Ember reassures her with a smile.

"My mother, does she suspect anything?" Lavender asks, chewing on her nail.

"I'm not sure what she knows, but she suspects something. What is the last thing you remember?" Violet asks.

Lavender grabs her husband's hand and squeezes.

"We ran away. I wanted to raise you in that big purple house. We both did. Thought we could unite the shifters and the witches with both of the successors marrying and welcoming a child. Atticus was on board, but my mother wasn't. We knew we had to run.

THE MARRIAGE HEX

We were young, only eighteen, and neither of us were a match for my mother, not to mention we didn't have much money to run away. We both love New Orleans and thought maybe we could join the coven and pack here. They don't have the same feuds."

"I heard of my father's death, and we packed up, ready to go north or west, wherever we could. It wasn't ever determined how he died, but I knew Aster did it," Oberyn says. "We had to keep you safe," he tells Violet, his hard exterior slowly crumbling as he looks at his thirty-year-old daughter. "Lavender gave birth to you on the side of Route 61. We could feel Aster getting close, like a noose tied around our neck," he says, shaking his head.

"I used every ounce of magic I had in me to tether your wolf to the necklace, I bought it just in case something bad happened," Lavender says through tears. "I didn't know what she would do. But I thought if she couldn't sense what you were, if no one knew, it would keep you safe. I just wanted you to be safe. I'm so sorry, Violet," she says with tears streaming down her face.

I can't help myself as I stand behind Violet, gently touching her shoulder. She surprises me as she squeezes my hand for comfort, not pushing me away.

"The last thirty years, we've been normal people, going to jobs everyday and never knowing you were out there or who we were in our previous lives," Lavender says.

"Your magic?" Violet whispers.

"I don't feel anything. I have to assume she did the same I did for you, tethering my magic, and Oberyn's wolf to an item. It can't be destroyed like that. She erased you, she took you from me," Lavender says.

Violet squeezes my hand tighter, as she takes a big sniff.

"That means…grand-mère is the one who surrendered me to Mander's," she says with the shocking reality.

Iris and Ember both gasp as Lavender looks away, the pain evident all over her features.

"I'm guessing she couldn't bear to actually hurt us. She probably wanted to make sure you manifested as a witch. Perhaps she tied it with your coming of age. I…I…fuck. I just need a minute," she says and Violet nods as her parents excuse themselves from the room.

Iris looks over at Violet, and grabs Ember's arm.

"We're going to clean up the living room and get the car packed," she says and I give her a gentle look, letting her know I have Violet covered, as I round the chair, getting down on my knees and gripping Violet's waist.

Her eyes are nearly crystalline from the tears she attempts to hold back.

"Vi?"

"She sent me there," she says, her face crinkling with emotion as she looks down at me. "She sent me there and then she acted like she was my savior. She took me away from my parents. She made them forget me. She took you away from me," she says, some rogue tears finally falling down her cheeks.

I wipe them away with my thumbs and hold her face tightly in my hands.

"What do you need, baby?" I ask her and she sniffs.

"She needs us to go back home and free Azure from the confines of that necklace before I rip her grandmother's throat out," Thorin snarls, ready for bloodshed.

"I want my parents back, I want my lost time with you back, I want this to not hurt so fucking much," she says, as I pick her up from the chair and press her against my chest, holding her tight.

I stroke her hair. The color making far more sense now, looking at her two parents. While her face takes after her mother, the split in her hair that she's never able to change is now clear as day. Her mother seems softer and gentler, and it's clear she gets her ferocity from her father.

Violet holds on to me like I'm the only thing keeping her tied to her sanity, and I shouldn't like it as much as I do. I want to wash away the pain, and frankly the truth, so that it doesn't hurt her anymore. But knowing that my mate, my wife, finds solace in my arms is a heady moment for me. I squeeze her even tighter, hoping that she knows I'll always keep her safe.

"We have to find where she's hiding their gifts. We have to band the coven and your pack around this. Taking Aster down isn't going to be easy," she says, and I pull her away to look at her face.

The tears have dried up and all I can see in her gaze is the need for vengeance.

"This is what you want?" I ask her, not wanting to vocalize how I feel about it, not until I know how she truly feels.

I cradle the back of her head with my hand as she looks up at me. "The coven deserves better. My mother deserves more. I deserve more," she whispers.

"You deserve everything," I whisper back.

"It's not going to be easy," she says. We both know this is true.

I knew Aster was a strong witch, but everything that's been laid out on the table here tonight goes beyond what I even imagined.

"You're not alone, far from it. We'll all take this on together," I tell her.

"For better or for worse, huh?" she jokes and my grip on her head tightens, making her lips part.

"For better or for worse," I repeat.

When I said my vows originally, they meant nothing to me, but as I look down at my wife, there's nothing that can stand between us.

She lifts on her toes and we share a sweet soft kiss, before the door behind us opens and her parents walk back in.

Lavender seems more put together, and Oberyn looks pissed.

"I take it you're the Alpha of Moon Walker Pack?" he says to me and I nod.

He takes a deep inhale and slightly bows.

"I have a list of shifters who can help," he says.

"And witches I know don't care for my mother," Lavender says.

"You're not coming back with us?" Violet says, her face falling slightly as her mother approaches her and grabs her hand.

"There's nothing I want more than to come home and get to know you better. But I can't do that, not without my magic, not without my mother finding out you know the truth. The moment she knows she's been found out I worry what she'll do. It's of the utmost importance that you do not let her even get a whiff that we're conspiring against her. Assuming that's what you want," Lavender says.

Violet's lip tilts upwards. Even after everything her mother's been through, she's giving her daughter the choice. Even after all these years of not knowing she was out there or who she was, she loves Violet beyond anything. She's letting her decide.

"I'm getting your gifts back and I'm righting the wrongs of our coven," Violet says proudly, a sharp confidence slipping out of her that's refreshing and has me falling for her even more.

Lavender smiles, and Oberyn looks proud.

"Then we have some planning to do before your trip home," Lavender says.

So we make a plan. One that I fucking hate, but it will keep us safe.

Chapter 35

VIOLET

The moment we arrived home, we started putting our plan in place. Part one is the thing I hate the most, and that's Silas and I going minimal with our in person contact, which is already weighing on me.

Not the same way as before. It's not like my body physically aches if I'm not near him. I just genuinely miss him.

I feel stupid for ever having doubted Ember and Iris. Not when Ember's mother and grandmother have already agreed to side with us, and not as I sit across from Delphine, Iris' grandmother.

She clutches her cane, as her unseeing but all telling eyes glance over at me. She may be blind, but she knows far more than I realize.

The older witch looks similar to Iris, the same umber skin, amber eyes, and relative height. Her hair is buzzed close to her head and her large gold earrings jingle as she closes her eyes, her chin pointing up to the air as she takes a deep breath.

A slow, calming smile takes over her face, before she laughs, all of her jewelry clanging with the motion.

Iris glances over at me, more used to her grandmother's quirks.

"How is your mother?" Delphine asks, and my mouth parts as I glance over at Iris.

"Devoid of magic," I say and she nods.

"I fear this is my fault," she says, her hand gripping her cane to the point where her knuckles nearly turn white.

"Mawmaw, what does that mean?" Iris says, asking the question for me.

The older woman sighs, rising from her seat she heads toward her bookshelf. Even without her sight, she knows what she wants as a small box flies through the air and lands in her hand. She comes back to the table and opens it.

"There's only so much I can say," she says, and Iris and I glance at each other.

A vow of secrecy. It's why no one in the coven ever talked about my mother, why each and every one of them had the same story to tell.

"Iris, take the purple one out," Delphine says to her granddaughter, which she does.

It's a small pearl. I don't understand what it is, but Iris does with a gasp.

"A prophecy?" Iris says and Delphine nods.

"I should have kept it to myself. But we were all worried when Atticus Collins became Alpha. He was unlike the ones before him. He had initiative. We were already scared. I'm sorry Violet. You have my support in this. You and your wolf, you're on the right side," she says, standing up from the worn wooden chair and walking away without a word.

I look over to Iris, who inspects the small pearl between her fingers. She hands it to me and it seems inconspicuous enough.

"Crush it between your fingers," Iris says in a whisper. "You'll be able to see what she saw thirty years ago."

I look at the pearl and back up at my best friend, who gives me a small smile.

"It's alright. Go ahead," she says, grabbing my hand so that we can do this together.

I crush the pearl in between my fingers as a vision plays before me. It's lightning fast, almost hard to keep up with. The vision starts with a baby wrapped up in a lilac colored blanket, its small fist clutching a rose gold chain as it coos. A moment later, my grand-mère, or a younger version of her, is picking up the child. Right before her eyes, the baby morphs into a large wolf, so quickly I can hardly make out the details. My grand-mère yelps, but before the sound is even clear, the wolf bites down sharply into her jugular, sending her bleeding to the ground. The wolf quickly transforms back into a baby that cries endlessly, no one is around to pick it up and soothe the poor child covered in blood.

My vision comes back to normal as I breathe heavily.

"She thought I was going to kill her?" I gasp as the reality of what we both witness hits me.

"See what I said about visions being confusing? That could mean anything, not literal death, but it's clear she took it that way," Iris says.

"I don't want to kill her," I whisper and Iris squeezes my hand.

"I know you don't. But Aster isn't the kind of witch you just let go, Violet," Iris says, and I know she's right. I know that we can't just rip her coven away from her, expose the truth, and let her go. There have to be consequences. Steep ones.

I toss and turn in my bed. It feels too big, too empty without Silas here.

"Take a sleeping potion, you're being annoying," Walter hisses.

"You're being annoying," I tell him with a huff, shoving my face into my pillow.

He chirps, jumping off my bed to go sleep in the guest room. He's been in a mood since he learned the whole truth. He's having a hard time dealing with the fact that the High Priestess isn't the witch we thought she was. I also think he's wrapping his small little cat brain around the idea that Silas will be a permanent fixture in this house once everything is resolved.

I can't sleep. There's this endless ache for Silas I can't curb. It's heavy in my chest among all the other aches plaguing me as of late. There's so much to do, so much pressure on my shoulders. All I want to do is forget. Just a moment where I'm not me and the weight of the world isn't on my shoulders.

I glance over at my nightstand. The necklace feels like it's beckoning me. While I know that now isn't the time to be messing around with this other side of me, it would almost feel like a relief to not be for a few moments.

My hand grips the brass handle, tugging the drawer open as I grab the nearly glowing necklace.

I should put it back, take a sleeping potion like Walter suggested. But there's also this nagging feeling of wanting to get to know Azure, to let her out and get to know this part of me that's been repressed, that's been hidden from me.

Haven't I given enough? Hasn't Azure?

I take a deep breath and stop arguing with myself as I place the necklace around my neck. The metal is cool and I hope that Azure doesn't rip out of me right away.

So I talk to her out loud, just like I do with Walter.

"Azure?" I ask.

It's almost like a yawn in the back of my head as she replies. *"You've kept me away from him. You're ashamed of me,"* she says and I shake my head.

"No. I was just scared. Kept you from whom?"

"My mate! You've kept me asleep and away from my mate," she says, irritation riddled in her tone.

I swallow thickly and panic laces through me. Mate?

Someone is our mate?

Fuck. Silas would have said something, I would have known. No, it can't be someone else. I can't give up Silas if this is what accepting my wolf's side means. I go to rip the necklace from my neck and the wolf sighs.

"Wait."

I hold the grip on my necklace, worried she's about to take over and with Silas not here, who knows how I'll get back to my standard form. This was such a stupid idea.

"Thorin. The man, Silas. They are our mate. He told me to keep it between us for now."

I press my tongue to the side of my cheek.

"Thorin or Silas?" I say, knowing if Silas told my wolf to not say anything, I'm going to wring his thick neck.

"Handsome, perfect, Thorin. He said you weren't ready, that the man wasn't ready," she tells me.

"If I keep the necklace on, do you promise not to shift?"

She groans in the back of my head, like she's a caged animal wanting to get out—I suppose she is.

"Is this the beginning of us becoming one?" she asks.

"Only if you're okay with me teleporting to the pack lands right now and giving our secret keeping mate a piece of my mind."

Excitement fills me, but it's not my own. Getting used to sharing thoughts and words with a wolf inside of my head is going to be a new experience.

"For the both of us, but I accept. Only if you promise I get to see

my Thorin soon. I miss him."

Fine.

The pack lands are not where I should be right now, especially not with this sizzling anger that's plaguing me. But how could he keep this from me?

Not only have I been worried about him possibly having a mate out there, but why have I been worried about this stupid fucking hex when we're tied together in this way, anyway? Why did he keep this from me? How long has he known?

The more I think about it, the more pissed that I get.

He lied to me. He asked me to stay as his wife, that we're in this together and he's been keeping this huge secret from me.

I slide on my boots, not giving a shit. I'm just wearing one of his massive shirts to sleep in as I take a breath and think about where he is. I don't care if he's inside somewhere. I'm risking teleportation.

I scoop my wand up from the vintage nightstand top and concentrate, popping right in front of my dear husband.

Unfortunately for me, he's shirtless, standing in a circle where another man is trembling, about to shift, while the entirety of his pack stands in a circle watching on.

The crisp air whips against my face as my jaw drops and a lot of the rage I felt before slips away.

Silas looks pissed, and the lot surrounding me look like they want to slice my throat.

Perhaps this wasn't the best idea.

"Violet," Silas' deep voice chastises me as the people around us eye their Alpha suspiciously.

"Fuck," Jonas hisses, grabbing my elbow and pulling me to the side.

Everyone eyes me suspiciously and I wonder if they can tell that

THE MARRIAGE HEX

this is Silas' shirt, like I smell like him.

I try to take a deep inhale, but it seems like I don't have that particular shifter trait.

"You think you're fit to lead the pack when you bring a fucking witch to the pack lands?" the man across from Silas spews.

Silas doesn't look at me, but I can almost see that Thorin is begging to come out.

"What the fuck are you doing here?" Jonas hisses under his breath.

"Did you know I was his mate?" I ask, and the man sighs next to me.

"You should go home."

"Do not let her fucking leave," Silas points over at us, but doesn't stop staring across the way at the man challenging him. It's an open field, the autumn night air crisp as the birds chirp and the shifters watch on like this is the most entertainment they've had in years.

"You two are honestly the messiest individuals I've ever met," Jonas complains.

I roll my eyes.

"Where is your mate tonight?" I ask, not looking away from Silas.

"Safe, at home with our baby boy," he says proudly, and I smile at that.

"What do you have to say for yourself, bringing a filthy fucking w—"

His opponent doesn't finish his sentence as Thorin comes rippling out of Silas' body so fast it happens in a blink of an eye. His jeans and shirt ripped to shreds on the ground.

It's nearly embarrassing how quickly Thorin jumps on the man, his paws pressing against his chest.

"God dammit," Jonas says.

"What?"

"There's no fucking way Thorin is going to let him live."

"*Good*," Azure purrs in my ear and I swallow as I watch that happen.

I came here thinking I was going to give Silas a piece of my mind, but it appears it might just backfire on me completely.

Especially as soon as Azure sees her beloved wolf. I can feel her pushing against my mental walls, begging to come out, begging to reunite with her mate.

Before I can speak, before any of the other wolves has a chance to degrade me any further, Azure rips her way out of me, breaking her promise, ripping Silas' shirt and taking over.

There's a short minute where I'm aware, but it's brief. The last thing I remember before losing myself is a deep rumbled purr that sends a shiver up my spine.

"My mate," it says, and I know without a doubt it's Thorin, greeting Azure with nothing but happiness.

I suppose my confrontation with Silas is going to have to wait.

Chapter 36

SILAS

It's all a blur. The last thing I remember is Violet popping into existence the exact moment that dumb motherfucker was challenging me. He called her a filthy fucking witch, and all I saw was red.

The only consideration I had was keeping Violet safe, protecting her honor, and making that fucking asshole pay.

I groan as I run a hand down my face. My hair is wet, and there's no crusted blood from the challenge on my face—it's really rather disgusting when Thorin does that. I blink away the aches and look around, seeing that I'm in the Alpha cabin, and there is a very pissed off, also wet, Violet glaring down at me.

She has the knitted blanket from the couch wrapped around her body as she glares at me.

"What happened?" I groan, sitting up, not giving a fuck that I'm completely naked.

"Which part? Where you've been lying about me being your mate, or when our wolves took over and did, Hecate knows what, in the woods together," she says, pulling a leaf out of her wet hair.

Instead of answering, I just lie back down on the floor.

"Fuck," I groan, and Violet nudges me with her foot.

"That's all you have to say?"

"Yeah, or else I'll wind up yelling at you," I tell her, and she scoffs.

"Yelling at me?" she says, an irritated pissed off look takes over her pretty face.

"The entire fucking pack knows what you are now, Violet. If one of them slips up, we're fucked."

Her mouth gapes open, and she promptly shuts it, knowing that I'm right. She just exposed us. While I might have a handle over most of the pack, along with their respect, there are other factors in play.

"I was being challenged tonight. There are still people in Moon Walker that don't want me here. They can ruin everything we're trying to do with this information."

She rubs her hand over her face, sitting on the couch as I stay lying on the floor, contemplating how we got here.

"I wasn't thinking. I just wanted to not be alone, not be me for a few moments, so I thought I would talk with Azure. She told me she had a mate, and I panicked, and then when I found out it was you, all I saw was red."

I stand from the floor and walk over to the laundry hamper in the corner, grabbing a pair of briefs and sliding them on.

"Well, now everyone there tonight knows you're a hybrid," I say angrily. Part of me is pissed at Violet for being reckless, but most of the anger is knowing that someone could use this information to hurt Violet.

She stands up, nowhere near matching my height, as she glares up at me. "Why didn't you tell me? Why did you lie to me?"

I wave a hand at her and head to the kitchen to get a glass of water, her feet pad across the hardwood, following me.

I go to open the fridge and she slams it shut, making all the condiments on the shelf rattle with the harsh closing.

"Why?" she asks.

I lean against the sad white refrigerator and look at her. Some of my anger falls away as I look at the saddened expression on her face.

"It was my problem, not yours," I say.

"Fucking idiot," Thorin says as soon as the words slip out of my mouth.

Violet laughs sardonically as she goes to my laundry basket and grabs a shirt, dropping the blanket and tossing it over her head.

"Did you ever consider that I've been wondering if you had a mate who would take you away from me? That maybe information has been withheld from me my entire life?" she says, and I shut my eyes and take a deep breath.

"I didn't mean it like that."

"Do you want me as your mate?" she says. The vulnerability of the question is nearly dripping off of her as I take a few quick strides toward her and grip her face.

"Violet, I want everything from you."

"Then why did you lie?" she asks.

"I didn't lie—"

"Don't even start with me, Silas. We're married. You said you wanted me to stay your wife. You took my virginity out in the woods, but you couldn't tell me this?"

"You weren't ready," I tell her.

"You're really fucking this up," Thorin says, and part of me wishes I could strangle my own wolf.

Her eyes harden on mine, and she grabs my wrist and pulls it from my face. Her wand materializes out of nowhere as she heads for the front door of the cabin.

SARAH BLUE

"Violet, stop," I say, following after her.

As she goes to open the door, I place a hand well above her head and slam it shut. She spins on her heel and shoves the tip of her silver wand into the center of my chest.

"I'm sick and fucking tired of people keeping secrets from me. I expected more from you."

I swallow thickly and look down at my incredibly pissed witch, who looks too hot for her own good when she's angry. I grab her wrist that holds her wand and place it above her head, holding it still as I grab her other wrist until both of her hands are secured above her head with my palm.

"Tell me, little witch, what really has you so angry? Was it the thought of me with someone else?" I ask and she glares at me, and I can't help but to smirk. "There could never be anyone else. All my life it's been you, Vi."

"You lied," she says and I lean in and kiss her cheek, which she tries to tug away.

"I didn't know if you would be able to feel the mating connection with your wolf not being a complete part of you. There was a lot going on. I didn't plan on hiding this forever."

"When, then? When were you going to tell me?" she asks.

My face falters, because I didn't really have a timeline.

She sighs. "Let me go, Silas."

"No," I tell her. Invading her space more and crowding her. "I'm sorry, little witch. Let me make it up to you," I say, my breath caressing the side of her face.

She softens ever so slightly, but I can tell she's pissed. But there's no fucking way I'm letting my mate, my wife, walk out of that door now that she's in danger, now that she's been exposed.

"Let me go," she says, but there's not enough heat with it.

I hold her wrists with one hand as I use the other to slide down her body and grip her hip.

"I wouldn't have killed him if you weren't there, you know? When he said that about you, I haven't lost control like that in a long time. Do you know why?"

"Why?" she whispers.

"Because you're my mate, my wife, my fucking everything, Vi. I would do anything to keep you safe, to protect you. I think that's part of why I didn't tell you. This hex, the circumstances, I wanted you to choose me the same way I've always chosen you. It's always been you."

"How do I know you want me for real?" she whispers. I tighten my grip on her wrist and press my body against hers.

"I loved you when I didn't have a wolf present, and I'll love you till the day that I die, Vi," I tell her softly.

Her big blue eyes search my face as she licks her lips.

"I love you too," she says softly.

As soon as the words slip out of her mouth, there's a gentle sensation that slithers its way through me. It's strong enough to give me pause and to loosen my grip on Violet's wrists.

She must have felt it too, with the way she relaxes against the door. Her brows furrow, and she blinks rapidly as she tries to escape my hold. When I tighten, not letting her move, she groans.

"See if you can take off your wedding ring," she says and confusion hits me. That is not where I saw things going after confirming our feelings for each other. "Just try it. You can put it right back on," she says with a smirk.

I let her wrists go, and they fall to her sides as I reach over and grip the tungsten carbide ring between two fingers and pull it off of my finger.

"What the fuck?" I say.

She smiles and shakes her head. "Of course," she says, clearly not passing the revelation on to me. "The hex. We gave it what it really wanted."

Still confused, she shakes her head at me like I'm an idiot.

"We did what we promised when the hex was cast on our free will. It's broken now," she says, looking over to the kitchen as she wraps her arms around herself.

I slide my wedding ring back on and grip her chin.

"Violet Delvaux, will you stay my wife?" I ask her.

It's like I'm forcing the smile on her face, but she nods anyway.

"I'm still mad at you," she says, which just makes me grin, as my fingers dig into the soft skin of her face.

"I'll make it up to you," I say and she glares at me, which is too precious. So I lean forward and press my lips to hers, kissing her cute little pout away.

"Silas," she whispers my name against my lips, and I shiver. She might still be pissed, but I plan on fucking the anger out of her.

"Hmm?" I ask, as I bend down, kissing the soft skin of her neck.

"You can't seduce me out of being angry with you."

"No?"

I slide my hand over her pussy, cupping her there, where I can already feel she's wet.

"You know, we're not fully mated?" I ask her and her brows furrow as I slide a finger over her wet lips, grazing gently over her needy clit.

"What?" she says in a breathy moan.

"You're my mate, but we're not fully mated until my mark is on you. Do you want my mark, baby? Do you want to be mine in every way?" I ask.

I'm not sure how I turned being scolded, to feeling my own frustrations, to shamelessly begging her to let me mark her, but here we are. I can't contain this beast that's been riding me since

THE MARRIAGE HEX

the day she walked back into my life.

She licks her lips, the back of her head thudding against the aged front door.

"You're mine, Violet. It's why we both waited to feel this fucking good. Let me sink my cock and teeth into you at the same time to prove it," I plead. It's slightly pathetic, but I don't care.

I know as soon as I really mate with her, seal her with my bond mark, that I'll always know she's safe.

"Do I…do I mark you too?"

I groan, rubbing my hard cock against the soft skin of her stomach as I grab her waist and fist the back of her hair, protecting her head from the door.

"You want to sink your teeth into me and mark me, little wolf?"

She shivers at the mention of her wolf and bites down on her plush lower lip as she nods her eagerness.

"Take my cock out," I tell her.

Her hands shake as she grabs the waistband of the underwear I just put on as she shoves them down my thighs and I kick them away. I grab the hem of my shirt and tug it over her head. She smells like me, she's married to me, but she's about to belong to me in every sense of the word.

I grip her ass and heft her higher against the door as her legs wrap around me. Her dripping pussy grinds against my length as she wraps her arms around my shoulders and her lips crash against mine.

The kiss is hungry, hurried, and everything I've ever wanted. Violet kisses me like I'm her oxygen and I kiss her back, knowing that she's mine.

Adrenaline, want, and need are coursing through my veins. I'm about to have the thing I never thought possible. The woman I've always wanted, but couldn't have, is about to be mine in the way that matters most to an Alpha wolf like me, and she's giving it freely.

The scent of her arousal is heady and has a moan of desire ripping out of my throat.

"Silas," she whispers my name, her fingers tangling in my hair as her legs squeeze me in tighter.

"Are you going to take all of me, Vi?"

She swallows as I slide the head of my shaft against her wet pussy and I can tell there's some apprehension there.

"Will it hurt?" she asks, and I smirk.

"No, baby, it was made for you," I say, thrusting deep inside of her.

She moans loudly, her nails digging into my shoulder and scalp as I slide in and out of her, letting my knot press against her entrance, but not giving it to her yet.

I lick and suck on the skin on the side of her neck, feeling eager and impatient about giving her my mark, about giving her everything.

"Are you going to take my knot, little witch? Are you going to take it all?" I ask her.

"Fuck. Yes," she says, her body banging against the door with each thrust. My fingers dig into the soft flesh of her ass, the tips of my fingers feeling the way her tight hole shifts every time I fuck her.

I want her there at some point, too.

"Where do you want me to mark you?" I ask her, hoping and praying she lets me put it on her neck, where everyone can see.

I need everyone to know that she's mine.

She tilts her head to the side, showing off the pink marks from the way I've been sucking on her throat, and I groan, fucking her harder.

Her mouth parts on a moan, and I quickly silence it with my own mouth. Nothing else exists right now. We have no problems, nothing to work through.

Right now it's me and Violet and the rest of the world doesn't matter. At this moment, I feel more peace than I have in my entire life. I'm consumed with her scent, the way her skin is pressed against mine, and the delicious way her cunt grips my length.

This is the most transformative moment of my life and I haven't even claimed her yet.

Chapter 37

VIOLET

Silas holds me against the door like I weigh nothing. His strong hands gripping my ass as he fills me completely, whispering sweet promises in my ear.

I didn't come here with this intention, or maybe I did. Maybe I needed to be reassured that Silas is all in, that he wants me to be his mate, that he wants me to be everything.

Was it reckless? Undoubtedly.

But with Silas' strong hands on me, I can't even think about my stupid actions. All I can think about is how good I feel right now.

My necklace bounces between my breasts as Silas pushes into me harder, kissing and sucking the side of my neck. My heart rate is out of control as I wait for what's coming. Not just his mark, but his knot.

His grip on my ass tightens, his fingers grazing my back entrance, making me moan.

"You're making a mess on me, mate," he says, licking up the side of my throat and his teeth grazing my ear. "Are you going to take my knot like a good little witch?" he asks.

"Yes," I pant out as he slows his thrusts.

"Perfect. Made for me," he says as his amber gaze meets mine.

I can already feel the stretch as the larger base of his cock presses into me. The whimper that falls through my lips is involuntary, but his eyes glow with the sound.

"That's it, baby. Fuck," he says, as his gaze glances down, his gaze completely focused on where my pussy is swallowing his knot.

I press my head against the door, letting myself take in the foreign feel of the stretch. There's a slight amount of pressure tinged with pain, but it slowly starts to dissolve into pleasure.

His thighs begin to shake and he curses, tugging me away from the door, carrying me like I have a feather light spell on me as he slowly sits on the massive, worn leather chair. My knees are pressed into the sides of the armrests as I shift against his cock.

Silas grabs my face as I balance my weight on my legs, and he kisses me fervently. Those same butterflies that happen every time he kisses me flap wildly in my stomach again.

It hits me then. My body has always known he was my mate, even from that very first kiss. Even before Thorin was freed. I tangle my hands in his soft, still wet hair and kiss him with even more rigor.

I slide down his length, taking more of his knot and he moans into my mouth, making my pussy flutter against his length and knot.

He holds the back of my head with one hand as he grips my ass with another, spreading me wide. It's obscene in the most delicious way I've ever experienced. My body shocks me by taking his knot, more than taking it, enjoying it.

When I finally have all of him in me, the stretch almost too much, Silas begins rutting up into me from where he sits.

The sounds that leave me are wild and completely out of my control, but nothing has ever felt close to this. No amount of self-stimulation, no fantasy could ever compare to the way this feels.

I have to part from our kiss, but Silas' mouth stays on me, sucking and licking anywhere his mouth can touch; my neck, my jaw, my breasts. Meanwhile, he holds my hair in a possessive fist.

"Let me come. Let me mark you," he says, almost begging, and it breaks something inside of me. I'm not sure how I have power over this six-foot-seven beast of a man, but yet I do.

"Please, Silas," I say and I swear the smallest whimper escapes him as he thrusts into me hard, making me scream out from the stretch. All the while, his lips part and his teeth sink into the side of my throat while his cock fills me with cum.

I expect pain, and there's a short moment of being uncomfortable, but it's quickly replaced with the greatest sense of bliss I've ever experienced.

My pussy gushes around his length as it all clicks into place. The life altering orgasm takes the forefront of my mind, nothing but pure pleasure. But then slowly something else creeps up. A feeling stronger than what the hex felt like. It feels like he's lassoed my heart and tethered it to his own.

It feels like everything, all the hurt, all the suffering, was worth it for this very moment.

I feel whole.

I feel safe in a way I've never experienced before. Silas loves me in a way I didn't know was possible. It's clear in this monumental moment that until right now, I never knew this kind of cosmic love existed. But now that I do, I'll never let it go.

Silas licks my neck, the place he left his mark, the pain already receding completely. There must be some sort of wolf shifter magic in play here, as he pulls back and looks me in the eyes.

"Mark me," he says and I swallow thickly.

Silas' teeth are sharp, not as sharp as a vampire, but compared to mine, my teeth are basically blunt.

"Please," he says, gripping my hair and tugging my face toward his own neck. His knot is still deep inside of me as I ride this euphoric wave.

I'm not sure what I expect as I kiss his throat and part my lips, digging my teeth into his neck. But it's not as feral as I feared it would be. It's sensual as I bite down. Silas grips my hair and ass roughly, moaning as his cock twitches inside of me, filling me with his cum for a second time.

I do the same as he did, licking the mark, and watch with fascination as it heals immediately, only the silver indents of my teeth left behind. It's beautiful.

I pull back, and his amber eyes are glistening, and he looks softer than I've ever seen him. He cups my face with his two large hands, his thumbs brushing my cheekbones as he just stares at me for a long few moments.

Instead of words, he brings his lips back to mine.

I go to adjust on his lap, noticing that his knot has us still locked in place. Silas moans at the movement as he kisses me tenderly. This isn't the same impassioned kiss from earlier. This is tender and soft. It says all the words between us that are too impossible to say.

"I love you," he says and I sigh.

"I love you, too."

For a short moment, everything is perfect as I rest my head against his broad, masculine chest, listening to his heartbeat, and holding him close. He strokes my hair and kneads my muscles as we both just lie there, enjoying the feel and moment with one another.

"How long will we be stuck like this?" I whisper, and he laughs, jostling me on his knot, which he's rewarded with a moan.

"I'm not really sure," he says and I pull back.

"What do you mean, you're not sure?"

He smirks, looking handsome and cocky as fuck. I can't even blame him.

"It's something only Alphas have and only with their mates. It's rare," he tells me as I graze my nails through his beard.

"Maybe one day we'll be incredibly ordinary."

"No fucking chance," he says with a smile, wrapping his big arms around me and holding me close.

I feel small in his arms, but I also feel cherished in a way I didn't know existed. I thought the love of my coven was all I needed, and don't get me wrong, I'll never turn my back on my fellow witches. But this level of protection, intimacy, and care is something I don't think I could ever live without, now that I've experienced it.

Silas makes me feel safe, and I'm not sure I've ever felt that before.

"You should stay here. The moment your grandmother finds out that you know you can shift, I don't know what she'll do."

I swallow. "We still need to find the objects she hid my mother's and father's abilities in," I say.

"Keeping you safe is more important right now."

"You're not mad?"

"I really want to be. But how can I be when my knot is deep inside of you, my mark on your neck," he says, his thumb trailing the mark with tenderness and affection. "I don't like that the pack knows about your ability and that it could put you in danger. But no I'm not mad. What about you, little witch, are you still pissed at me?"

I sigh, because unfortunately I'm not. I was really hoping I could ride this irritation a bit longer.

"More so at myself. I shouldn't have stormed over here."

"I should have told you," he says, which makes me smile.

I feel his knot go down, fluid dripping out of me as he slides his hand between us, pushing his cum and my release back inside of me.

"I'm still on a potion," I remind him.

"Don't care," he says, his fingers toying in the mess and over my clit.

"Do you think the wolves are happy?" I ask him, a wide wolfish grin takes over his face.

"More than happy," he says, removing his fingers and bringing them to his own mouth.

It shouldn't be as hot as it is, but I find myself leaning forward and pressing our lips together, before sliding my tongue against his, reveling in the taste that is wholly us.

Tonight, everything is as it should be.

Tomorrow is another story.

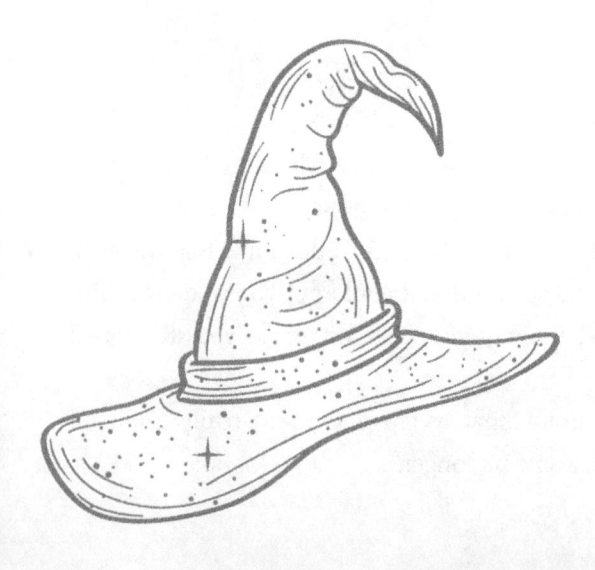

Chapter 38

VIOLET

I'm nervous as hell, but Silas thinks that by being honest and upfront with his pack, it might help protect me and get the pack on our side with the plan.

The amount of eyes on me while I stand next to the podium is overwhelming and making my skin itch, but Silas commands his pack with a no-bullshit attitude. He clears his throat, making it clear he's ready to speak.

"If you weren't at the challenge last night, I assume you've already heard about Violet's unexpected appearance," he says, and low chatter fills the space. "Violet is my mate, and Violet is half wolf. Anyone who wishes her any harm is not welcome in this pack. She is a descendent of Alpha Collins and she deserves respect not only as a pack member, but as the Alpha's mate. If you have any issue with this, please feel free to leave the pack lands immediately," he says.

There are a few people who stand up.

Too bad they don't know that Ember and Iris are waiting outside and washing away their memories of the last few days, along with a bus ticket to get the fuck out of town.

After the defiant pack members leave, Silas looks around the hall.

"We're entering a new era. One where witches and shifters work together. One where supernaturals help each other, not allowing one another to flounder. Violet is a huge part in making this happen and brokering peace with the Celestial Coven. When I took over this pack I was told peace was impossible. I'm standing before you today telling you it is possible and it will, in fact, happen. I know I wasn't raised here, I know there are probably those of you who are still skeptical and have a lot of distrust for witches in your heart. But I'm asking you to keep an open mind. I'm asking you to think about the future of your children and how you want the rest of your lives to look like."

He grips the podium, and I shouldn't be as turned on as I am now. Silas Walker is one hell of a leader, and the way he speaks to his pack proves that.

"I suppose I will claim the man too," Azure says in my head, almost startling me.

I smile and Silas gives me a look from the corner of his eye before looking back out at his pack.

"Part of ensuring this peace deal is making sure that Violet's heritage does not leave the pack lands. Right now we have the advantage of surprise. If the High Priestess knows Violet can shift, this will all be for naught. I'm asking you not only as your Alpha, but as someone who wants this pack to thrive, to swallow your pride and really think about what is best for the pack."

"What if she just angers the High Priestess even more and then we wind up with the coven at our doorstep?" someone shouts. I squint and realize it's Kit. She's glaring at me, and I notice some other female shifters are.

"Then I hope you're willing to fight for what is rightfully ours.

If it comes down to it, are you all bark or are you ready to stand up for the pack?" Silas barks back.

"There's never been a hybrid," she retorts.

"Well, now there is, and she's my mate," Silas snaps back.

Yeah, he's definitely getting head tonight.

Kit folds her arms and sighs, glancing me up and down, clearly not impressed. But nonetheless, she nods her head and slightly bows to her Alpha. I smirk to myself, knowing that the man they all fear would eagerly get down on his knees for me and do whatever I ask.

The power I have over this man is getting to my head.

"Do not leave the pack lands unless absolutely necessary. All communication is strictly pack business."

I expect some kick back, but to my surprise, everyone nods or bows in some fashion. In a short time Silas has improved their lives by so much, they've seen what he can do, and they believe in him.

So do I.

"If you need anything else, you know where to find me," Silas says, grabbing my hand and leading me to the back of the building before stopping in the hallway and grabbing my jaw, forcing me to look up at him. "Something have you turned on, little wife?" he says with a cocky smirk.

"You know, it's really not fair that I don't have the whole scent thing," I say, and he leans in and kisses me.

"I don't want you to go," he says, his thumb tenderly rubbing my face.

"I have to. We need my mom to do this," I tell him and he nods, even though he doesn't want to agree with me.

"Iris and Ember are sure that they can keep Aster occupied for long enough?"

"Absolutely. If Aunt Daisy can't help, then I'll leave. I'll come right back."

"You have to promise me, Violet. The moment anything feels wrong, you teleport right to me. You don't take any fucking risks."

I use my hand to cross my heart. "No risky business. I'm going to see if Aunt Daisy can help me find the items holding their abilities, and then I'm out. I'll come right back here. Well, after I pick up Walter."

His nose scrunches in distaste and I grab his wrist, playing with the calloused tips of his fingers.

"We have to act fast. As soon as the coven realizes my mother's back, and what really happened, it's over," I tell him and he sighs.

"Doesn't mean I have to like it."

I fist his shirt, and he places a hand above the wall, crowding my space as he kisses me softly.

"Be safe," he says and I kiss him one more time, before exiting the building and meeting up with Iris and Ember.

They're both dressed casually in jeans and a t-shirt, looking ready to raise hell and I smile.

"How was the memory erasing?" I ask.

Iris grins and Ember shrugs.

"That magic feels wrong," Ember says with a shiver.

"It's supposed to, so we don't use it. But I gotta admit, it felt nice to be a little evil, especially because it was protecting you."

I smile and hug them both, taking a deep breath.

"Are you two ready?" I ask and they both nod, even if there is some fear there.

Iris and Ember go to Goddess Apothecary while I manifest right outside of my grand-mère's house, waiting for her to leave. I hear the crack of her teleportation, knowing that Iris called her to let her know a potion went array as I sneak into the house, my great aunt Daisy, sitting in her same worn chair.

I don't waste any time getting on my knees before her and touching her far too skinny legs.

THE MARRIAGE HEX

"I don't know what she did to you, Aunt Daisy, but I'm trying to make things right. I found my mother and father. Do you know where she put my mother's magic?" I ask her.

Her eyes search my face as her aging hand cups my face. She summons a book that comes whipping through the air and lands with a thud on the table. It's worn, nearly ancient looking with the way the leather is colored. She flips a hand, and it opens. It's not a book at all, it's a box housing two rings.

I pick them up and I can feel it. It feels like the same magic I felt when I put on my necklace for the first time.

"What did she do to you, Daisy?" I ask.

Her eyes are soft as her hand caresses my cheek.

I grab the rings, and there's a soft click of a door. My heart races and I'm barely able to think. The most important thing right now is to get these items to someone I can trust, someone who she wouldn't suspect. The only way to teleport myself physically out of this house is when I'm holding my grand-mère's hand. She warded her home that way. It never felt odd until now. But physical objects are a whole other story.

I take a breath and transport the rings to someone I know can keep them safe, someone who my grand-mère will never suspect.

As soon as they're out of existence, Daisy shuts the book and returns it to the shelf.

Her eyes clash with mine again and for the first time in my entire life, I hear her speak.

"Run," she whispers.

I hold her eyes for a brief moment, panic filling me as I run for the front door and swing it open. The moment it's open, a wand is placed at my throat.

My grand-mère's pinched expression and disappointment is evident as she uses the tip of her wand to toy with the necklace.

"I see you've found the truth out about who you are, grand-daughter," she says, eyeing the necklace cautiously.

I can't slip up. I'm not sure how much she knows.

"I found it in the house. You knew what I was?" I say.

"It's why your mother ran away. She knew I would not approve. I also assume it's why you ripped your magic from her in the womb. At least she had the foresight to pull this disgusting part of you out. You are a witch, Violet. A future High Priestess. This just won't do."

I'm sliding my wand out of my back pocket as she sighs. I'm stunned on the spot, and everything goes black.

Chapter 39

WALTER

I'm enjoying a sunbeam on the porch, as one does, when two wedding rings appear on my collar.

I can sense the magic immediately and sigh. I had plans to do nothing today, but it appears my dearest witch has gotten herself in a bit of a bind.

Using magic in this form is exhausting, but somehow I persevere, knowing what I need to do.

I meow with irritation after the teleportation; I haven't done that in ages. The stench of wolf is disgusting as I trot down the dirt road, sensing my witch's large shifter husband.

I scratch on his door hard enough to leave marks and smile as he opens the door and looks down at me with furrowed brows. I sigh and meow, batting at my collar.

He bends down and sees what I have, his gaze turning lethal, as he looks at the rings on my collar.

"Fuck," he curses.

He lets me into the home as he tries to call the coven members who've always supported my witch. As he does so, he puts out a cooked piece of salmon for me. Perhaps the man isn't so bad after all.

Still smells like a dog, but at least he has good food.

"Do you know where your mistress is?" he asks and I concentrate.

No, I don't know where my witch is, and for the first time in my enduringly long life I begin to panic.

Chapter 40

SILAS

I pace the cabin, fear licking up my spine.

Aster knows something, and I'm not sure how much she knows. All I know is that my witch is not back and Iris and Ember haven't answered my calls.

There's a knock on my door, and I quickly rush over to answer it.

I'm not sure who to expect, but an older woman with a cane and a ridiculous amount of jewelry stares at me.

"The rings, son," she says, holding out her hand and I blink at the woman.

"What?"

"Give me the rings. A witch is needed to give them their abilities back," she says and I just stare at her and she sighs. "You're a good man, I've seen it. I've seen what happens. Give me the rings," she says and then I realize the connection.

"You're related to Iris?"

"Yes, my dear granddaughter has no memory of the past few weeks. I can only assume what happened, but I know where I'm needed," she says.

I'm so scared for Violet's life that I go over to Walter and remove the rings from his collar. He doesn't even protest as I hand them to the woman.

"What do I do?" I ask her, feeling vulnerable and truly afraid for the first time.

She hands me a small pearl and closes it in my hand. "Find my granddaughter and give her this. Get your wolves ready."

"I need to find Violet," I tell her.

"Aster is many things, but a murderer is not one," she says.

"Atticus Collins," I reply, and the woman shakes her head.

"That was pure dumb luck. She wouldn't do that kind of harm to her family."

"I've seen the harm she's done to that family," I reply, and the woman gives me a soft smile.

"Aster doesn't have all the pieces, only whispers of a disgruntled wolf. I will go to New Orleans, ask upon the Salvador Coven for help. You will band your wolves and give this to my granddaughter. I will return tonight," she says.

Walter rubs his head against my shin and looks up at me with his creepy yellow eyes. He's telling me to trust this witch. It's against everything I feel in my gut, the need to find Violet and make sure that she's okay. But I nod, the witch smiling at me and tapping her cane, before popping out of existence.

"She better not be betraying us," I say, and Walter chirps with agreement.

I have a witch to find and a rat to kill.

Surprisingly, finding the wolf that betrayed us is easier than I thought.

"I told you we should've killed him," Thorin says in my head. He's

THE MARRIAGE HEX

just as anxious as me, pacing around my mind, worrying for Violet and Azure.

The man is on his knees. Jonas' grip on the back of his neck is fierce.

"That's my son. This is my fucking pack," he snarls.

"Ah, but he's mine. Paige is my mate. This pack never wanted you, Silas is ten times the Alpha you ever were," Jonas snarls in his face.

"Paige, baby. I'm sorry I left. I can make things right. I'm making things right," he says.

Paige shakes her head, holding her small newborn son to her chest.

"Hoyt, what have you done?" she says, looking at Jonas with sad eyes.

"I did what I had to. What I need to do," he says and I tilt my head and get on my haunches and look over his face.

I thought he was crazy before but he looks deranged right now. I couldn't piece together why every Alpha since Atticus Collins has been a nightmare, but when I look at his gaze, something is wrong.

"Paige?" I ask, and she approaches, but doesn't get too close with her son.

"Yes, pack leader?" she says respectfully. I've come to like my best friend's mate. She is sweet and soft, just what Jonas needed.

"Have his eyes always looked like this?" I ask.

A growl erupts from Jonas and his grip tightens on the man's neck as his mate inspects her former lover's face. I'd be the same way, but you'd have to be obtuse not to realize the way she's looking at him isn't with affection but hate. He wasn't just a terrible Alpha, but a horrible man.

"No, they changed after he became Alpha," she says.

"Thank you. Why don't you take the baby home?" I tell her and

I can see that Jonas is filled with relief over the idea.

"That's my son! Paige, get the fuck back here, you ungrateful fucking—"

Jonas snaps his neck. I can't blame him. The man's body falls to the floor and my best friend sighs.

"Sorry about that."

"We already got everything out of him anyway. I'm surprised no one knew he was still creeping around on the property," I say.

"He only knows what he saw from that night, that Violet can shift, and possibly that she's your mate."

I have to keep my temper in check. I almost wish the hex was still plaguing me, that I could find her in that way, but there's nothing. I know she's still alive. I can feel that through our mating bond, but other than that, I feel hopeless.

I can't go knocking down the High Priestess' door or else I'll wind up getting killed myself. I just have to follow the guidance of the witch from earlier. So that's what I do, making my way to Goddess Apothecary.

Downtown looks slower than usual as I open the door to the business, the chime overhead dinging at my arrival. As soon as I walk through the door, Iris gives me a disgusted look.

Right, she likely doesn't remember me.

"Can I help you?" she asks with an attitude that she absolutely does not want to help me.

"I was told to give this to you," I say, holding out the pearl and her brows furrow.

"Who gave this to you?"

"Older woman, cane, lots of jewelry."

Her furrow deepens as I place the pearl in her outreached hand.

"Mawmaw gave this to you?" she asks.

"She didn't give me a name. She said to give this to you and you would know what to do—I'm praying you do. Violet's in trouble," I say.

"Violet?" she echoes, her fear palpable as she looks down at the small iridescent pearl.

"I fucking hope you know what to do with this thing and can help me. Might not seem like it right now, but I gotta tell you we were on the path to becoming friends," I tell her, which makes her more suspicious.

But she puts the pearl between her two fingers, crushing it, her eyes going white for a second and she takes in a strangled breath. I watch in horror and fascination as her eyes roll and I just wait.

She takes a deep inhale of breath, clutching the table in front of her as she blinks at me.

"Fuck," she curses, grabbing her wand and grabbing my wrist.

She turns the store sign to closed and locks the door, her grip on my arm impressive as she glances over at me.

"We've got to reverse this spell on Ember and get to Violet quickly."

"Do you know where she is?" I ask, wanting to get back to Violet as soon as possible.

"No, but I know if we don't figure it out soon, there might not be much of her left," she says.

Before I can answer, everything is going black. It feels like I'm being whipped around in a tornado of smoke before I fall promptly on my ass in front of a cottage covered in florals. There are a million toadstool statues scattered around the gardens, with multiple appearances of frogs. I swear I hear little bugs or whisperings, but I ignore them as I glance over at the witch who brought me here.

"Hurry up," Iris snaps, as I get off my ass and dust myself off as Iris flings the door open.

Ember yelps and clutches her hand to her chest.

"Holy Hecate, you scared the fuck out of me. Don't you knock?" Ember says and Iris sighs.

"Violet needs us. High Priestess fucked with our minds."

Ember looks between the two of us.

"Who's he?" Ember asks.

"Not totally sure, but mawmaw trusted him enough to give me a vision. Then I realized time is missing, don't you feel it?" Iris asks Ember.

The redhead's eyes look over her friend and she's contemplative as she nods. "You're right," she says with a gasp.

"I guess now is as good of a time as any to fill you in?" I say.

"Not necessary," Iris says, holding out her wand and pointing it to Ember's temple. The other witch winces, but gasps as all her memories come back into her mind.

She returns the favor, holding the wand to Iris' head, and then they both turn and face me.

"She must have been quick with making us forget, the spell was nowhere near as strong as Violet's mother's," Ember says.

"Let's just be glad we didn't need another witch to get this done. Did Violet get the magical items?" Iris asks.

"She sent them to Walter. I don't know how. Your mawmaw is headed to New Orleans to reinstate Lavender's magic and Oberyn's wolf."

"We're going to need more witches to take on Aster. She's too fucking strong," Iris says.

"I think your mawmaw might have us covered there," I say.

Iris nods, clearly trusting her mawmaw's ability.

"We need to find where she took Violet," Ember says and I groan.

"We're doing a seance, aren't we?" I ask.

"Best we do it at Violet's house," Iris says. I just hope I don't find myself trapped in a room again, and that Atticus Collins will lead us to his granddaughter before anything unrepairable happens to the woman I love more than anything.

Chapter 41

VIOLET

It feels like someone is taking an ice pick to my head as I crack open my eyelids. I have to blink away the blurriness and the dryness in my eyes as I look around.

I go to lick my lips, but I can't.

I go to lift my hand, but I can't.

Even when I open my mouth to speak, nothing comes out.

"It's okay, it's okay. Grand-mère is here. I'm going to make everything right again."

I stare at her. The feeling of tears running down my face feels foreign, almost like I'm disassociated from my body.

My grandmother pets my face. "Don't worry, you won't remember. Now that I have this," she says snidely, pointing to my necklace that hovers above her work table. "I can make you what you were always supposed to be." She grabs my chin, tilting my face to the side, the tip of her wand pointing right at my bond mark. "It will only hurt for a moment."

She whispers an incantation, and the scream that wants to rip out of my throat is constrained. There's nothing I can do but sit here in painful silence while she breaks me apart. It feels like my skin is being burned off. It feels like she's stealing a part of me that I love.

It feels like she's erasing Silas.

There's a scent of burning flesh, and I'm close to passing out again when she puts a salve on my throat, petting my hair back.

"It's okay, Violet. It's okay. Now everything will be how it was supposed to be."

She turns her back on me, going back to whatever magic she's doing to my necklace, and I mourn in silence. What if she destroys Azure? What if she just ruined my mating bond with Silas?

What if…what if she makes me forget?

That has me attempting to move, with no success.

"At least Lavender came to her senses and ripped this out of you," she mumbles. "It's unnatural. You were never meant to be this. You're a witch, that's all you are. You're my granddaughter, my progeny. You're not one of them."

But I am. Half the pack may hate me, hate that I'm mated to Silas, but I'm still one of them. I'm both. I'm a witch and I'm a wolf shifter and I don't want her taking away this part of me. I hardly even got a chance to know.

"It's alright, darling, you won't remember the pain. Being a High Priestess means sacrifice. I sacrificed having my daughter so that you could be what you need to be. The Celestial Coven needs to stay in the hands of the Delvaux family. It can not be tarnished."

She sounds nearly manic as she speaks to herself, while I'm forced to be here and endure.

I look as far to the right as my eyes will allow. At that moment, she drips my necklace into a bubbling cauldron. The pain I feel as she pulls out only the top of the chain, the rest of the necklace destroyed. It's like a piece of me dies.

My grand-mère takes a sigh of relief, inhaling deeply and looking at the ceiling before coming back to me. She wipes my tears from the sides of my face.

"I'm sorry your mother did this to you. But don't worry, everything will be as it always should have been," she says, bringing her wand up to my temple. She kisses my forehead as she begins the memory spells, and I'm pretty sure a piece of me dies right then and there while I lay paralyzed in her shed.

Chapter 42

SILAS

The seance proves less than fruitful. Iris looks pissed and Ember looks like she's about to cry as I wince, and clamp a hand over my neck.

"What the fuck?" I hiss, and Ember approaches me with her head cocked to the side.

"Move your hand," she tells me, and I do.

She gasps and clamps a hand over her mouth, looking at me with tear-filled eyes.

"Your mark. Your mark with Violet. It looks like it's been burned off."

I stare at her a moment before going to the powder room. I click the gold plated light and look into the oval filigree mirror and my mouth drops. It looks just like someone took a hot rod and removed my mating mark.

I search deep into myself, and I don't feel her at all. The connection has been severed.

My grip on the porcelain sink is so tight I worry that I'll break the lip of it. What is she doing to Violet?

What has she done to my mate? Who is no longer my mate? My

hands shake against the white sink, as I tremble with fear, Thorin whining in the back of my mind. I look into the mirror and the man staring back at me is a disheveled mess.

My neck looks burned and a horrorowing sense of dread fills me.

What if Aster is capable of more than we thought? What if… no, I can't think like that. I splash water on my face, but it doesn't clear my thoughts. Violet can't be gone, her wolf can't be gone.

Thorin is crying and the reality starts to hit me. I can't live without Violet. What if she's suffering? Hurt? And I'm not there for her?

I stare back at my face, my eyes red from tears I didn't know I was shedding. I can't lose her, not after finally having her. Falling into a pit of despair isn't what she needs, I need to be strong and bring her home.

There's a loud crack that sounds like lightning hitting the backyard as I pull myself together and head through the back door.

It's not just Violet's mom standing in the yard, it's nearly a dozen people. Iris' grandmother, Violet's father. The three witches who gave us access to Lavender's home, and other witches I've never seen before. They're all here to make things right, to save Violet.

Lavender looks different, and I can scent the wolf on Oberyn, who still seems a little uncomfortable with me, but he says nothing as Lavender approaches all of us.

A few of the witches seem less than enthused to be around Oberyn and me, but not scared, it's almost like they know something we don't.

"You found your wand," Iris says to Lavender, who gives her a quick smile.

"I'm already a little spent helping Daisy and getting my wand back, but we need to act fast. We need to find where Aster is holding Violet."

"Must the wolves be here?" An older redheaded woman says.

"Hush, Grandma," Ember snaps at the woman, but surprisingly she does shut her mouth and shrug.

Lavender looks tired, and Oberyn seems worried for her, but she's clearly committed to finding Violet. I'm watching this all happen trying to swallow down my own fear over the situation. Lavender gives me a small smile, it doesn't mean much, but it also means everything.

These witches are gonna help me get my girl back.

"Witches in a circle," Lavender says, not wanting to waste another moment, the other witches follow suit.

Oberyn and I stand to the side and watch as each of the witches uses a knife to cut their palm before holding hands and chanting. The wind in the backyard picks up, blowing branches and whipping the witch's hair.

They chant repeatedly, all of them with their eyes closed, focusing on the task at hand and I just watch in awe. My experiences lately with witches have only proven that this feud has been superficial. No side is inherently bad or good, we're all just people who want the best for those we care about the most.

I know that no matter what happens, the pack and coven will find a way to coexist after this, but the fact is, if I don't get Violet back, I won't be around to see it.

Suddenly, all the witches' heads turn up, staring up into the evening's sky, still continuing to chant. Until everything suddenly stops, the breeze dies immediately as the witches hush. They're still holding hands as a whisper tickles my ear. I glance over at Oberyn, who clearly felt the sensation as well.

The witches part hands and almost bow before turning and looking at us.

"We know where they are," Lavender says, her face crestfallen as she looks at the burn mark on my neck, her face full of pity and sadness. "She's alive."

The relief that fills me is cataclysmic as I take in a reassuring breath.

I swallow thickly as Ember and Iris each grab one of my arms and I'm quickly teleported to a garden. I have to clench my knees for a moment to shake off the nausea.

Oberyn claps my back and I pull myself together as we all stare at the shed before us. Lavender puts a finger over her lips as I watch as the Salvador coven use salt to circle around the shed.

They all stay stationed in a circle, chanting in a whisper as I follow Lavender, Oberyn, Iris, and Ember through the front door.

"You're too late," Aster croons. Her wand is fisted in her hand as she stares at Lavender. "She's perfect. Just how she always should have been. Just like you were."

I glance over at the table. Violet's eyes are closed and her hair is now completely light blonde. The inky black color that matches her fathers, that makes her uniquely her, is gone.

"I couldn't save you, Lavender, and you may hate me for it. But I did what had to be done. It was unnatural. It would get her killed. The coven needs to be strong."

"What have you done?" Lavender asks, and as I go to approach Violet, Aster points her wand at me and her eyes narrow.

"She's no longer yours. She's mine," Aster says and I pause for a moment as I look down at Violet's neck, where her grandmother burned our connection from one another.

"*Kill her,*" Thorin says, my body vibrating with the need for him to come out and seek vengeance.

Violet doesn't feel like my mate anymore.

I look down at her and still love her, still need her. But that deep

THE MARRIAGE HEX

ache of possession is gone. She's killed her wolf.

Thorin whimpers and cries in my mind and I don't know what to do, how to soothe either one of us.

Aster goes to grab Violet's wrist but Iris and Ember both point their wands at the older witch.

Aster laughs. "Just the two of you? Please," she says, the idea of Iris and Ember being powerful enough to stop her is comical.

The door behind us creeks and Aster straightens her back.

"Daisy, go back in the house," she says to her sister.

The older woman uses her cane, walking past me, and holding out a wand, giving it to Lavender.

"Go fuck yourself, Aster," Daisy says, holding her own wand.

A united front of four witches stands against the High Priestess, yet I can barely look away from Violet. What has she done to her?

I stand next to her, keeping a grip on her wrist. Wherever she goes, I go too.

"I'm still the High Priestess. I did what had to be done, what was necessary."

"You stole my baby from me, made me forget who I was, stole my magic, and had my daughter sit in an orphanage because you were afraid of what she would become," Lavender says, her tone thick with sadness.

"You trapped me in myself," Daisy says.

"It was for your own good," Aster says and Daisy holds her wand higher, pointing it at her sister. "You're the worst kind of witch, sister." Aster laughs and sighs. "One day, you'll realize what I did for this coven."

She goes to teleport and then realizes she can't; her face dropping, her thin lips forming a straight line when she realizes she's been bested.

"What now? Tell me? How, even with the help from outside, do

SARAH BLUE

you plan on dealing with me?" she asks, like she has a plan.

"Undo what you've done to my daughter and we'll let you live," Lavender says sternly.

A slow grin takes over Aster's face as she shakes her head. "That can't be undone. I've made sure of it," she says, holding up the chain of Violet's necklace.

The anguish that floods through me on Thorin's behalf nearly has me falling to my knees. I just hold on to Violet's wrist, grounding myself to her, that she's still physically here.

"What? None of you have the gall to kill me," Aster says confidentially.

"No, far worse," Lavender says.

A spell whips out of her wand and I watch as Aster falls to the ground, incapacitated.

"Get the rest of the coven here immediately. We need to do this now," Lavender says.

I just hold on to Violet's hand, feeling out of place and fucking helpless.

"What about Violet?" I ask.

"Stay with her, be there when she wakes up. We will have to run a diagnostic to see what Aster did to her so we can reverse it," Lavender says, barely looking at her daughter, and I wonder if she blames herself like I do.

"What are you going to do with her?" I ask. Trying to push back how bad Thorin wants to kill that woman right now.

"Something far worse than death," Lavender says.

Iris and Ember both stay in the shed with me for a short moment, touching their best friend. Ember wipes the tears away from her eyes.

"We'll get her back," Iris promises, all of us knowing when she wakes up she won't be the same. "Take care of her, we'll be back soon," Iris says, holding Ember's hand and leaving the shed.

It's quiet in here, only the sound of the nearby bugs and Violet's shallow breaths filling the space.

I rub small circles on her soft hand before kissing her palm.

"You'll be okay. We'll get through this. We get through everything."

She doesn't answer and I rest my head against her arm and consider praying to a being I don't believe in.

"Violet. I need you to wake up, okay?"

Nothing, just silence. I just rub her hand and plead with any force that will listen to bring her back to me in whatever form they can.

"I don't know if I can go on," Thorin says to me. His anguish is deep and harrowing.

We don't know that Azure is gone.

"I can't... I can't feel her in any way."

Remember what Lavender said? Someone's magical essence isn't something that you can just destroy. She's not gone, I don't believe it. We'll get your mate back.

"If they're both gone?" Thorin asks.

Then we join them in whatever afterlife there is.

This appeases my wolf as I stand fully and push the blonde hair out of Violet's face. I hate it. It's not who she is.

"Baby, come on, wake up."

Suddenly, two glacier blue eyes are staring back at me. No longer with the warm affection or teasing nature I've come to love.

No, Violet stares at me like she hates me.

She quickly sits up, pointing her wand at my neck.

"Get the fuck off me, wolf," she grimaces.

"Violet?"

The cold tip of her wand presses harder into my neck as her

head tilts and she stares at me, before looking around the shed.

"What have you done to me?"

"Nothing, it was your grandmother. I'm trying to get you out of here. Your mother is outside. Iris and Ember are outside."

"I don't have a mother," Violet says and I take a deep breath.

"You had some darker magic cast on you. Let's get you home where you can rest and we can figure this out."

"I'm not going anywhere with you," she says, a look of disgust on her face.

She slowly stands from the bench, her wand pointed at me the whole time.

"Violet, it's okay. I'm your husband, remember?"

She scoffs, her nose scrunching.

"Now I know you're lying. Where is the High Priestess?"

"Outside. But I don't think—"

She cuts me off, swinging open the door as she watches the witches circling around her grandmother as the older woman's eyes roll back into her head.

"What are you doing?" Violet yells. "Let her go. What the fuck is wrong with you all?"

The witches ignore her, continuing their magic as I stupidly grab Violet's hand. Immediately, my hand wells with blisters as Violet turns and glares at me.

"Don't you ever fucking touch me," she says, nothing but malice in her eyes. "Let her go," she yells again, staring at her coven.

Her mother breaks apart from the group, and Violet winces as Lavender approaches her.

She cups her daughter's face.

"I'm sorry," she says, before pulling out her wand, and Violet starts to pass out. I catch her before she hits the floor. "Take her home. It's going to take some time to have enough strength to undo what's been done," Lavender says, pocketing her daughter's wand.

"What if she never remembers?" I ask, emotion clogging in my throat.

Lavender does the same loving gesture to my face, something a motherly figure has never done.

"I lost thirty years. There's no way in hell I'm losing any more. We'll get her back, no matter the cost," she promises me.

So, I do as she says, bringing her back to her home, lying her in her bed. I sit there, hoping for a miracle.

Chapter 43

VIOLET

There's a heavy weight on my chest, and I shove it off, sharp nails digging into my skin as an irritated voice trickles into my head.

"Don't tell me the old hag made you hate me too," Walter says.

"Ugh, why are you talking so loud?"

"I didn't say anything," a deep voice says, as I quickly open my eyes to see the massive man from earlier.

He's in my bedroom, staring at me.

I pull the soft purple comforter up to my chin and stare at the man for a moment. He's huge, not bad looking…okay, he's handsome, but he's definitely a wolf. Why in the actual fuck would a wolf be in my bedroom right now?

I feel for my wand. Nothing.

I cast a quick wordless spell for my wand. Still nothing.

"Your mother took your wand for now," the man says, and I can't help but to slightly sneer at him. I'm not sure why I hate him, but it's irrelevant.

"I've never met my mother. Why are you in my house?" I ask him.

His blunt nails drag against his beard. The sound is soothing. No, it's annoying.

"If I were to tell you I was your husband and that your grandmother erased me from your memory, would you believe me?" he asks, his glowing amber eyes looking at me with sadness and hope.

"No," I reply honestly. "I'd never marry a wolf," I say.

The man laughs even though it's evident that he doesn't find it funny.

"Unfortunately, he may stink, but he doesn't tell lies," Walter tells me and I furrow my brows as I stare into his yellow eyes.

Walter is crotchety and irritable, but he's not a liar. If anything, his dedication is solely to me. Why would he lie?

"And what he said about grand-mére?" I ask Walter, the man watching in fascination as I talk out loud to my cat.

"Sadly, true. The High Priestess may have done more to your mind than we realize," Walter says, and I take a moment to think.

What memories do I remember? I remember my grand-mére always being there for me, raising me as her daughter. I remember growing up with Iris and Ember and the coven. The Celestial Coven is everything to me. I've never had a relationship, never even had any interest in anyone romantically.

I'm not married. My grand-mére wouldn't do something like this, not to me. She loves me more than anyone. I'm the future of the coven. She wouldn't.

"Get out," I tell the man in front of me.

"Silas," he says. "My name is Silas. We were best friends for sixteen years, growing up in an orphanage together. A few weeks ago, I moved to town and a hex you cast on your sixteenth birthday forced us to get married. We didn't like it at first, but once we gave in the hex was lifted. We're far more than husband and wife, Violet. I don't care how long it takes for you to remember, but I'm not going anywhere." He stands up and looks at me. "I'm going to give you your space right now, but I'll be back later," he promises.

I watch him leave and then fall back into bed. I want to wake up from this messed-up alternate reality. I also want my fucking wand.

It's been hours of me pacing around my house, waiting for someone familiar to come by and tell me what's going on. Instead, there's a massive brown wolf pacing my backyard, nearly making a trail with the way his paws dig into the dirt as he walks around my yard.

"This is all so weird," I say out loud.

"Trust me, I wish it weren't reality either," Walter sighs, plopping down against the back window where a stray sunbeam glistens through.

"Where is everyone?"

"Dealing out justice, I suppose," Walter says.

"What does that mean?" I ask.

Walter just sighs, licking his paw, and not answering me. Typical.

The wolf doesn't stop pacing, he seems restless, and almost anguished? No, surely not, he's a beast, nothing more.

There's a tap at my door and I take a sigh of relief, hoping it's someone with real answers.

The same woman from earlier who looks just like me with bright blonde hair and my two best friends flank her, along with a prim calico cat that walks closely to the older woman. They almost look scared to approach me.

"Violet," Iris says.

I narrow my eyes at her.

"Where's my wand?"

"I have it. Can we sit down and talk about what happened? Give you your memories back?" the woman I only somewhat recognize as someone who could be related to me says.

"Who is the beautiful feline?" Walter says, threading through my own legs and I ignore him.

"Where is the High Priestess?" I ask.

Ember winces and grabs my wrist, which I quickly tug away. There's hurt written on her pretty features, but she doesn't say anything as she drops her hand.

"What have you done with her?" I say in an accusatory tone.

"Violet, will you let me show you a few things?" Iris says.

She pulls out her phone and opens up her camera reel, showing me pictures of us. With my hair two toned, a bright smile on my face. I grab the strands of my bright blonde hair between my fingers.

"Did I color it?" I ask.

"No, you never could, no matter what spells we tried," Iris says with a light smile. "Can I show you some of my memories from the last week?" she pleads.

I look at Iris, and search my memories. Something lingers at the back of my mind, telling me I can't wholly trust her. But that doesn't make sense? How can she be my best friend and someone I can't trust? Feeling like I have nothing to lose, I nod in agreement.

She smiles, interlacing our fingers and pressing our foreheads together.

The memories whip through my mind. The way we stood just like this as she granted me protection, and I made her take a vow of secrecy when I told her everything Silas told me. There's a vision of going to New Orleans and making my mother regain her memories, of admitting what I am at the table to everyone. I gasp as that memory flies by. The last memory is of my grand-mére telling them that it's too late, that I'm perfect now.

I pull back, my eyes wide as I look at her. I can tell her memories are real, but I don't feel them myself. I have no memories of any of that happening. I glance over to the woman who's my mother, who gives me a tear-filled smile.

"Will you let us bring your memories back?" she says.

I look back over at Iris. "This isn't some big trick?" I ask her, and she shakes her head.

"Let us try and I'll give you your wand back," the woman—my mother—says.

If I wasn't already motivated, that definitely pushed me over the edge as I sit on the floor, the three witches surrounding me. I take a few deep breaths as they chant, and I try to believe in what they're telling me.

They chant the same words repeatedly, the same ones from Iris' memory, but I don't feel any different.

Suddenly, a memory fills me. It flashes by so quick I almost miss it.

"I'd be the best husband, and you know it. We'd be one of those couples who wanted to spend all of our time together. You wouldn't be able to resist me. Honestly, the more I think about it, the sillier this pact is, because I think I'm going to convince you to marry me well before then anyway, Violet."

The voice isn't as deep as the one from the man in my bedroom, but yet, I can tell that it's him. It's hard to picture where we are, but I can hear his voice clear as day. As soon as the memory comes, I notice the chanting has stopped, and three concerned faces are staring down at me.

"The damage she caused in your memories is more vast than I realized. I think we'll need the entirety of the coven," my mother says and I look over at Ember, who is openly crying.

"Oh, Ember," Iris says and Ember shakes her head, her wild strawberry blonde hair landing around her face.

"She was just so happy. I can't believe she would take that away."

"I was?" I ask.

Ember sits down on the floor, her bare knees hitting the wood as she cups my cheeks.

"You were. He makes you really happy, Violet. You were doing everything you could to make things right with the coven and the other supernaturals. You're our best friend. I love you. I just want you to be you again," she says.

I can't help but to wrap my arms around her, as guilt consumes me. I care for Ember; I know that's true. But I don't feel the same way as she does, and I know it's wrong.

They aren't lying. Something is wrong with me.

"When can the coven convene?" I ask, holding back my emotions. "They don't need to know these conflicting feelings going on in my mind. Once we have the power of the whole coven, this will all be a distant memory… right?"

"The full moon," my mother says. "We're going to need all the help we can get."

I sigh in agreement as I look down at the floor where the two cats are sussing each other out. "This is my familiar, Marie. I didn't think she'd be able to find me after this time," my mother says lovingly and I look down at the cat, not feeling anything.

"*Beautiful*," Walter says, nuzzling his head against the unfamiliar cat, but I suppose everything is somewhat unfamiliar right now. "Can we keep her?" my crotchety familiar nearly begs.

The multi-colored cat bats him across the face and Walter looks startled.

My mother laughs and I stand there, feeling completely out of place.

"I think I'm in love," Walter says, the other cat sits primly, turning her head and ignoring him.

Days pass and I still feel indifferent to everyone around me. Deep down, I know I have feelings for these people, but there's a wrongness I can't shake.

I stare out the window.

Silas is back. Well, I suppose he barely leaves. He's either in my backyard chopping wood to build Hecate knows what in my backyard, or he's pacing around in wolf form. His presence is never ending and feels like a guillotine over my head.

I catch him glancing at the house every now and then, hopefully staring at the purple monstrosity like I'll wake up and everything will be back to normal.

He seems sad and pissed off every time he swings the axe on a new piece of wood.

I shouldn't be gratuitously staring at him, but he did just get hot and took his shirt off. He's supposedly my husband, after all. I should at least be able to take a cursory glance here and there.

His large muscles flex each time he brings the axe down. He wipes his brow with a rag as he moves them over to the lake. There's a small base of something that used to be there. It looks like he's adding on to it.

Why? I have no clue. All I know is that every day, he comes here, works on his project and pouts. Then his wolf takes over at night.

The longer I look at his face, the more I realize he's exhausted. Dark circles are heavy under his eyes and his beard is unkempt.

Why can't I feel this connection we supposedly had?

Why can't I feel anything?

My mother comes over for dinner. She does this every evening, like she's trying to win my affection through my stomach. She also brings Marie, which makes Walter happy. At least someone in this house is enjoying themselves. Even if the female cat seems to make her disinterest known.

Today Lavender brought red beans and rice, which does help sway things in her favor. She takes a plate out to Silas and they talk for a few moments, and she pats him on the arm before heading back into the house.

I have a fork full of food headed toward my mouth when she speaks.

"Aster is at a facility for aging humans, and that's where she will stay. She will live the rest of her life believing she's a human, one of the very things she always hated. She will not have visitors, she will wither away in her own version of hell," she says, not even an ounce of sadness in her tone.

"She's your mother," I chastise, sitting up straight.

I can flash through Iris' memories, but I just can't believe her memories over my own. I'm still having a hard time understanding how my grand-mère could do something so malicious?

"She raised me. She was there for me when you weren't. You're the one who left. All she ever did was look out for the coven," I say, and my mother gives me a sad smile.

"The full moon is in two days. All will be well," she says, but there's still a furrow in her brow.

"Which assisted living facility?" I ask.

"It's in Ohio," my mother says with a smirk.

Grand-mere *did* hate any place above the Mason Dixon Line, especially a place like Ohio. It's everything she would loathe.

"I think I've lost my appetite," I say, excusing myself and going to my room and staring out the window.

Walter joins me and sighs as I pet his fur. Marie curls up next to him, and I swear my crotchety old cat smiles as she gives him some affection. But it doesn't make me smile, it doesn't make me feel anything. I feel wholly broken.

"*I miss you, Violet,*" he says, rubbing the top of his head against my jaw, before resting with his new kitty girlfriend.

How much of myself have I lost, and will I ever get it back?

Chapter 44

SILAS

Sweat is dripping down my back as Oberyn approaches me; I still haven't gotten a good read on him, he's not a man of many words.

"Need a hand?" he says.

"Sure," I reply as he helps me put in another post in the gazebo.

I don't know why I'm building this fucking thing, but it's better than just sitting on her porch acting like a pathetic watch dog. So, to keep myself busy, I'm rebuilding this god damn gazebo that has caused me even more suffering.

"Lav and I got married in this thing. I didn't know Aster destroyed it, or that she even knew we officially got married," he says.

"We're sure Aster isn't coming back?" I ask.

The man huffs, helping me make sure the post is level.

"Lavender is sure she won't. You know, a part of me always thought Aster was more afraid of Lavender ascending too early than she was about us being together."

My brows furrow, and confusion laces through me.

"Fuck, she hasn't told you?" Oberyn says. He uses his foot to shift the post before placing the joints in place. "The moment Aster's magic was lifted from her, Lavender ascended to High Priestess. It's a done deal. Even if Aster were to somehow get her magic back, she wouldn't be a match for Lav or the coven."

I look over at the house, glancing at Violet's window, the curtain slightly jolts and I smirk, knowing she was watching us out here.

"I think Violet was under the impression she was going to be the next High Priestess."

Her father looks concerned, glancing over at the house, and then turns back to me.

"Do you think she'll be upset?"

"Once she's back to herself?" I say, hoping that she gets her old self back. I don't mind coming here every day and working on wearing her down. But every time I see her and suffer her lack of recognition, a part of me wants to die. "No, I think she'll be relieved. She wanted what was best for the coven above all, she was ready to take on the role, but I don't think she really wanted it."

"Good," Oberyn says. He swallows and sighs. "Listen, I'm no good with this shit. Lavender isn't my mate in that way because she's not a wolf. But my parents were mates. Is your wolf alright?"

"No," Thorin nearly whimpers in my head.

"Far from it," I tell him honestly.

"Two more days till the full moon, she'll be back to herself," he says, but I can tell he's trying to convince himself just as much as I am.

We spend the rest of the afternoon building the gazebo and talking about the pack.

Once the posts are all in place, we sigh, knowing the roof is going to be an absolute motherfucker.

"You're the right Alpha for the pack," he says, surprising me.

"What?"

"My place right now is supporting Lav, getting to know Violet

THE MARRIAGE HEX

and just fucking existing. You're young, you're sure. And hell, I feel like if I challenged your wolf you'd kick my ass."

"*I would*," Thorin says solemnly.

I smirk and toss the hammer into my tools. "I'm working on making a council. I think I'd like for you to be a part of it," I tell him and he smiles.

For the first time since meeting him, I see the resemblances between him and Violet and it makes my heart pang even more. I look back up at her window and no one is there. I feel empty and all I want to feel is some hope.

"How many members do you think would be willing to help you get your mate back?" he asks.

I look at him confused and he shrugs.

"Lavender thinks having both sides of Violet during the ritual will help bring back her memories and her wolf. Aster destroyed the necklace, but you can't destroy someone's essence," he says.

"I'll get as many as I can," I tell him honestly.

I've given this pack financial freedom, released them from the pressure of the witches. This is all I want in return. I'll lay my life down for my pack, but there's no life worth living without Violet.

The night air is almost unseasonal with a bitterness that feels like a bad omen. There's already a circle of candles glowing in the cold night air as witches and shifters alike start arriving.

My heart swells with how many members of my community showed up tonight, even those who showed a distaste for me being married to Violet. Jonas, Paige, Maddox, Bruce, Kit, and so many others came out here even while tensions are still relatively high.

Promises by Lavender and the Celestial Coven at large have dissipated some of the mistrust, but old habits die hard. Yet, they're all here in the hopes that their presence can help bring my girl back. Bring Thorin's mate back.

The witches are all busy, setting things up, making everything just right as Violet sits in the center, her arms wrapped around herself in a shiver. I take off my flannel jacket and walk over, placing it over her shoulders.

"Thanks," she whispers.

She looks afraid, withdrawn, and not herself.

I thought moments of my life were painful, but watching the woman I love slip away takes the fucking cake.

"Are you nervous?" I ask. Even the smallest conversations with her have been uncomfortable.

But as she thumbs the collar of my jacket and lightly inhales my scent, it's the first time I've felt hope in a really long time.

"What if they can't get my memories back. What if I'm not a wolf anymore?" she asks me, her emotionless face is startling as I drop down to my haunches.

"Then we'll just have to start over."

She shakes her head and looks around as everyone is busying themselves getting ready for the ritual.

"What if I never feel again?" she asks, this time fear is nearly wafting off of her.

"Everyone here cares about you; if you think this is the last resort, you're wrong. We just all want you to be safe and happy," I tell her.

"You were happy with me?" she asks, wrapping my jacket firmly around her body.

I smile at her. "The happiest I've ever been."

She looks down at the ground, her boot rubbing into the dirt.

"I hope I remember you," she says, and I swallow thickly, not wanting to think of the alternative.

"Me too, little witch."

She clears her throat at the pet name as I walk over to Lavender. She's bossing everyone around, clearly anxious for this to work.

"What do you want the wolves to do?" I ask.

She gives me a small smile. "I think it's best for you to stay in this form, but Oberyn and I agree that the magic might be more powerful if the pack is shifted. Members of the Salvador Coven are coming as well. I won't stop until the harm my mother caused is remedied, until Violet is the vibrant witch she once was," she says.

I look back at Violet, who looks so out of place, so small and lost.

"I'll go talk to the pack."

The High Priestess nods, and as I'm walking toward the pack, a hand grips mine. One covered in bangles and bracelets. I recognize her before she even speaks. Delphine, Iris' grandmother.

"A word, wolf," she says, and I turn to face her.

Her hands clasp over her wooden cane, as she looks nowhere in particular.

"No matter what happens tonight, it's important you don't breach the circle, not until the ritual is complete."

I tilt my head at her and she sighs.

"If you can't promise me that you'll stay out of the circle, I can subdue you," she says, it's not in a mean tone, she's being extremely serious.

"Why would I want to break the circle?" I ask.

"Violet's mind and body are about to go through what may be a painful transformation. I understand your protectiveness of her as your mate is unparalleled. No matter how much she screams or her body trembles, you can not break the circle. Breaking the connection of witches could ruin everything."

"I won't break the circle."

SARAH BLUE

"She'll be fine, I've seen it," she says, before turning and joining the witches.

I reiterate what Lavender told me, and watch as my community undresses, piling their clothes in a safe area as they all shift. I take a moment to not let fear and hopelessness fill me, because what I see right now is magical.

Two groups who have hated each other for centuries are here today, working together to strengthen this truce. No, it's far more than a truce. It's the dawn of a new era—one where we work together to protect our secrets and the families we care about.

It's evident in the people here today. Kit, who clearly has not had an issue pissing off the witches at every opportunity. Maddox who was vehement about peace not even being a possibility. Even some of the old timers who have been here for the worst of the worst, like Bruce, are here tonight.

Even on the witches side, I can sense some unease being around the wolves. Ember's grandmother still seems a little off-kilter, but she's still here. Other witches are uncomfortable being present, but regardless they're here to help Violet, the coven, and relations between our two groups.

It's something I never dreamed possible, but we're all here. We've been brought together by a common thread, my beautiful wife and mate.

Hope is blooming in my chest as I breathe in the fresh air and take in the echoing howls around me. They're thanking the full moon for its blessing and the gesture nearly brings tears to my eyes.

Together. Two sides of a coin that have had their fair share of hate have been brought together, and this ritual is going to tie us together regardless of what happens to Violet. Though, every single fiber of my being is hoping that this is enough.

The wolves create a larger spaced out circle around the witches. I find myself in between, standing there, staring as Violet lays herself on the ground, my jacket still wrapped around her.

The witches link hands and as soon as they do, there's a breeze ripping through the air. The silence is deafening before they begin chanting.

The wolves all look on with rapt fascination, for most of them this is the first time they've seen magic of this magnitude. Even for me, it's still as impressive as when Violet lit the pumpkins on her front porch.

Bright candle flames rise as their volume rises, and my eyes don't leave Violet. Her eyes are squinting in pain, and even from here I can see her body vibrating. It takes everything in me to not run over to her and make sure she's okay. But I resist. I stay the course, standing in place and watching with hopeful eyes.

The witches raise their joined hands, nearly shouting their chant at this point as Violet begins to whimper in pain, her body shaking as a pained scream rips out of her throat. My fists are balled so tight to keep my control, to not shift, and to not ruin the ritual.

Violet is whimpering, tears streaming down the sides of her face, as I notice it. The change is gradual, a few strands at first, before even more start turning black, bringing back the noticeable hairstyle she's always had. The one that signifies the two halves that make her whole.

Despite the change, the witches don't stop. They continue repeating the spell. Some wolves howl. I'm not sure if it's on their own accord or if there's something in the air telling them that Violet is part of this pack, that she needs us.

The full moon is bright overhead, glistening in the sky, reflecting off Violet's sweat covered skin. Her body is still trembling, but she isn't vocally in pain anymore. Her hands clutch against my flannel jacket as the wind subsides, the thick cream-colored candles going back to a standard flame.

Each of the witches slowly bow their heads, whispering an incantation I can't even hear, before dropping their hands.

As soon as the circle is broken my steps are quick.

Violet seems like she's asleep as I approach her and wipe away her stained cheeks. Her face is cold, but I feel it.

"My mate," Thorin coos in the back of my mind.

I smile, pushing her hair from her face. I still don't know if her memories are back, but it's clear the ritual linked her back to Azure. Her wolf is no longer trapped in a necklace as I wait with bated breath.

Her parents and coven all hover close as we wait for her to wake up. It feels like time is endless as we wait for her eyes to finally pop open.

What if she doesn't remember?

"Then you're going to have to work on your personality to make her like you again," Thorin says, and despite myself, I smile.

Bright blue eyes open, staring at me as she gives me a soft smile.

"Hey there, wolf man," she says.

I stare at her, not sure if that means she remembers or if she's fucking with me.

"Violet?"

"Oh, not the full name. Stick to Vi, wife, mate, baby, or little witch, please," she says, fully grinning at me this time.

I'm rougher than I should be, pulling her to my chest. Her arms wrap around me as I hold her tight.

I feel whole again.

Chapter 45

VIOLET

The rest of the evening is overwhelming as everything comes crashing back to me, and how I felt during these last few days that I wasn't myself. I know it's not my fault, but there's still major guilt for how I treated everyone.

I talk to Ember and Iris, hugging them both close and apologizing profusely for how cold I was.

"Hey, stop it. You weren't yourself. We don't blame you, we're just so happy you're back," Ember says, squeezing me tight.

"Seriously, Vi. You did nothing wrong. How are you holding up?" Iris asks.

I search my feelings and they're all so complicated I don't know where to start. There should be no conflicting thoughts about my grand-mère, yet, I still have an ache in my chest. Even though she hurt me, even though everything was a lie. It's a harsh reality when someone you loved and trusted can hurt you so profoundly.

She deserves to be where she is. Her punishment may even

be too light. It's hard to combine the woman who taught me everything about magic, who showed me love and gave me my coven—with the woman who left me in an orphanage, left her daughter magicless, and only cared about witches.

Iris rubs my arm. "Hey, we don't have to talk about it right now."

"Thanks." I look around and a slow smile spreads across my face as the wolves mill about, ready to take their full moon run.

Witches and wolves came together to bring me back, to give me my family and my mate back.

"Oh, just forget about me, huh?" Azure says with sass in the back of my mind, and I smile even wider.

I look around and just think about what I want to say to her instead of saying it out loud. "I could never forget about you. I missed you."

"As you should. Let a girl run free, would ya?"

"Just give me a minute", I tell her as I approach my mother. She seems tense, and nervous. I don't speak, instead I wrap my arms around her, trying not to cry. But as she holds me back and I'm reminded of all the time I've missed with her and my father, some of the guilt goes away. Grand-mère's love was conditional, but the people around me, they would have loved me either way. That broken shell of a woman I was before the ritual, and the true me.

My mother pets down my hair and kisses the side of my face.

"I'm so sorry, Violet," she says.

"It's not your fault."

"I just wish I could have protected you when it mattered all those years ago."

I pull back and gaze into the bright blue eyes that mirror mine. "You did everything you could. You brought me back now, you were there when it mattered."

My mother smiles, looking over my shoulder.

"Let's have brunch tomorrow. But go ahead," she says.

I furrow my brow. "Go ahead and what?"

She cups my face. "Go be with your pack. I know your father is ready to run with the wolves again. Let her free," she says.

The warm feeling of acceptance fills me. Something I wasn't sure was possible. I look around the coven, and they all give me nods of approval. I was so scared that they wouldn't love me or accept me once they found out what I was. But here they all are, supporting me in the way only a true family does.

"Thank you," I say, and she kisses my cheek one last time as I search around for Silas.

It doesn't take long. He gave me some space so I could thank and greet everyone who came here tonight, but I can feel his gaze on the side of my face. I walk over to the outcrop of trees.

The wolves are nearby, my father included, I assume.

Silas stands up straight from the tree he was leaning against as I approach. He's cautious with me, and I don't blame him. I can't imagine what it was like on his end watching me slip away, or the transition during the ritual.

"Are you tired, do you want to go home?" he asks.

I smirk, tossing his flannel jacket, grabbing my shirt at the hem and tossing it on the ground. He looks at me with wide eyes.

SARAH BLUE

"Well, are we going to go on our first run as a pack together or what?" I ask.

Azure is nearly prancing around in my head, ready to be let out, ready to see her mate.

The smile that takes over Silas' face is devastating, and I fist his shirt and bring him closer to me.

"What do you say, dear husband?" I ask.

His grin is still wildly in place as he kisses me and brings me behind a tree. I guess modesty is still a thing kept between mates as he helps me undress and he does the same to himself. The cool air of the night tickles my skin as I appreciate the naked man in front of me.

He takes a step in front of me and cups my face with both hands and looks at me like I'm his world. I could have lost the love of my life. She made me forget him. More of the guilt washes away as he kisses my forehead and holds me close.

"Stick with me, okay?" he says.

I can feel Azure roll her eyes. *"Yeah, I'm just going to wander off from my mate. Idiot,"* Azure says.

I smile and kiss the center of Silas' chest. It's then I see his neck, my thumb dragging along the scar that matches my own and my lips part in shock.

"We're not mated anymore?"

Silas just smiles. "It seems the universe didn't think we were rare enough. Looks like I have the pleasure of marking you all over again."

"He's smooth. I'll give the man that," Azure says.

"Azure is getting antsy," I tell him.

"Thorin has been screaming at me since the moment you recognized me," he says. "Should we give them what they want?"

"I think they deserve it," I say as Silas backs up, his big beautiful wolf taking his space.

He takes a few steps toward me, nuzzling my collarbone as I pet his fur.

"I missed you too, Thorin, are you ready to see your girl?"

He makes a chuffing noise and backs up as I willingly shift for the first time. The pain isn't as rough as before, and Azure lets me stay in the background as she and Thorin are reunited.

Both of their heads nuzzle on another as they see each other for only the third time. Thorin is delicate with her, even though he's so much larger.

It's then I hear Thorin's deep, demanding voice for the first time.

"My mate, how I've missed you," he tells Azure, who preens at the attention.

They play, yipping at each other's legs as we meet up with the rest of the pack. What I can see is limited, but I know the large black wolf with deep brown eyes is my father. He bows his head slightly at Thorin.

The other wolves, all different colors and sizes, glance our way, and there's no conflicting feelings. They recognize Thorin as their Alpha and me as his mate. It's freeing in a way, being a visitor to this experience. It doesn't last long as Azure kicks me out to frolic with her mate, but I feel whole.

Pieces of me may have gotten dinged off over the years. But slowly, with Silas back in my life, finding my parents, and making the coven what it should have always been, I have more than hope in my heart. I have everything.

Chapter 46

AZURE

"I've missed you," my magnificent large wolf tells me, pressing his head against mine.

We've both pushed the pesky humans out of our minds. They make everything so complicated.

When it's me and Thorin, everything is perfect.

"I missed you, too."

"These wolves, they're our pack now. They bow to you, sweetness," he tells me.

I feel shy for a moment as his tongue swipes out and licks my face.

"Don't be shy, you're better than everyone and they should know it," he says. I nip at him playfully as he laughs in that wolfish way he does.

"So, what do we do on a pack run?"

"We just have fun, whatever the lady wishes," he says with very salacious undertones.

He begins to run, not too fast, so I can catch up.

I have my pack, I'm fully a part of this connection with Violet. I'm finally free.

Chapter 47

VIOLET

My skin is sweaty and my heart is thrumming in my chest when we get back to the place where we discarded our clothes. Some of the pack just went home while others came back to get their garments.

Azure pushed me out for some festivities, but I feel alive. I didn't think it was possible to find more family outside of my coven, but after tonight I think I've made the right steps with the pack.

Silas and I are dressing, the other shifters around are the only reason I don't jump his bones right now. He smirks, like he knows it. Man is too good looking for his own good.

"Let's go home," he says, tightening his flannel jacket around me as we walk over to his bike that I somehow haven't been on the back of.

He gets on first, and I wrap my arms around him tightly, taking in his scent and the feel of his body pressed against mine. He hands me a helmet, and I put it on, even though I place a safety enchantment over us in hushed tones.

Silas starts the engine and squeezes my thigh.

"Ready?"

"Yes," I reply with a squeeze as he drives us into the night.

It's freeing and fun, but doesn't come close to how it felt to shift and run tonight. The moon shines ahead of us, the sign of a new beginning as he pulls up to the house. I no longer need to hide his bike as he parks and I hop off and hand him the helmet.

"Can I show you something?" he asks and I nod, taking his hand in mine as we walk around the side of the house to the backyard.

My mouth drops as I take in the gazebo he built alongside my father. He painted it purple to match the house and added lights.

"Your mother spelled the lights," he says as we approach and I step onto the gazebo, where I notice the blankets and pillows waiting for us.

I cast a spell so we aren't eaten alive with bugs as Silas sits and I straddle his lap, running my nails against his beard and looking into his eyes.

"Thank you for this."

"Had to keep myself busy or I would have gone crazy. Thorin was already halfway there."

"I never—"

"You didn't do anything, Violet. All that matters is you're here now, you're in my arms, you're you again."

"Do you really think you could have made zombie me fall in love with you again?" I joke and he smirks.

"I had plans in place. Maybe some hexes, some impromptu trips to the courthouse. I would have made it happen," he says.

I keep touching his face because he's pretty, and I missed him.

"What now?" I ask.

"Honestly? I need my fucking mark on you again, Vi. I don't think I can wait."

I smile at his impatience, only because I feel the same way. His large hands are spanning my waist as he holds me. It almost feels reminiscent of the first time we bonded, our wolves having their fun and leaving us with the fallout, but this time it's less charged. It's softer and more intimate.

Especially as we sit in the gazebo he made, the full moon glinting against the lake as the frogs bellow and the peaceful fall air surrounds us.

"Now what kind of wife would I be if I said no?"

"A cruel one," he says.

I lean forward and his lips meet mine, his hand on my ass as the other tangles in my messy hair.

He moves me over his jeans, his cock hardening as he slides his flannel jacket off my shoulders. His touch is warm and comforting and I don't know how I could have ever lived without feeling his touch again.

I know what to expect now, and I'm not scared. I'm eager. Even after the hell we've been through, being able to relive one of the best moments of my life is priceless.

I shift my hand between us, unfastening his pants as he shimmies them off his hips. I laugh as he unsuccessfully takes off his pants, and I stand.

He pushes up my shirt, kissing my stomach, and I toss it off my head, before he unbuttons my pants and pushes them down my legs. Silas kisses my lace-covered pussy, before dragging his tongue over the material. He has a momentary loss of control as he grips the side of them and shreds them in half.

He grips my ass, bringing my center to his face, holding me at the juncture of my thighs and cheeks. He lavishes my clit with his tongue. I rake my fingers through his hair, keeping him where I want him. He moans and I realize he's stroking himself while touching me, which only makes me even more turned on.

SARAH BLUE

My legs tremble and he holds me in place while I nearly tug on the dark strands of his hair.

A whimpered moan falls out of me as he sucks on my clit, sending me over the edge. I shiver with my release as Silas pulls his pants off, using his feet to toss them in the corner.

He holds my waist as I sit back on his lap, my wet pussy sliding against his hard cock.

"You were pretty confident we would end up here tonight, huh?"

His hands cup my face, our gazes locked in on one another.

"It doesn't matter. All that matters is we're here now. Let me bond with you again, let me be the husband you deserve."

"You already are," I tell him, bringing our lips together.

The same butterflies are still there, even after all this time and sacrifice.

His hands leave my face, holding me up as he slides himself into me. I unbutton his shirt, sliding my hands over the broad expanse of his chest as I slide down his length.

There's no comparing our two bondings, but this feels more intimate, more purposeful as Silas' eyes meet mine, nothing but love in his golden gaze.

"Mark me over the scar," I tell him and he glances down at my neck.

I want to take this awful thing and make it beautiful again. I slowly ride him as I push all my hair to the opposite side, giving him my neck.

Silas is barely hanging on beneath me, and I know the moment he knots me I'll be done for.

"You're mine, Vi, in this world and the next," he says, his tongue licking a stripe up my neck as he thrusts from below, pushing his knot into my entrance.

THE MARRIAGE HEX

I scream my pleasure as he sinks his teeth into me for the second time. The euphoric feeling of the bond taking place again and the way he fills me up perfectly is almost too much.

I'm whimpering as he ruts me from below, licking the spot he just re-marked and I push through the exhaustion and do the same for him. Marking him in that same spot I claimed not so long ago.

Relief floods through me as I feel our previously severed connection.

His knot is still in me even as his cum threatens to spill out and he holds me close.

I rest my head on his chest and he soothingly rubs circles on my back.

Never in a million years did I see myself here. Never dreamed the first boy I kissed would end up being my last. That the man who was supposed to be my enemy became my everything. Yet, here we are.

"What now?" I say, pulling back.

He smiles, his eyes slightly hazy with lust. "We live the life we always dreamed of," he says.

I stroke his face and press a quick kiss on his lips.

"I can live with that."

"Good, because I'm not going anywhere."

My first friend, the boy I used to love, is now the man I love unabashedly.

Epilogue

SILAS

October 11th, the following year

I stand in the gazebo with Jonas at my back. Delphine stands between us as the crowd waits in foldable wooden chairs, staring at me. I could have never imagined this would be the crowd at my wedding. Not only do witches and shifters sit next to each other, but add in a vampire and other interesting supernaturals, I never could have imagined. But this is how it was supposed to be.

"It was meant to be," Delphine whispers. She still scares the shit out of me sometimes. I never know exactly what's a vision and what's reality, but one thing is for certain, I will never get on her bad side.

"Gotta say, I never thought I'd see you in a suit man," Jonas says, as Paige walks their son down the aisle. He's the flower boy, but his walking is a little messy. "God, he looks fucking cute," Jonas says and I smile, watching my nephew.

"You did good."

"Paige and I want to try again soon," he says.

Everyone coos at the little boy as he waddles his way up to the gazebo, grinning with only a few baby teeth as I hold out my arms. He eagerly lets me pick him up.

"Uncle Si is your favorite, isn't he?" I ask him as Jonas tsks behind me.

"Give me my son," he says.

"Oh, but you don't want that. You want me to hold you throughout my wedding ceremony, don't you?"

Jonas rolls his eyes, and I hand him his son as the music plays.

Candles float above the crowd, and purple petals are randomly tossed about the aisle.

Next, Walter and Marie prance down the aisle, both of their noses high and proud. The ring box jingles against his collar as he walks it down the aisle. When he reaches the gazebo I bend down and unlatch it, scratching his chin and then Marie's. He gives me an eyeroll, and Marie bites his ear, but there's no heat to it. I've been feeding the little bastard small scraps here and there until he eventually gave up on hating me. At least Marie has made him somewhat less of an asshole. I guess love will do that to a man.

Ember walks down first wearing a cinched deep purple dress. She smiles widely, blowing a kiss at her plus one as he sits there covered head to toe in black, sunglasses covering his eyes and an umbrella clutched in his gloved fist.

She takes her place across from us and I smile at her as Iris walks down the aisle next, her smile not as wide, but still genuine as she walks toward the gazebo. A very cautious glance at her plus one who was purposely sat in the back row.

Iris takes her place next to Ember as the music softens and Violet walks down the aisle, her mother and father on each side of her.

Her dress is a cream silk that wraps around every delicious curve of her body. It's nearly reminiscent of that ridiculous nightgown she wore when we got married at the courthouse.

"*Beautiful,*" Thorin says, and I smile down the aisle as my wife approaches.

Her hair is in loose curls, clearly protected by magic as a crown of dark purple and forest green leaves rest on top of her head.

Violet's smile is radiant and her mother and father look proud as they bring her to the gazebo.

Oberyn and Lavender kiss her cheeks. Watching their relationship grow over the last year has been a blessing. They've built a home in between the pack lands and the center of town, but they come over often.

Lavender has been mentoring her to be High Priestess in the right way, and I know when Violet's time comes she'll be ready, but for now we get to live. Oberyn and I have gotten extremely close. Jonas is still my second in command, but Oberyn is a close second. He spearheaded the council and we've brought Pack Moon Walker into a new era.

Oberyn takes Violet's hand and places it in mine, before slapping my shoulder and they take their seats.

The witches place their wands in the air and we watch in complete magnificence as the area surrounding us darkens, only the tremendous amount of candle and fairy lights shining in the space.

Violet smiles, squeezing my hands as Delphine starts the ceremony.

There are no hard as hell circuit court benches, or unenthused witnesses. No, this is the wedding Violet deserves. The people who love us the most surrounding us as we take new vows to one another.

Delphine directs Violet to go first, and I do my best to keep my shit together.

"Silas," Violet starts, her eyes watering, but she holds back tears.

"You were the first person I ever loved. My first kiss, and really my first friend. I don't remember what was said that night all those years ago when we were both hoping for a better life, but I don't think either of us could have ever dreamed of this. You make me a better person, and I've never been happier than I am when I'm in your arms."

"You make me the best version of myself. I vow to love you, to honor you, and to be there for you always. I promise that our life will be filled with adventure and trust, and that there's nothing that could ever break this bond between us. We're eternal and I love you so much," she says, sniffling and smiling at me.

"I'm going to fucking cry," Thorin says, which has me laughing and trying to hold back my emotion.

"Silas," Delphine says.

"I don't know how to follow that," I say, and the crowd laughs as Violet wipes her face and takes my hands back in her own. "It's always been you, Vi. It's always going to be you. Fate brought us together, and I couldn't be more thankful. You're the best part of my day, and I've never smiled more in my life. I promise to keep you safe and protect you always. I promise to spend all my years loving you and making sure you never have a single doubt. But most of all," I say with a grin.

"I promise to be the best husband, and you know it. We'll be one of those couples who spend all of our time together. You won't be able to resist me."

Violet's jaw drops, and the crowd seems confused. But not Iris. She helped me dig up that memory so I could recite it tonight.

Her smile is radiant.

"You may kiss your bride," Delphine says, since this is really a vow renewal.

I place a hand at the small of Violet's back and cup her face as

THE MARRIAGE HEX

I dip her low and kiss her. We both can't help it as we smile when we kiss. My stomach dips, as it always does when I'm with my wife.

The crowd cheers, the nighttime sky drifting back to evening as purple petals fall from the sky and we hold hands to our reception area.

The party is filled with drinks, music, and dancing.

I dance with Lavender while Violet dances with her father for the father-daughter dance.

"Thank you for this," she whispers. "I've missed so much. I needed this, especially here," she says, the same gazebo where she and Oberyn got married.

I hug Lavender, the most motherly figure I've ever had in my life as she pats my cheek.

"Thanks, Mom," I tell her and she smiles. She grabs her husband's arm. "Stop hogging the bride," she tells him, and Violet smiles as she watches her parents go dance together.

Other couples, unlikely or not, join the dance floor.

Violet smiles up at me as I hold her waist.

"Happy Birthday, little witch," I say, and she beams.

"Did you see there's a wedding cake and cupcakes for my birthday? It was Ember's idea," she says, glancing over at her sunshine friend who's shrouded by an umbrella.

"I did, it's perfect. You're perfect."

"Finally, you've got it right," Thorin says.

"Thorin agrees," I tell her out loud, and she smiles.

"Tell Thorin, Azure and I think you are both pretty perfect, too."

"She's not wrong," Thorin purrs.

"I have a surprise for you," I tell her, pulling the envelope out of my suit pocket and she takes it, opening it carefully with her purple manicured nails.

A smile takes over her face as she reads the note.

SARAH BLUE

"Banff?" she says.

"Thorin thought you might want to run in the mountains instead of the swamp."

"How sweet of him," she says, grabbing my lapels and bringing me in for another kiss.

"Thank you for marrying me, for real this time," I tell her.

"You know, I need to make a birthday wish," she says with a dark, arched brow. "Should I tell you what it is?" I tilt my head at her, and she leans in to whisper in my ear. "I wish you could keep up," she says, shoving my chest.

My eyes widen as I reel back, as I watch as my wife playfully runs away in her wedding dress.

All I can do is chase.

I'd chase my wife to the end of the world, and I'd never have it any other way.

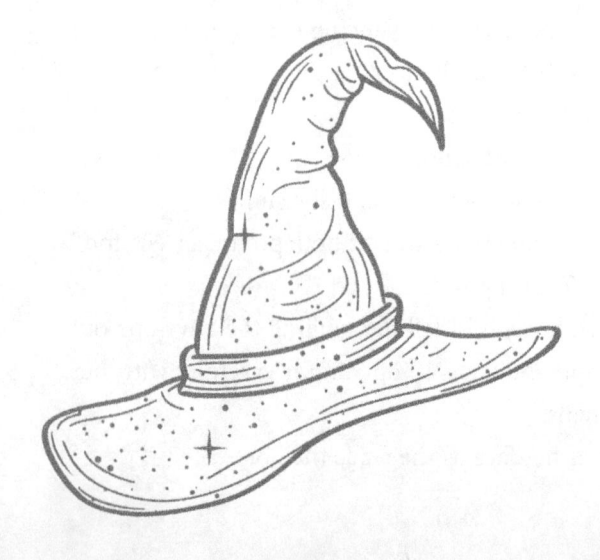

Bonus Chapter

VIOLET

Silas was adamant that we over pack, and I suppose he's right. Now that I've been fully connected with Azure for a year, I go through a lot of clothes. Sometimes that needy little wolf just can't control herself.

"You've seen my Thorin, have you not?" Azure says as Silas carries the suitcase and we enter our stay for the next two weeks.

The air is crisp against my skin and I can't help but to be in absolute awe of our surroundings. I didn't leave the south much, and the lake and mountains that were out in the distance were mesmerizing. The lake is a shade of blue I've never seen, and the mountains are larger than I could've imagined.

I can feel how happy Azure is to be here, almost as much as I am. While Silas and I spend a lot of time together, it's not often we go days without someone needing something, whether it's the pack or the coven, or some other supernatural craziness.

"What do you think?" Silas says, and I rest my head against his big arm, taking it all in.

"It's perfect. How many people stay at this place?" I ask as we walk up the pristine driveway and I don't see another car.

"What do you mean? The whole place is ours?" Silas says with a smirk.

Sometimes I forget my husband is rich.

"You mean that we're rich," Azure says, and I shake my head.

But she's not wrong. He's my mate, and there was no prenup involved. His fortune also is mine. He spent more than his own fair share fixing up the estate; the entirety of the mansion is now restored. Both of us have our own offices, a whole side of the house is dedicated to a clinic where I help both witches and shifters, and maybe on the occasion a few other supernaturals.

Life is good, and this vacation is just what we needed.

"Thought it would be best if no one was milling about seeing two strangely beautiful people shift into wolves," Silas says and I furrow my brows at him.

"Did Thorin tell you to say that?"

"No, he said beautiful people who shift to even more stunning wolves," he says with a grin as we enter the mountain retreat.

It's modern, while still holding that rustic mountain home charm. A fire is already crackling in the fireplace as I take off my scarf and jacket and put them on the back of a chair.

The back of the home is all windows, showing nothing but snow-covered mountains and a pristine lake.

Silas comes up behind me, wrapping his large frame around mine. I melt into him, loving how warm and comforting he is. I hold his forearms tight as he kisses the side of my head.

The sun is slowly fading beyond the mountains as he holds me.

Life lately has been far less complicated, and I've never been happier. Sometimes I miss my grand-mère in a way that old memories have a way of making you reminiscent, but I know she's where she belongs, and so am I.

THE MARRIAGE HEX

My mother is an excellent High Priestess, and someone I learn from every day. Getting to know my father was a bit more difficult, but over time, I learned how similar we are, and he's taught me so much about the Moon Walker Pack.

Ember and Iris are still my sisters. We're closer than ever, even if we love keeping one another on our toes with our love lives. But one thing is for sure, no matter what, we always have each other to depend on.

Then there's the man who loves me so effortlessly and completely. I don't know how there was ever a time I didn't have him in my life.

"I love you," I whisper, and he kisses my hair again, both of us swaying slightly.

"I love you too, little witch. Now, why don't you get that tiny bikini you packed while I get the wine and cheese and we get in the hot tub?" he says.

I smile as he runs his nose over my hair. I'm still a bit bitter that my senses are never as good as his.

"Mmm. I can scent that you want to," he says.

"You're a rotten cheat, Silas Walker."

"You only say that because you don't know how sweet you smell when you're turned on," he says.

I turn out of his arms, grabbing his shirt as he smirks down at me. I love this big, romantic, sweet man so much that sometimes my chest aches. How did I get so lucky?

"You better have gotten white wine," I say.

"Don't insult me."

I shove at his chest as he watches me grab the suitcase and roll it into the massive primary bedroom. It's also at the back of the house, with a stunning view. The bed isn't as large as ours at home, but it'll do. The sheets are a crisp white and there are purple petals splattered all over the bed.

I smile to myself, pulling out my wand and opening the suitcase. With a flick of my wrist, I send all the clothes to the closet or their drawers, tugging out the requested tiny black bikini.

My grin widens as I grab the custom swim trunks for Silas, that have a repeating pattern of my face on them, and head back out toward the kitchen. He has a cheese board, wine glasses, and a chilled bottle on the counter.

I twirl the swim shorts around my finger as Silas greedily takes in my body. Does this happen to everyone? Feeling continuously in love and turned on no matter how much time passes? Or is it a mate thing?

"Is your face on those shorts?" he says and I grin.

"Think of it as a mark of ownership."

Silas narrows his eyes at me, but his eyes glow ever so faintly. At least I know Thorin enjoys my taste.

I toss them at him, which he easily catches. His eyes don't leave mine as he undresses. God, he looks good. Silas is all man and I'll never tire of it. He slides the shorts on and looks down at them.

"You can never have me close enough, can you, baby?"

"Never," I reply, grabbing the wine bottle as he grabs the tray.

I wrap my arms around myself, not used to the cold as Silas flips the lid to the hot tub and starts the jets. He places the tray on the ledge and I do the same with the glasses as he gets in. Water spills over one edge as he holds out his hand. I take it and his brows furrow at me.

He tugs on his shorts and comes up with a piece of fabric, and I can't help but to laugh.

"What did you do?"

"I maybe spelled them to disintegrate in water," I say.

He narrows his eyes at me and grabs my waist, planting me on an impressive thigh.

"You're a menace sometimes, Mrs. Walker."

I grin, and rest my back against his chest, loving the conjunction of the warm water and crisp air as the sun falls and we take in the scenery.

"You wouldn't have it any other way."

"You're right, I wouldn't," he says, kissing my shoulder. "I don't have magic. But I do have teeth," he says, biting the strap of my bikini, making my top fall off.

All is fair in sexual warfare.

Especially as he cups my breasts with his large hands, his thumbs playing with my piercings.

"Tell me, wife. Do you love torturing me?" he says, pieces of his bathing suit floating up in the bubbles making me grin as his hard cock rubs against my ass.

"I'm pretty sure that's what a wife is supposed to do," I say as one of his hands slides in the water, untying my bathing suit bottoms on both sides, before he fists those and they splat against the massive deck.

"My pretty wife. My perfect mate. Sent here to torture me for eternity," he says, one hand palming a breast while the other spreads my legs wide as he toys with my pussy.

"You know, we seem to have a penchant for fucking outdoors," I say with a slight whimper as he rubs my clit.

"Can't help it I like fucking you with a pretty view," he says, a quick lick against my neck, before sucking his mating mark between his lips. "But nothing compares to my pretty wife."

This man is too good with words.

I raise up ever so slightly, and he sees my intention as he fists his cock, helping me get the right angle as I slowly sink down on his length. He brackets my chest with one strong arm, while his other fingers stroke around where we're connected, touching my entrance and his hard cock.

The water splashes even more as I shift up and down his length. The back of my head rests on his shoulder as he whispers dirty, sweet things in my ear.

"Such a sweet little witch when you're getting fucked, aren't you?"

"Mmm."

"My sweet little wife needs to come, doesn't she?"

I nod my head as Silas takes over, showing off his strength as he fucks me from below while toying with my clit. His knot is hitting my entrance, but I don't think he would want to knot me in the hot tub like this.

"Don't worry. I plan on living inside of you during this trip. You'll get your knot," he says, like he can hear my thoughts.

Or maybe I was audibly begging for it. Who truly knows?

"Right there," I hiss, digging my nails into his forearms, leaving little crescent indents in his skin.

He fucks me hard while he sucks on our mating mark and it sends me over the edge. My pussy fluttering against his length as a deep moan slips from his lips and I can feel his cum pulsating inside of me.

His heart hammers against my back as he pulls out, keeping me on his lap and wrapped in his arms.

He kisses my neck as we come down from the high and enjoy the speckling of stars peaking out in the night sky.

"What do you say we let the wolves have their fun?" he says and I laugh.

No doubt Thorin is hammering against his mind, asking to see his girl.

"It's only fair," Azure says in my mind, and I smile.

THE MARRIAGE HEX

So we get out of the hot tub, shifting and letting our wolves run through the crisp autumn air.

When we shift back, all the cheese and wine is nowhere to be seen and we laugh. I rest my hand against my stomach, feeling full as Silas grabs my hand and leads me to the bathroom.

We shower off the night and easily fall into the bed.

I turn to face Silas, dragging a hand down his face and scratching his beard.

"You know, I'm pretty happy sixteen-year-old me made this all happen," I say with a smirk.

"Oh little witch, we both knew this was inevitable," he says with a smile.

He kisses me goodnight and I fall asleep happily and content, cuddled next to my husband, who I've been lucky enough to marry twice.

Our little marriage hex just might have been what put this in motion, but he's right. You can't escape fate.

THE MARRIAGE HEX

Acknowledgments

This book was such an undertaking and there are so many people to thank for getting this book published.

Sandra, Kay, Val, Marie MacKay, and Amarna, my team who made this cover, interior, and editing of this book happen.

My Alpha team, Leisha, Marielli, Jess, and Jade, thank you so much for being able to read as I write, always giving me encouragement and helping me make my books the best that they can be. All of you are so amazing and I'm so lucky to have such a great Alpha team.

My Louisiana rep team Amber and Dani for checking for representation of your fine state.

My sensitivity team, Kaylah & Ava for always being amazing and willing to read my work for diversity.

Sam, K.L Mann, Lindsay, Stephanie, Cecelia, Hailey for reading early to check for errors and to help get me hyped up for this release. Thank you for letting me pester you and always supporting my journey.

Also by Sarah Blue

Paranormal
Celestial Witches
The Marriage Hex
The Fang Arrangement - Coming Soon

Charming Series
Charming Your Dad
Charming the Devil
Charming as Hell

Love in the Veil
Petty Cupid
Lucky Cupid
Daddy Cupid

Omegaverse
High Roller Omegas
Queen of Hearts

Dead Palms MC
Nobody's Darlin'

Pucked Up Omegaverse

One Pucked Up Pack
Don't Puck With My Heart
Puck Around & Find Out

Heat Haven Omegaverse

Heat Haven
Omega's Obsession
Protector's Promise
Too Tempting
Heat Haven Holidays

Lavender Moon

Lavender Moon
Lavender Moon Meets Las Vegas

The Carlson Brothers - Contemporary Romance

Swallow Your Pride
Forget Your Morals

SARAH BLUE

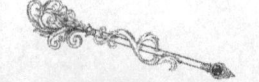

THE MARRIAGE HEX

About the Author

Sarah Blue writes contemporary sweet omegaverse, erotic, why choose romances. She loves romance in nearly any genre. When she isn't writing you can find her nose buried in a book or lit up from her kindle. She loves the sweeter side of romance and creating interesting characters while adding adventure and spice. Writing strong female characters and male characters willing to show weakness is something that makes her gooey on the inside.

Sarah lives in Maryland with her husband, two sons, and two annoying cats. If she isn't reading or writing she is probably working on a craft project or scrolling on Tik Tok.

www.authorsarahblue.com
@sarahblueauthor on Instagram and TikTok
Sarah Blue's Reader Group on Facebook

Printed in the USA.
CPSIA information can be obtained
at www.ICGtesting.com
LVHW091219141124
796623LV00026B/73